I t
just as she entered the kitchen.
I raised my camera, flicked the switch
to continuous exposure and pressed.

As the lens click-clicked, she stopped abruptly, frozen. I heard a quick intake of breath and saw a flash of tightening jaw through the viewfinder. Then she let out an unearthly shriek.

"Arnie!" She ran into the kitchen, out of my sight for a moment. "No! No! Arnie!"

The hairs on my arm rose at her tone, and I ran into the kitchen myself. I froze for an instant, too.

On the floor by the stove lay Arnie, staring upwards, blood puddling beneath and beside him on the yellow tiles. Jolene knelt in the blood, shaking him, calling him, trying to rouse him.

She would never succeed.

Books by Gayle Roper

Love Inspired Suspense

See No Evil #39
Caught in the Middle #50
Caught in the Act #54

GAYLE ROPER

has always loved stories, and as a result she's authored more than 40 books. Gayle has won a Romance Writers of America's RITA® Award for Best Inspirational Romance and finaled repeatedly for both RITA® and Christy® awards. Several writers' conferences have cited her for her contributions to writer training. She enjoys speaking at writers' conferences and women's events, reading and eating out. She adores her kids and grandkids, and loves her own personal patron of the arts, her husband, Chuck.

GAYLE ROPER

Caught in the act

REVISED BY AUTHOR

Steeple
Hill®

Published by Steeple Hill Books™

STEEPLE HILL BOOKS

Steeple
Hill®

ISBN-13: 978-0-373-44244-7
ISBN-10:   0-373-44244-0

CAUGHT IN THE ACT

This is the revised text of the work which was first published by Zondervan in 1998.

Printed in U.S.A.

When I am afraid, I will trust in you.
—*Psalms* 56:3

For my brothers and sisters
at Calvary Fellowship Church
"I thank my God upon every remembrance of you."

ONE

"Merry, could you drop me at my parents' after work?" Jolene Meister asked as we left *The News* office for lunch. "My father brought me in this morning."

I'd only have to go out of my way a couple of blocks, so I said, "Sure. No problem."

And that easily and innocently I precipitated my involvement in murder.

Again.

Jolene and I walked to Ferretti's, the best eating our small town had to offer. The winter wind on this dingy December Tuesday bit through my new red coat, and I suspected my nose was turning almost as rosy as my wool blend. The two scars on my nose that I'd gotten in a bike accident when I was eight years old would be turning a contrasting blue.

Ah, well, I thought. If I smile, I can have a patriotic face: red nose, white teeth and blue scars.

Gene Autry was serenading downtown Amhearst about Rudolph the Red-nosed Reindeer over a tinny public address system by Santa's little house. How come a cowboy had made millions off a deer's red nose and all I got from mine was a color scheme?

"Hey, Jolene." Ferretti's hostess, a brassy blonde named Astrid, seated us with a smile, then left.

It never ceased to amaze me how everyone in Amhearst knew everyone else. As a recent arrival I found it both cozy and unnerving. "How do you know Astrid?"

"I went to school with her younger sister, Elsa. She's a real dingbat."

"Who? Astrid or Elsa?"

"Both."

Knowing Jolene as I did, that probably meant that the two women were very nice and rather intelligent.

"Does anyone ever move away from Amhearst?"

"Sure." Jolene indicated our waitress whose name tag read Sally. "Sally's daughter Caroline moved to California to be in the movies, right?" She looked at Sally.

"Yeah," Sally said. "But she moved back home last month. Astrid's sister, Elsa, got her a job as receptionist at Bushay's. Elsa's Mr. Bushay's administrative assistant."

Didn't sound like dingbat territory to me, but it sure sounded like Amhearst.

I ordered a Caesar salad and Jolene ordered a huge plate of eggplant parmigiana.

When Sally disappeared with her order pad, I looked at Jolene.

"And how do you know Sally?"

"She and my mom were in the PTA together."

"And you know Caroline, the would-be movie star?"

"Sure. She was three years ahead of me in school."

"See? Weird."

Jolene shrugged and pressed her hands to her cheeks. "Do I look flushed to you?"

"Like you're getting sick, you mean?" Jolene was a hypochondriac.

I looked at her big brown hair and bangs, her bright brown eyes, her flawless skin. "You look great to me." In an overblown sort of way.

Our lunches came, and I looked from my salad to

Jolene's spicy, cheesy dish. "How can you eat that and not gain weight? It's swimming in oil. It's not fair."

"Fair?" She leveled a forkful of dripping eggplant at me. "Is it fair that you have two gorgeous men chasing you?" She snorted, a noise that sounded decidedly odd coming from her delicate nose. "Don't give me fair, Merrileigh Kramer. I'm not listening."

I grinned. I'd never in my life had one man chasing me with any real enthusiasm, and suddenly I had two. It made me feel nervous and powerful. It made me giggle.

It also made me check over my shoulder constantly because I hadn't quite figured out how to break the news to my new boyfriend that my old boyfriend, suddenly ardent, had come a-courting. And what was worse yet, old Jack didn't even know that a warm, delightful and charming man named Curt Carlyle existed.

"So Jack just showed up at your door on Sunday?" Jolene buttered a piece of Italian bread with real butter.

I crunched a particularly large chunk of romaine. "You go with a guy for six years, and he refuses to make a commitment," I began.

"Six years?" Jolene's voice squeaked with disbelief.

I held up a hand. "Don't ask. Just accept my word that he's charming and I was stupid. Anyway he's hardly contacted me since I moved here in September, and boom! There he is. Although I guess it really wasn't boom, was it? Four months is hardly boom."

"Merry Christmas, my Merry," he'd yelled when I opened my door Sunday afternoon. He pushed a giant silk poinsettia into my hands, smiling broadly at my confusion. Then he grabbed me and hugged me tightly, crushing the poinsettia painfully between us.

"What are you doing here?" I demanded, ever gracious.

"Is that any way to greet your sweetheart come this great distance just to be near you?"

Just four months ago I'd have swooned with delight if he'd deigned to call me his sweetheart. Now all I felt was an incipient case of heartburn.

"I've moved to Amhearst," he said, taking off his coat without an invitation. "At least for a while."

I think he thought I was paralyzed with delight, but it was horror as I tried to imagine him fitting into the new life I'd found when I fled my old in despair over him.

He threw his coat across the back of the chair. A sleeve flopped down and slapped my dozing cat, Whiskers, in the face. He sat up with a sleepy scowl and decided right then and there he didn't like Jack. When Jack saw the cat, I could tell that the feeling was mutual.

Bad sign.

"You've moved to Amhearst?" My voice was heavy with disbelief. "Why?"

"To be near you, sweetheart." His eyes went soft and dark.

"But—" I sputtered. "Your job. You didn't quit your job!" Jack was a CPA with a large firm back home in Pittsburgh.

"Of course I didn't. I'm here doing an audit on Bushay Environmental, and it'll take weeks at the very least."

I planted my fists on my hips. "Your company sends you here, and I'm supposed to believe that indicates undying affection for me?"

"I campaigned for this assignment," he said earnestly.

He reached for my hand, and I suddenly saw him as a giant vacuum cleaner, ready to suck me up and spit me back into the past. The image terrified me. I dodged him, leaned over and filled both arms with Whiskers, who immediately began to purr.

Jack either didn't understand my move or made believe he didn't. He kept on talking as if he always reached out and found nothing, as if it didn't matter that I preferred a cat to him.

"Amhearst isn't exactly a desirable location," he

informed me. "It's out here in the western edge of Chester County miles away from anything."

I scowled at him as if he'd insulted me. I liked Amhearst, and part of its charm was its rural setting. And Philadelphia was only an hour away, for heaven's sake.

As usual he missed my reaction. I used to wonder if his lack of response to how I felt was a power play designed to get his own way, or if he was just too dense to see what was in front of him. As I watched him in my living room, I decided he was just dense. That idea made me sad.

"I asked to be sent here instead of Atlantic City and a casino audit." He reached over Whiskers and touched my cheek. "I gave up a plum assignment, and all for you."

Atlantic City in December didn't sound all that plum to me. Cold, damp, depressing.

Jack continued to recount his campaign for the Bushay job, trying to convince me of his ardor. "'You've got to send me to Amhearst,' I told Mr. Proctor. 'I want the Bushay job even though it means weeks away from home to complete it.'" He smiled impishly. "I didn't tell him about you."

I raised a skeptical eyebrow as Whiskers jumped out of my arms.

"But I knew you were my reason." He reached for me again. "My girl."

I dodged his grasp again by grabbing my coat from the clothes tree in the corner and throwing it over my shoulders. "Well, I may have been your reason for coming here, but I'm not sure I'm your girl anymore."

And I walked out. I had absolutely no place to go, but I knew I'd never again have such a wonderful exit line. And six years of no commitment was a long, long time, no matter how you looked at it.

As I finished my tale, Jolene eyed me with something like admiration. "So where'd you go?"

"To *The News*. Where else?" I crunched more Romaine.

"Was he there when you got home?"

"I didn't get home until ten-thirty, and Jack can't stand waiting for five minutes, let alone five hours."

Jo's eyes widened. "What did you do for five hours?"

Suddenly I felt embarrassed because I knew what her response to my answer was going to be. I cleared my throat. "I had a date."

"What?" she shrieked, just like I knew she would. She started to laugh so hard I thought she'd choke on her eggplant. "This guy moves all the way from Pittsburgh for you, and you go out with someone else? Merry, my estimation of you has jumped off the charts. You are a wild woman after all."

My mind tried to comprehend me as a wild woman, but the idea was as impossible to grasp as a soap bubble from a wand was for a child.

"You're so lucky," she said. "I haven't had anyone chasing me in years." Her lovely brown eyes looked forlorn beneath her brown bangs.

"Of course not. You've been married."

She shrugged carelessly—which said volumes about her view of marriage. "But I'm not married now."

"True and false. You're not divorced, either. Maybe you and Arnie will get back together yet."

Again the careless shrug. Poor Arnie. I hoped he wasn't pining for her because it looked like he'd waste away to nothing before Jolene returned.

She mopped up the last of her eggplant with the last of her bread. "So what did Curt say when he heard Jack was here?"

I concentrated on corralling the last of my salad. "He doesn't know yet."

"What?" She laughed until I thought for sure her mascara would run.

I looked at her sourly. Clowns in the center ring didn't give the laughs I did. "I plan to tell him next time I see him."

Her smile was a mile wide. "You're afraid to tell him."

I stuck my chin in the air and gave my version of her snort. I wasn't about to admit she was right.

"One thing I want to know," Jolene said, making one of her patented changes of topic. "How can someone who looks so much like a football player be an artist?"

I smiled, picturing Curt's dark curly hair and glasses and shoulders so broad he could block an entire movie screen at thirty paces.

"I think I'm falling in love with you," he told me recently.

"No, you're not," I said in something like panic. "We hardly know each other. Love takes time to grow." I knew because my mother had told me so all my life.

Still, when he looked at me a certain way, my knees buckled, I had trouble breathing and my heart barrumped in time with the Minute Waltz.

"Things between Curt and me are fragile," I told Jolene. "New. Too new. I don't know how to tell him."

I must have looked as disconsolate as I felt because Jolene patted my hand. "It'll work out. Don't worry." She grinned at me. "Just keep me informed, you hear?"

We took our checks to the cashier by the door. Jolene eyed me while she waited for her change.

"You didn't tell Curt about Jack. Did you tell Jack about Curt?"

I made a big deal of buying one of those little foil-wrapped mints.

She snickered. "You're better than any movie I ever saw, girl. And I want to be around when they meet."

Perish the thought!

"I have to visit the ladies' room," she said. "Come on."

I followed her into the cozy, well-lit room, admiring her black leather and faux-fur coat and black boots. The lady had style if not class.

I looked at myself in the huge mirror over the sink. My short, thick, spiky black hair was drooping a bit as usual. I wet my fingers and ran them through it, trying to wake up the mousse that was supposed to keep it sticking up in what the beautician had assured me was a very stylish do when she cut off my almost waist-length hair back in August.

Sighing, I gave up on my hair. I stared instead at the Christmas candle sitting on the vanity.

Christmas. My first in Amhearst, and I was facing it with some excitement (two men) but also with much misgiving. For the first time ever, I wouldn't be with my family for our warm and wonderful celebration. No fat Christmas tree with Grandma Kramer's heirloom angel gracing the top bough. No hot mulled cider that Dad tried to foist on everyone. No marvelous turkey smells and no Aunt Sissy's famous pumpkin pie.

Jolene would have a warm, cozy family Christmas with hugs and presents and all that stuff. She wouldn't sit alone all day, staring at her cat. That would be me.

Every time I thought about my holiday solitude, I suffered mild depression. As a result my little apartment on the first floor of an old carriage house sported only a wreath on the door. I hadn't gotten myself a tree or put electric candles in my windows like everyone else in Amhearst. Of course I now had a silk poinsettia sitting on an end table.

It was my job that prevented a trip to Pittsburgh and home. I had only Christmas Day off, if being on call means "off."

"Someone has to be available in case a big story breaks," said Mac, my editor at *The News*. Then he grinned. "I guess you've drawn the short straw, Merry." He didn't even feel sorry for me.

I kept telling myself that I didn't mind. I was an independent career woman, pressing on with my new life. I didn't believe myself for an instant. But, I reminded myself before I started weeping on the spot, I was the one with two men!

Not that I needed or wanted two. One would certainly

be more than enough since monogamy was my preferred lifestyle. I just had to decide which one.

"Hey!" Jolene said as she came out of a stall. "You're smiling. Which one are you thinking about?"

"Not telling." I swung my purse strap back onto my shoulder and slammed the bag itself into the blonde woman walking out of the other stall.

"Oh, I'm sorry!"

She smiled at me, her gray eyes crinkling at the corners. "Don't worry about it. It's o—"

Her voice faded to nothing, and her face lost its pleasant smile. She stared past me with a sudden look of great distaste. I blinked and turned to see what she was looking at, and there stood Jolene. Her face had also lost all its charm and warmth.

"Well, well," Jo said. "Look who's here."

"Hello, Jo," the woman said in a tight, tense voice. "How are you? And how's Arnie?"

"We're both fine." Jolene matched icy politeness for icy politeness. I could get frostbite just standing here.

"Tell him I said hello," the woman said.

"Like he cares," Jolene spat the words like little pellets flying from a straw to land stinging blows on the back of an unsuspecting neck.

The woman sighed in disgust. "You haven't changed a bit, have you?"

Jolene bristled. "Watch it, Airy. I don't like being in the same room with you any more than you like being in the same room with me."

My eyes widened. I am Polly Peacemaker, and if I'm caught in conflict, I never know what to do. But it appeared I was the only one uncomfortable here. These two women were obviously sluggers, though Jo was clearly batting champ.

"Believe me," Airy said, "if I'd known you were going to be here, I'd have avoided Ferretti's at all costs."

Jolene, face haughty, sniffed. "My coworker and I were having a business lunch."

Airy sneered. "Don't give me that snotty attitude about your job, Jolene. People at your level don't have business lunches."

Jolene glared. "You just think you're so smart."

I looked at Jolene, disappointed. Certainly she could do better than that worn-out old line.

"Tell me." Airy's voice dripped acid. "Which of us graduated valedictorian? Um? It certainly wasn't you."

What? At twenty-five years old or so, she was bringing up high school? What was next? Elementary school jealousies?

"Like test grades show intelligence," Jolene scoffed with a wonderful disregard for the entire educational system. "I'd rather have my social smarts than your boring IQ any day."

"You used to be nice, you know." Airy nodded slightly as if agreeing with herself. "Up until about third grade. It's been downhill ever since."

Yikes, I thought. Elementary school.

"And you've been jealous of me ever since."

"Oh, pu-lease! I'd kill myself before I ever became like you."

A woman pushed the ladies' room door open and froze halfway in, caught by the nastiness of the voices. She locked eyes with me for the briefest of seconds, then withdrew, condemnation in every line of her body.

Not me, I wanted to tell her. I'm an innocent bystander. I know better. I have class.

Jolene and Airy hadn't even noticed her. They were too busy pouring out a lifetime of vituperation.

Suddenly Jolene turned sly. "By the way, Airy, how's Sean?"

All color drained from Airy's face. "Don't you even mention his name," she hissed. "Don't you even think about him."

Jolene just smiled. If I'd been Airy, I'd have been tempted to sock her one for her arrogance.

"How do you like his new mustache?" Jolene asked innocently. "I think it makes him look quite debonair, don't you?"

"His new mus— How do you—?" Airy was so angry that she was sputtering. And scared? She shut her eyes and took a deep, calming breath. Then she said in an urgent, passionate voice, "Sean is off-limits to you. Don't you ever, ever come near him."

"Oops. You mean I shouldn't have had lunch with him yesterday?"

Airy looked as if she had turned to stone. She didn't even appear to draw breath.

Jolene did everything but smack her lips at the reaction she had gotten. "Why don't you just settle for Arnie? You and he would make a great pair. The leftovers." And she turned away.

Airy reached out and grabbed Jolene's arm and spun her around. Jo blinked in surprise. The guppy was taking on the shark.

"I mean it, Jo. *Stay away from Sean.* You may have taken Arnie away from me once upon a time, but not Sean. Not Sean! He's mine."

Jolene raised an eyebrow and looked down her perfect nose. "Only if you can keep him, sweetie." She shook Airy's hand from her arm as if she was flicking garbage off a plate and strode out of the room.

I was left staring at my toes, unsure what to do. What did one say to the loser in a catfight? It was one of life's little lessons that Mom, usually so good at preparing me, had neglected.

I heard a soft sigh and glanced up. Airy looked so sad.

"I'm sorry," I said, even though I had nothing to do with any of it.

Airy nodded and smiled weakly. "You'd think I'd have

learned to deal with her by now, wouldn't you? I mean, I've known her since I was four years old. Princess Jo."

She pulled a packet of tissues from her purse and wiped ineffectively at her nose.

"Merry Christmas," she said and walked out without looking back.

When I left the ladies' room, I looked to see if Airy was still in the restaurant. She wasn't but Jolene was, standing straight and beautiful and haughty as she waited for me.

It was a silent walk back to *The News*.

TWO

"Merry, come here!" My editor, Mac Carnuccio, cocked a hand at me as soon as I came in from lunch.

Mac was king of our little world. His style was exactly the opposite of our previous editor, the erratic stacks of paper littering his desk being but one instance. Still, in the short two weeks that he'd held the job, he'd put out a paper as good as or better than our former editor.

And he clearly loved being in charge, taking a kid's pleasure in the subtle perks of power, especially the enormous desk by the enormous window.

"I love sitting here," he'd told me last week as he leaned back in his new ergonomically correct executive chair. "I feel like I own all of Amhearst."

I'd looked out on Main Street and agreed it was an impressive sight. "Monarch of all you survey, eh?"

Mac smiled broadly at an iridescent gray pigeon taking its afternoon constitutional on the other side of his window. Then his face sobered.

"I'm not really editor, you know." He glanced at me. "I'm only acting editor. The rag's for sale, and who knows who will buy it and what will happen then. Ever since I saw Cary Grant in *His Girl Friday*, I wanted to be a suave, fast-talking editor. And—" his grin returned "—for now I am."

Now this suave, fast-talking editor was waving to me, his Rosalind Russell.

As I hurried through the newsroom, I zigged and zagged as necessary to avoid being eaten by the spectacularly healthy plants that Jolene insisted on growing here. The huge grape ivy that sat on the soda machine had been joined by a gigantic red poinsettia, one of several that sat about in case we forgot that Christmas was a mere week away. On the great windowsill of the picture window African violets bloomed pink and purple and variegated in spite of the time of year, and Jolene's Christmas cactus in a teeth-jarring shade of fuchsia hung nearly to the floor.

Mac's policy was the same as our former editor's: ignore the greenery and maybe it would die.

"Have I got an assignment for you, Beautiful," Mac said when I stood before his cluttered desk. "You'll love it!"

"Yeah?" Whenever Mac told me I'd love something, I got nervous. We were so different that most things he thought were great, I thought were vulgar, profane, and/or without redeeming social value.

"And if you don't love it," he said, "the penalty is dinner with me. Alone. At my place."

"I can tell already that I'm going to like this assignment a lot." I smiled to let him know I knew he was joking about the dinner, though I wasn't certain he was. He asked me out with great regularity, and I refused with equal regularity. The last thing I wanted or needed was an office romance with a guy like Mac. Besides, a third guy would definitely be more than I could handle.

"I already assigned you Longwood Gardens at Christmas, right?"

I nodded. Longwood Gardens was a local wonder that I was to do a piece on for the December 26 issue, something I could write ahead, an informative filler that wouldn't change, unless, of course, the conservatory decided to burn down or something.

"Good." He nodded. "Don't forget."

I scowled at him. Like I'd forget an assignment.

He fumbled through one of his multiple stacks of papers. He grunted with satisfaction as he pulled a sheet free. "You know about His House?"

"Whose house?"

"His House."

I looked at him blankly.

"You know. Like in God."

"God's house? Like church?"

"What's church got to do with anything?" Mac looked as confused as I felt.

"Church is God's house."

"Oh, yeah. I guess it is. But I'm not talking about church. I'm talking about His House."

We were back where we started.

"His House is a place for girls in trouble."

"Ah," I said. "In trouble with the law? With pregnancies? With their parents?"

"Probably all the above, but mostly with pregnancies. I want a tearjerker story on some of those girls. I want to wring the readers' hearts."

I nodded. I could do that.

"I want your story to be so compelling that our readers will admire these girls, no, will love these girls for their courage to carry their babies instead of terminating their pregnancies. I want heartbreaking stories of desperation and blossoming maternal love, of perseverance in the face of abandonment by families and, most terribly, by the babies' fathers." He rose from his seat, carried away by his own rhetoric. "I want the readers to cry!"

I stared at him in astonishment. Where had all this emotion come from?

He grinned sheepishly as he noticed not only me but Edie Whatley, the family page editor, staring at him.

"Lapsed Italian-Catholic guilt," he explained as he sank into his new chair. "I'm conflicted over abortion. I'm conflicted over the Church. And Christmas always makes it all worse. I mean, what if Mary had aborted Jesus? Did you ever think of that?"

"Mac!"

"And then there's all the other seasonal questions. Should I go to midnight Mass on Christmas Eve? It sort of makes me feel good to go, you know? But isn't that hypocritical if I never go any other time? And shouldn't you go to church to talk to God, not to get a warm seasonal buzz? But it'd make my mother happy. The question is: would it make God happy? And why would he want to see me after the way I've acted the rest of the year? If there is a God."

I couldn't help laughing at his expression, but I realized he was asking some very serious questions.

"Come to church with me on Christmas Eve," I said.

"Are you asking me for a date?" He looked much too eager.

"Absolutely not, but you could sit with me."

His eyes lit up.

"I wouldn't want you to feel awkward in strange surroundings," I said primly.

"Too kind, kid. Here." He handed me the sheet of paper.

I read Dawn Trauber, Director, His House, followed by a phone number.

"Call her," he instructed. "Set up an interview."

I nodded. "Thanks. I agree with you. This will be a great story."

"It better be, Schweetheart," he said in his best Humphrey Bogart. "I may not go to Mass, but consider me the Little Drummer Boy bringing my gift of the story to the manger. You're the drum I'm beating on, pa-rum-pa-pum-pum."

I went to the file cabinet along the wall, slid the gigantic jade plant—now festooned with an equally gigantic red bow and white fairy lights—to the rear of the cabinet, and dived into the *H* drawer. Certainly the clipping service had something for me on His House. I pulled the information out.

I carried the file back to my desk by way of the soda machine. As I walked past, I tossed my head. Just that quickly I was attacked by the great grape ivy. Its tentacles reached out and wrapped themselves about my spiky hair, twisting and twining themselves until I was imprisoned against the dollar slot.

My file fluttered to the floor. I gurgled in outrage and began struggling, though I didn't want to be too rough because I was more afraid of Jolene, the mad gardener, than I was of the plant. But I didn't want to be dinner for a carnivorous organism, either. So I pulled and twisted, and no sooner did I get one spike free than another fell prey to the shoots.

I could just see the headline: "Reporter Vined to Death. 'But it seemed such a nice plant,' friends say."

As I struggled, a tendril reached down the back of my collar and wound itself around my neck. I felt it begin to choke me.

"No!" I lashed out wildly. I felt my feet slip on some downed leaves just as Jolene and Mac reached me. I grabbed for them to keep from slamming to the floor, but they calmly sidestepped me and grabbed the falling grape ivy instead. I hit the floor with a great thud, but all I heard was, "Thank goodness! We caught it just in time." That was Mac.

"Merry! What were you thinking? You might have harmed it." That was Jolene.

As I sat there with my skirt around my ears and my hip announcing its fury at my inconsiderate treatment, Mac and Jolene patiently unwound the vines from my hair and with a great show of concern put the plant back on the soda machine.

"Poor thing," Jolene murmured as she patted the villainous tendrils of green.

Snarling, I grabbed my fallen file, pulled myself to my feet and limped back to my desk.

A minute later a laughing Mac stood beside me offering a peace Coke. The absurdity of the whole thing struck me just as I took my first swallow. Mac had to swat me on the back several times to prevent me from choking.

"You made my day, Merry," he said as he walked away. "You made my day."

In the work situation, all I ever wanted was to be a consummate professional. Well, professionals are people who please their bosses, right? I perked up a bit.

I went into our e-files to supplement the His House paper file, which wasn't exactly fat, and between the two sources found several news articles, many of them about local church women's groups who had showers and ingatherings to benefit the House. There were several pictures of smiling women sitting behind stacks of hand-knit baby sweaters and blankets while boxes of diapers rose like block towers beside them. There was a picture of the House itself, a huge, old Victorian just east of town.

I looked carefully at a picture of the director, Dawn Trauber, woman around thirty who reminded me of Katie Couric. Same nice face. Same warm smile.

According to the article that chronicled her coming to His House, Dawn had wonderful credentials. She had a degree in social work from Philadelphia Biblical University and an MSW from Temple University in Philadelphia. She had worked for several years as a houseparent at a children's home near Lancaster. According to the article, she had now been in Amhearst three years.

There was nothing in either file about any of the girls who stayed there.

As I thought about it, I wasn't surprised. If I had to stay

in a facility like His House, I didn't think I'd want my story and picture splashed all over the local paper. Obviously I couldn't keep my situation a secret. I might not even want to. But to let a bunch of strangers in on it was another whole issue.

Well, Lord, you're going to have to help me find a way to do this story. I don't think it's going to be easy.

I called His House and asked to speak with Dawn Trauber. When she came on the line, I explained who I was.

"I'd like to do a holiday story about some of your girls. You know. Coping with extraordinary circumstances at a time of year that's often difficult in the best of situations."

"Well," Dawn said, drawing the word out. I could hear the reluctance. "Certainly you can speak with me and certainly you can find out all you want about how we operate. As far as talking to the girls themselves, though, I don't think it's a good idea."

"What if one or two are willing to speak with me?"

"We'll see. Come out and let me meet you. I need to assess whether I can trust you."

We made an appointment for the next morning, and I hung up uncertain whether this drum was going to rum-pa-pum-pum.

Suddenly Jolene stood at the side of my desk. I looked at my watch. Exactly 5:00 p.m.

"Ready?" she asked. She smiled sweetly if somewhat vaguely at me, the very picture of a lovely, somewhat ditzy woman without a care in the world. In other words, she had returned to the woman I worked with each day. Gone was the mad gardener who let me fall while she saved her plant or the shrew who so masterfully dissected Airy at lunch.

Airy. What was it short for? Arianna? Ariadne? Arabelle? Certainly not Aristotle.

"What's Airy's real name?" I asked as I tucked all the clippings into the His House file and slipped it back into its place in the *H* drawer. "And how does she spell it?"

"Airy?" She sounded as if she'd never heard of anyone by that name.

"You know," I prompted, "the woman we met in the ladies' room." Though come to think of it, I hadn't met her. No one had been in an introducing mood.

"Oh." Jolene nodded in "sudden" remembrance. "Valeria."

"Valeria?"

Jolene nodded. "Valeria Lucas Bennett. Sounds high society, doesn't it?" And she laughed sarcastically.

I shrugged my red coat on, and we left *The News* by the back door. Jolene talked as we crossed the parking lot behind the building.

"She was Val until I started calling her Valentine's Day when we were in first grade. Valentine's Day, go away. Don't come near for another year." Jolene sang the rhyme. "She decided she didn't like Val anymore. I suggested Larry from Valeria. She said that was a boy's name. Then I told her she should be A-i-r-y, like a breeze floating wherever she wanted to go. Airy, Airy, quite contrary, How does your garden grow? With weeds and seeds scratching your knees and ugly prickers all in a row."

I shuddered for poor Airy as I unlocked my car doors. We climbed in and I cranked the heater as high as it would go.

Jo loosened her scarf. "Airy and I sat next to each other all through school. Lucas and Luray—that's our maiden names. By the way," she said as I turned toward her parents' home, "I need to stop off at my house for a minute."

"Oh." I thought of her very upscale condominium in the new development on the old Greeley farm south of town, fifteen minutes from here. How like her to neglect to mention this little detour until now.

"I don't mean the condo," she said, reading my mind, a

trick of hers I found very disconcerting. "I mean my house. I need to see Arnie, and he's there."

"You have a house and a condo?"

She looked at me as if to say, "Doesn't everyone?"

"How long will this take?" I knew I was committed no matter how long it took. After all, she was already sitting in my car.

"Not long. No more than fifteen minutes."

"To get there or to talk with Arnie?"

"Yes."

Sighing softly, I told myself that I wasn't being taken advantage of, that I liked going miles out of my way. After all, I had nothing better to do, unless you counted eating dinner, petting Whiskers or relaxing a minute before running out again to take a picture of the committee for the Amhearst Annual Christmas Food Project, or AAC-FOP as Mac called it.

Fifteen minutes later we pulled up before a gorgeous, gigantic mansion—I couldn't think of any other word for the glorious vision in front of me. "This is your house?"

"Yeah, it's mine." She climbed out of the car.

"Wow!" I wondered about Jolene with her cloying lily of the valley perfume and big hair. Thoughtfully I glanced at her coat. Maybe that wasn't faux fur after all.

The house drew me. Light streamed in wide ivory ribbons from Palladian windows and picture windows, bow windows and plain old regular windows, casting a golden glow on perfect shrubbery and a winding brick driveway and front walk. Through one large window a Christmas tree trimmed in little white lights twinkled from its place next to a sofa bigger than my entire apartment. A chandelier that looked like it would fit in well at the White House shone through the great window over the double front door.

"Look at all those lights," Jolene said in disgust.

"They're wonderful," I said, mesmerized.

She gave her unladylike snort. "Arnie loves lights. When he was a kid, they didn't have any money. I mean none. His mother would only let them have one light on at a time, and that was a sixty watt. Now he puts on every light in the house, all a hundred watt. You need sunglasses at midnight! 'I can afford it,' he yells. 'Don't you turn a single switch off!'"

I grabbed my camera from the backseat. At least I wouldn't have to worry about using a flash.

"Has the paper ever done a feature on this place?" I asked. I could see it as the first in a series of Great Homes of Chester County, some new like this, some historic, some remodeled places like the barn over on Route 322. I'd have to talk to Edie Whatley, the home page editor. This was more her territory than mine, but I'd love to do such a series.

I stopped halfway up the walk and stared at the magnificence of it all. "Why live at your condo when you have this?"

"Because Arnie goes with this."

I'd never met Arnie, but how bad could the man be if he could provide all this electricity? "Why did you two break up, Jolene?"

"Irreconcilable differences."

"Yeah? What about?" I leaned to the left, peered into the dining room and admired the crystal chandelier over the mile-long cherry table. I stared at the silver tea service sitting on the sideboard. Like Jolene ever served tea.

Suddenly I could hear my mom, loud and clear.

Merrileigh Kramer! What are you doing, asking such personal questions about the demise of Jolene's marriage? How rude can you get? Apologize right this instant!

It's the opulence, Mom. It threw me.

It's greed, Merry. And poor manners-which you never learned from me.

I placed a hand on Jo's arm. "I'm sorry. I had no right to ask what went wrong. That's your private concern."

"I don't care," she said. "Everyone asks. Even my parents." She turned and opened the door.

I blinked. Even her parents? If I ever separated from a husband, should I ever actually get one, my parents would be first in line asking why. And I'd better have a very good reason, too.

I followed Jolene inside, my heels click-clicking on the parquet floor of the entry foyer. Ahead of us, rising to the second floor in a great curving sweep, was a staircase worthy of Scarlett and Rhett.

The foyer walls were covered with a yellow and cream floral sateen with thin navy stripes running through the pattern. I reached out a finger, and it bounced on the batting beneath the fabric. This was real class.

Jolene ignored the beauty of it all and kept talking. Of course she'd seen it all before.

"Arnie and me had differences over everything." She waved at the foyer chandelier. "Electricity. Me working. Eating dinner at my parents." I knew Jolene ate there every night. "Where to go on vacations. What wallpaper to pick. Can you believe he hated this?" She pointed at the fabric.

Arnie was obviously a philistine.

"Then we couldn't decide whether to buy a weekend place down the shore or up the mountains. And he couldn't decide on fidelity."

I was so busy photographing the yellow living room with its pale yellow carpeting and its accent wall of navy paper patterned with white daisies that I almost missed Jolene's last comment.

I lowered my camera and looked at her with compassion and sympathy, but she was stalking across the foyer toward the back of the house, apparently uninterested in my commiseration.

"Arnie!" she bellowed. "Where are you? I haven't got all day. Dinner's waiting and you aren't invited."

I followed her, my head swiveling as I walked. Suddenly I stopped before a painting of a Chester County stone farmhouse surrounded by snow-laden evergreens. I checked the bottom right corner, though I already knew what I'd see. Curtis Carlyle. GTG.

"Jolene, you've got an original Carlyle! How come you never told me?"

She stopped and turned to look at the picture. She shrugged. "I forgot. But I've got a question for you. What's that GTG thing in the corner after his name?"

"He puts that on all his work. It stands for Glory to God."

She looked at me without comprehension, then at the picture.

"It means that he's thanking God for the talent and opportunity to paint," I explained.

"Oh." She looked at the picture once more, shrugged again, and continued her trek across the vast expanse of foyer.

I stretched out my hand and traced Curt's name and the GTG. What a great guy he was.

I turned back to Jolene just as she entered the kitchen. In profile she was as beautiful as she was full on. I raised my camera, flicked the switch to continuous exposure, and pressed.

As the lens click-clicked, she stopped abruptly, frozen. I heard a quick intake of breath and saw a flash of tightening jaw through the viewfinder. Then she let out an unearthly shriek.

"Arnie!" She ran into the kitchen, out of my line of sight. "No! No! Arnie!"

The hairs on my arms rose at her tone, and I ran into the kitchen myself. I froze for an instant, too.

On the floor by the stove lay Arnie, staring upwards, blood puddling beneath and beside him on the yellow tiles.

Jolene knelt in the blood, shaking him, calling him, trying to rouse him.

She would never succeed.

THREE

Poor Arnie. He would never need all his lights on ever again.

I set my camera on the table, ran to Jolene and caught her by the shoulders.

"Jo, come on away from him," I said softly. "The police won't want us to touch him or move him."

"Merry, we've got to help him!" Her brown eyes shimmered with tears and pain. "CPR! Do you know CPR?"

I knelt and hugged her. I could feel the sticky blood beneath my knees. "Jo, it won't help. He's dead."

"No, he's not!" She reached for him again. "He's still warm."

I pulled her hands back. "He's dead," I repeated softly. "Someone has killed him. We don't want to move him or do anything that would cover up evidence."

She stared at me. "Someone killed him?"

We turned together and looked at Arnie. He stared blindly at the ceiling, gravity pulling his eyelids back into his skull. His shirtsleeves were rolled up to the elbows and one pant leg was crumpled about his calf. There was a round hole in the left lower chest area of his tan button-down shirt, not far below his heart. Blood had soaked his shirt front, though it wasn't flowing anymore. Arnie's heart no longer pumped.

I didn't want to think about the exit wound beneath him from which blood must have rushed in a torrent. It was hard to comprehend that the great pool of it covering the yellow tiles had recently flowed through his veins as surely as mine swept through my body.

"Come away, Jo." I stood and pulled her up with me. "We need to call the police."

I led her to the kitchen table and pushed her into a chair. I grabbed the wall phone and dialed 911.

"Jo," I said as I hung up in spite of the fact that the 911 voice wanted me to stay on the line. "Is there someone else we should call?"

She looked at me blankly. "Like who?"

Many days I wondered about Jo's mental acuity, but tonight I knew the slowness was shock. "Like Arnie's parents. Brothers and sisters. Pastor. Your parents."

"Oh." She shook her head. "He didn't have a family. His mom's dead and his dad disappeared when he was four. There are no brothers and sisters. And there's certainly no pastor."

She sighed in pain. "I have to tell my parents face-to-face. It's not telephone news, you know? My dad will be so upset. He loved Arnie. He was the son he never had." She shook her head. "Poor Dad."

I looked at the man on the floor. Poor Arnie was more like it.

Since Jolene had no calls to make, I quickly dialed *The News,* connecting with Mac's desk.

"Mac, I'm at Jolene and Arnie Meister's house where we just found Arnie shot to death."

He made a distressed sound. "Let me talk to her."

I gave Jolene the phone and listened to her murmur into it. Suddenly she held it out. "He wants you."

"You know what you've got to do, right?" Mac asked.

"Yeah, I know." A story by deadline tomorrow. *The News* is an afternoon paper of twelve to sixteen pages, and our deadline for news is nine, editing ten, and it's ready for delivery by noon.

I hung up and led Jo to the foyer, away from Arnie. "Come on. We'll wait in the living room."

She kept wiping her bloody hands down her coat again and again. I caught them and held them and felt them shaking.

She looked over my shoulder. "He has the tree up." She took a step toward the living room.

"Give me your coat before you go in there." There was no need to track blood through the house. I helped her slip out of it.

I took mine off, too, and we dropped them in a pile on the parquet floor. Then we sat awkwardly next to the beautiful Christmas tree on the sofa bigger than my apartment. But there was blood on our shoes and clothes as well as our hands, and we marred the pale yellow carpet and the huge sofa. Jolene never noticed.

She stood up almost as soon as we sat down. "I can't leave him alone on the kitchen floor." Tears wet her cheeks. She started unsteadily toward the kitchen.

I nodded and followed her. "We'll sit at the table."

"I want to hold his hand."

I remembered Sergeant William Poole of the Amhearst police saying to me once, "The first rule of any investigation is never touch anything at a crime scene. Never, never, never! It contaminates the evidence and makes convictions hard, should we find the perpetrator."

"I think we can't touch him, Jo. I'm sorry." I led her to a kitchen chair with a yellow plaid seat cushion.

She sat and laid her head on her arms on the table. I looked at her sadly, wishing I could ease her sorrow and knowing I couldn't.

I turned to the room. Putting my hands behind me, I made a slow circle, looking at everything and anything.

Who knew what would be important for my story? Or for the solution of the crime?

"Jolene," I said hesitantly. "I've got to take pictures." It seemed so intrusive to go flash, flash here and flash, flash there.

She raised her head. "For the paper?"

"Yes. But also to reconstruct the scene and look for possible clues."

She gave me a watery, wavery smile. "You've got the detective bug."

"Sort of," I confessed, blushing at the actual verbalizing of that thought. How pretentious of me, though I had actually solved another murder. "But I won't take any pictures if you don't want me to."

"The cops are going to photograph him, aren't they?"

I nodded.

"Then you might as well, too. Just don't put him in the paper like that."

"I'll tell Mac," I promised.

I picked up my camera and began circling the room. As I walked, I talked, as much for myself as to keep Jo from falling prey to greater shock.

"How'd you meet Arnie?" I snapped the refrigerator and the couple of notes that were held to it by magnets shaped like fruit. One note from a scratch pad said: Jolene—5:30. The other, an 8x10 printout on a certificate template, read: $50,000.00!

Jolene looked at Arnie. "We met the first day of kindergarten. He was this shrimpy little kid with big glasses and a bigger mouth. He liked to boss everyone around. I hated him."

I glanced at Arnie. "He's no shrimp now."

Jolene shook her head. "But he was all through high school. The littlest guy around. Mr. Brainiac. He and Airy were quite the pair. Two dweebs."

I thought of the beautiful Airy Bennett. "Dweebs? Airy? Arnie?"

"Hard to believe, huh? I hung out with Airy because I felt sorry for her. And people were nice to Arnie because he'd tell you all the answers or write your paper for you or whatever—for a price. He loved that kind of stuff. But Airy wouldn't even let you copy her homework. 'It's cheating, Jo.'" Jolene's voice took on a hard edge. "She was the most self-righteous thing!"

I'd never let anyone copy my homework either, but I thought I wouldn't tell Jolene that little piece of trivia.

In the sink I noticed two glasses with dark liquid dregs. I leaned over and sniffed. Iced tea. I looked for telltale lipstick on one of the glasses, hard to do since I couldn't pick them up for fear of disturbing prints. If Jolene hadn't been keeping Arnie company anymore, maybe someone else had.

I sighed. She, if there was a she, either wore that lipstick that never came off or she wore none. Or she'd wiped the glass clean of any evidence. Interesting thought, that.

I noticed a wastebasket tucked in the corner by a cabinet. I walked over and peered in. I saw crumpled paper towels with blue hearts and flowers on them, a clear plastic wrapper from some package, an empty half-gallon Tropicana orange-tangerine juice container and the box and plastic tray from a Lean Cuisine dinner, chicken marsala. No clues as far as I could see, but I took a picture anyway.

"If Arnie was such a brainiac dweeb," I said as I took a picture of the bullet lodged in the cabinet directly behind where he must have been standing when he was shot, "how did you two ever get together?" I glanced again at the man lying on the floor. "And how did he get to be such a handsome guy?"

"After high school he went away to college," Jolene said. "He'd earned all these scholarships and stuff. I didn't see him for about almost four years. Then I went to a New

Year's Eve party, and there he was. I couldn't believe it! He'd gotten so tall, and he'd started wearing contact lenses. And he pumped iron all the time. There's all kinds of weight equipment in the room down the hall."

She looked at me vaguely "He was gorgeous, wasn't he? I fell for him big-time."

"And he fell for you?" I prompted as I took a seat beside her. I pushed her purse, gloves and scarf away from the table's edge.

"Remember, he'd gone with Airy for years. It took me a couple of months to convince him to drop her."

I looked at Jolene. "Arnie had been going with Airy?"

"Since seventh grade."

"And you cut her out?"

"Yeah." Jolene unconsciously sat straighter. "It was easy."

I nodded as the ladies' room animosity suddenly made more sense.

"Would you say Airy was a late bloomer, too?" I asked.

"She's still waiting to bloom," Jolene said with more than a trace of the nastiness I'd seen earlier. I also recognized a case of wishful thinking. Airy had definitely blossomed.

The doorbell rang, causing us both to jump.

"I'll get it." I stuffed my camera in my purse and went to let the police in. I led the two uniforms to the kitchen where they took one look and phoned home. In a few more minutes, my friend Sergeant Poole of the Amhearst police arrived. A crime scene team from the state police followed quickly, as did the coroner. Even a fire truck showed up as part of the first-response team, even though I'd told the 911 operator we didn't need AFD personnel.

In no time Jolene and I found ourselves back on the huge couch again, our scarves and gloves tumbled in the pile of coats on the floor in the hall.

"What will I do about the blood on my coat?" Jolene asked, staring across the room at the collection of garments, fixing on a problem that had comprehensible ramifications. The busyness of the men in the kitchen and their purpose bewildered and overwhelmed. "I love that coat. Arnie got it for me before our troubles."

"Don't worry about it." I patted her hand. "I'll take it to the cleaners for you when I take mine."

She nodded and slumped back on the sofa. We sat silently in the brightly lit room and waited as we had been asked by Sergeant Poole.

Finally we were interviewed, though I didn't have much to say. I sat stiffly in one of the cherry dining room chairs, hoping I didn't appear guilty of anything because I wasn't. I just get a guilty complex around extreme authority. It probably went back to the time when I was a little kid and lied to my mother about where I got the candy bar I'd stolen. As I sat straight and still, stoically waiting my grilling, I studied the porcelain in the china cabinet on the far wall. One shelf was Royal Doulton figurines, their colorful images a contrast to the shelf of sleek, sophisticated Lladro porcelains. The top shelf was full of collectors' pieces of blue Wedgwood with rings of white flowers encircling them.

Where had the money and the good taste for those things come from?

Sergeant Poole sat across the table from me.

"How can I help, William?"

"How did Mrs. Meister get the blood on her hands and her coat?" he asked.

"She knelt beside Arnie when she first found him. She tried to pick him up and hold him. She didn't realize he was dead."

"Um," he said and waited. I waited, too, because I didn't have anything else to say. He knew me well enough to realize that if I had been trying to protect Jolene or if I had anything further to say, I would have blurted it when he waited. That authority reaction thing again.

Finally he asked, "What do you know about the victim?"

"Very little. I never met him. In fact, I never even saw him before tonight."

"Not a great way to make an acquaintance." And he smiled sympathetically.

I smiled back and relaxed a bit.

"Why did you come here today?" he asked.

"Jolene—Mrs. Meister—was supposed to meet her husband here."

"*Meet* him here? Doesn't she live here?"

"No. They were divorcing, and she lives in her own condominium."

His eyebrow rose. "Acrimonious divorce?"

"I don't think so." I knew exactly what he was looking for. The spouse is always the first suspect.

"Are you and Mrs. Meister good friends? Would she tell you if things were nasty between them?"

"Work friends, that's all."

He nodded. I could see my influence as a character witness shrinking faster than a blown-up balloon without a knot in the end.

"Why were they meeting?" he asked.

"I have no idea. She didn't tell me. She just asked for a lift."

"She doesn't have a car?"

"Her father drove her in to work today."

"She lives with her parents?"

I shook my head. "I told you. She owns a condo. Maybe she'd spent the night with them or something. Or maybe her father drove out to her place to get her and then drove her to work. Or maybe her car's in the shop."

"Was Mrs. Meister surprised when she found her husband?"

"Very," I said, picturing her reaction. "I think she was devastated." I paused, then asked a question I wanted answered. "How long do you think he's been dead?"

He raised his eyebrows, then said politely, "I'm not giving half-baked opinions to the press, Merry. We'll wait for the coroner's report."

"Don't get so testy, William. This isn't for publication," I hastened to assure him. "This is for me. I want to know how close you think we came to walking in on a murderer. I mean, nothing appears to have been touched or stolen. Is that because we arrived and scared someone off? Is there a very mad person out there who might not like Jo and me anymore?"

He studied me for a minute. "Okay, off the record. I don't think you scared anyone away. I think he's been dead for maybe three hours."

"Why do you think that?"

"You sure you want to know?"

I nodded, hoping I wouldn't regret this.

"The white, waxy condition of his skin, the flatness of the eyes indicating loss of fluid and the lividity."

I'd noticed the purple-blue on the back of his arms and on the underside of the exposed calf where the blood left in his body had gathered in response to the pull of gravity.

"And," he finished, "rigor appears to have begun in the smaller muscles."

"But he's still warm to the touch."

"The body cools slowly, a degree or two an hour."

"Dust to dust doesn't take long, does it?"

Sergeant Poole grunted noncommittally. "Where were you all afternoon, Merry?"

"Me?" I think my voice squeaked.

He nodded.

"At work. Lots of people saw me. Lots." And a cannibalistic plant. "You don't think I had anything to do with Arnie's death, do you?"

William Poole smiled slightly. He had an interesting lopsided smile which sat pleasantly on his furrowed face.

"Not really, but I have to ask. It's what I get paid for. Now what about Mrs. Meister? Where was she all afternoon?"

"At work, too."

"Do me a favor," he asked congenially. "Write down the times you had any conversation or contact with Mrs. Meister during the afternoon. One of my men will stop by for the list tomorrow."

"I'll have it ready." I'd be more than happy to provide Jolene's alibi.

"Do you know you have blood on your hands, Merry?"

I looked at them and shivered. The blood was dried around my nails. "I got it when I pulled Jolene away from the body. I know I have some on my shoes and on my coat from when I knelt beside her. Even my knees."

Shortly after that, I was dismissed. Both Jolene and I were in the living room waiting for permission to leave when an officer came to us.

"We're going to remove the body now," he said. "I wanted to warn you because I don't know if you want to see him carried out in a body bag. I'd like to give you the opportunity to leave the room."

I glanced at Jolene who looked horrified.

"A body bag," she whispered. "Oh, no!"

I heard the wheels of the gurney roll across the parquet. I grabbed Jolene, turned her from the door, and held her as they wheeled Arnie from his brightly lit home for the final time. I felt my eyes fill with tears, and I didn't even know the man. I couldn't imagine how Jo felt. Her shoulders were shaking.

When she and I were finally given permission to leave, I glanced at my watch. It was 8:30. We'd been at the house for about three hours. I was already a half hour late for the photos of the AAC-FOP committee, and I had to take Jolene home yet. I shrugged. Hopefully the committee had lots of last-minute plans to make and would still be there by the time I managed to make it.

We drove back to Amhearst in silence. I kept thinking that one second you're alive, and the next you can be dead. One minute your brain is zipping electrical impulses all over your body, the next it's flat line. One minute your blood is racing through your veins, and the next it's a pool all over the yellow tile floor.

A mystery, if ever there was one. What did you think about this phenomenon called death if you didn't believe that absent from the body was present with the Lord?

We drove through downtown Amhearst, past the cluster of brightly decorated stores open until nine in a mostly vain attempt to attract the Christmas business back from the malls. Shortly we pulled up before half of a double on Houston Street in the older, less prosperous part of town.

The light by the front door showed a porch covered with bright green indoor/outdoor carpeting and lined with black wrought-iron railings. In spite of it being December, two white molded plastic chairs sat on either side of a small white plastic table in the center of the porch. On the table was an arrangement of plastic greens and an angel whose head turned from side to side. A wreath of plastic greens with a mashed plaid bow hung between the storm door and the inside door.

I couldn't imagine anything more unlike the mansion we'd just left.

Jolene grabbed my arm. "Come in with me, Merry. I can't face my parents alone. They loved Arnie. They really did."

The last thing I wanted to do was help break the news of the tragedy, but I opened my car door and climbed out. We started up the steps as the door of the other half of the double opened. A man in a camel topcoat came rushing out only to stop short when he saw us.

"Jolene," he said and sort of reached for her.

"Reilly." Jolene nodded at the man but kept walking up the stairs, making it obvious that she wasn't stopping for conversation.

Reilly watched her with a hungry expression, but when Jolene kept moving, he went down the steps to a car at the curb.

"Who's he?" I asked as we reached the porch.

"Reilly Samson. He works with Arnie. His grandmother lives next door."

"Her?" I indicated the gap between the curtains next door where an eye stared at us. I smiled and nodded. The curtain promptly fell back in place.

"Old Mrs. Samson, the world's nosiest neighbor," Jolene muttered. Her face twisted. "Wait until she hears about Arnie! She'll probably celebrate."

"What?" I was shocked.

"She hated him."

"Why?"

"Who knows. She's just a bitter old lady who hates everyone."

"Even Reilly?"

"Sometimes I think so."

"Even you?" I couldn't resist asking.

"Especially me," Jolene said.

"Really? Why?"

"Because I got rich." With that, she opened the front door.

The house was a typical Amhearst double with two stories plus basement and attic. The rooms ran in a front-to-back pattern of living room, dining room, kitchen, and back porch on the first level with a large staircase in the front hall running to the second floor where a hall opened into three large bedrooms and a bath. The third-floor attic where the roof pulled the walls in would be a single huge room. A postage stamp of a backyard finished the property.

As soon as we came through the front door, an older man and woman rushed into the hall, swooping down on us and burying us in solicitude and questions about Jolene's tardiness. I was surprised because I hadn't realized that Jolene's grandparents lived here, too.

"Come in, come in," the man kept saying to me, beaming as he tried to take my coat. A slight Southern accent colored his voice. "I'm so glad Jolene brought a friend home with her!"

"Are you all right, Jolene Marie?" The woman scanned Jo's face and hugged her shoulders. "You don't look well, dear. Maybe we need to make it warmer for you? We can turn up the thermostat, can't we, Alvin? Or maybe you just want to come into the kitchen. I saved your dinner. There's plenty for your friend, too. Are you certain you're all right?" And she pulled Jolene to her bosom again.

Jolene pulled away from the smothering arms and said, "Mom, that's enough! Dad, make her stop."

Mom? Dad? Not Grandmom and Grandpop?

"Easy, Eloise," Jo's dad said, patting the woman on the shoulder. "We need to meet Jolene's friend."

Suddenly I was being stared at by two curious elderly gnomes, one with vague blue eyes, one with sharp brown ones.

"This is Merry Kramer, Merry as in Christmas. We work together." Jo made it sound as if I were a fellow escapee from a chain gang.

"Merry." Jolene's mother smiled sweetly at me. "What a lovely name, especially this time of year. Were you born in December, dear? I just bet you were."

"June," I said.

"Oh." She looked confused. "I thought Jolene Marie said Merry."

I must have looked equally confused because Jolene's father said, "The month of June, Eloise. Not the name."

The woman smiled sweetly. "Oh, of course. Silly me."

She looked older than my Grandmom Kramer by several years, though I knew she couldn't be. Grandmom

Kramer was seventy-nine, and there's no way she could have a daughter as young as Jolene. Of course the appearance of age could have been caused by this woman's determinedly gray hair and the too-tight permanent, the unbecoming glasses and the lined face.

As I smiled my sweetest at Jolene's mother and father, I searched my mind for Jolene's maiden name. Carlsbad. Mammoth. Jewel. It had something to do with caves or caverns. Ah! Luray!

"Mr. and Mrs. Luray, how nice to meet you." I shook their hands prettily. My mother would have been proud.

"Right this way, girls," Mrs. Luray said. "The food's waiting."

Mr. Luray was wrestling me for my coat while my stomach growled at the wondrous aromas that filled the air. No wonder Jolene came home for dinner every night. "I can't stay." AAC-FOP was waiting. "I'm sorry."

"I wish you would." Mr. Luray's fingers wrapped around my coat collar as he tried to drag it off my shoulders. He was bald, homely, wore thick glasses and had muscles on muscles. It was obvious he and Arnie had bonded over weights. "Jolene doesn't bring friends home much."

"Dad," Jolene said sharply. "Let Merry alone, for heaven's sake!"

Mr. Luray nodded pleasantly. "Okay." His hands fell from my collar.

Mrs. Luray peered first at Jolene, then at me. "You do look pale, Jolene Marie. You do. So do you, Merry, but then maybe you're always pale. I wouldn't know, would I?" She smiled vaguely at me, patting my hand.

I smiled vaguely back.

"But are you sure you girls are all right? Have you had a disagreement or something? I know that when I have a fight with Mrs. Samson, Dad can always tell because I look so pale." She smiled at me again. "Not that we have that many fights, you know. But that's how it shows when we do. Or maybe—" and her smile faltered as she turned to Jo "—maybe you had a fight with Arnie, dear? You didn't have another fight with him, did you, Jolene Marie? I can't stand it when you two fight." She looked as if she might cry.

Jolene looked at me in helpless frustration.

"Now, Mother," Mr. Luray said. "Don't get yourself so worked up. Your heart will start fluttering."

Oh, boy. A fluttering heart. Just what we needed with the news we were bearing.

"Do you take heart medicine, Mrs. Luray?" I asked.

"Aren't you sweet to be concerned," she said. "Yes. I keep it handy all the time in case I need it."

"Where is it?"

"In the kitchen on the windowsill over the sink. And upstairs both in the bathroom and on my night table."

"Mr. Luray," I said, "I think it would be a good idea if you got your wife's medicine."

Mr. Luray looked at me with narrowed eyes, saw something in my face, and headed for the kitchen and the windowsill.

"Bring a big plastic bag back with you, Dad," Jolene called. A muffled assent drifted to us.

"What?" Mrs. Luray seemed confused, which I now suspected was a normal situation. "What's wrong? Jolene Marie, why do I need my medicine? Oh, I knew it! You and Arnie did fight! You didn't hit him, did you, dear? Tell me you didn't hit him! Or throw something at him. It's so unladylike."

"Mom!" Jolene shouted fiercely. "Can't you ever shut up? I can't stand you when you run on like that!"

Mrs. Luray and I both stared at Jolene. I, in startled disbelief at her tone of voice, her mother with acceptance.

"I'm sorry, dear. I didn't mean to upset you, but then I can see that you're already upset, aren't you? Why, dear? Tell

Mommy. You'll feel better if you tell me. Don't worry. I can take it. Just tell me. You did fight with Arnie, didn't you?"

Jolene put her hands to her face in aggravation.

Mr. Luray appeared, a pill bottle clutched in his right hand and the plastic bag in his left. Jolene took the bag and handed it to me. As I held the bag open, she stuffed her coat in. "My scarf and gloves are still in the car."

I nodded, pulling the ties to shut the bag. "I'll get them."

"What's she doing with your coat, Jolene Marie?" Mrs. Luray asked. "It's a special coat because Arnie gave it to you. What's she going to do with it?"

"It's dirty, Mom," Jolene said through gritted teeth. "She's taking it to the dry cleaners for me."

Mrs. Luray's face lit with joy. "Why, how sweet, June," she said to me.

I opened my mouth to say "Merry," but refrained. She wasn't listening to me anyway.

"Daddy," Mrs. Luray said, her high voice tinged with sorrow. "Jolene Marie and Arnie had a fight. She's just going to tell us about it. Isn't it too sad?"

"What's wrong, Jo?" Mr. Luray said. His manner was stark and aware.

"Yes, dear." Mrs. Luray's hands fluttered with a life of their own, pale butterflies with age spots marking the wings. "Tell us."

Jolene took a deep breath, then looked steely eyed at her parents. "Arnie's dead," she said baldly. "He was shot."

Mrs. Luray gasped once, twice, three times, clutched her chest, and sank to the floor.

FOUR

I stared at the frail woman lying on the floor. "Should we do CPR? Call 911? Stick that medicine under her tongue or something?"

Jolene and her father looked at each other, then shook their heads in unison.

"Don't worry," Jolene said wearily. "She'll be okay."

"Jolene!" I fell to my knees beside the unconscious woman. "What if she dies right here on the floor?"

Jo and her father continued to ignore Mrs. Luray in favor of a conversation about Arnie.

"Is he really dead?" Mr. Luray asked.

Jolene nodded.

"Shot?"

She nodded again.

He hugged himself, and a tear slid down his wrinkled cheek. "Oh, Jolene! Why? Who?"

"I have no idea, Daddy." Jolene went to her father. She held him and rocked him like a mother might comfort a hurting child. His shoulders shook and his breath came raggedly. The man was heartbroken.

I was moved by his grief, but I kept looking at Mrs. Luray, lying there on the floor. I pulled a fuchsia and kelly green afghan off the back of the red sofa, and tucked it around the woman. I searched for her pulse, expecting to find a thready, thin, and erratic rhythm. I blinked. Her pulse was so strong you'd have thought a tympanist was in there whopping out the "wonderful, counselor, the mighty God, the everlasting Father, Prince of Peace" section of last week's performance of The Messiah at the Community Center.

"She's fine," I blurted.

Jolene released her father, and they both looked down at me.

"Always," Mr. Luray said. He sniffed and swallowed. "Come on, Jo. We'd better get her on the sofa. She'll be upset if she finds herself on the floor."

Jolene nodded. She and her father bent in unison and lifted Mrs. Luray, afghan and all, and laid her gently on the sofa. Jolene stuck a fluffy kelly green pillow under her mother's head. They'd obviously done this many times before.

"I'm sorry if you were scared." Mr. Luray held out a hand and helped me to my feet. "It's just Eloise's way of dealing with things she doesn't want to think about." He looked at her affectionately. "She's very delicate, very sensitive, you know."

I looked at Mrs. Luray. I wasn't certain *delicate* and *sensitive* were the words I'd have used.

She began to stir. "What happened? Where am I? Alvin?"

Mr. Luray sat on the edge of the sofa and opened the pill bottle. He slid a flat, white disk into his hand. "Shh, Eloise. I'm right here. Put this pill under your tongue, and you'll be fine in no time."

Jolene leaned toward me. "It's a Tums," she whispered.

I stared at Mrs. Luray. "Does this happen often?"

She shrugged. "Depends on how you define often. She was passing out several times a day when Arnie and I first separated. Now she can talk about it without any trouble. You saw that."

"Oh!" Mrs. Luray said suddenly and in great distress.

I spun around, expecting her to black out again as she recalled the terrible news about Arnie.

"Smell that!" she said. "Jolene, your dinner's burning!" She struggled to her feet and moved quickly to the kitchen. "I'll save it!"

Jolene watched her mother leave the room, then went to her father. "Are you all right, Dad?"

"Not really." He put his arm around her waist and they leaned into each other, sorrow etched on both faces.

I collected Jolene's coat and let myself out as Eloise Luray called, "Everything's all right, Jolene Marie. I saved your dinner for you."

Bone-weary, I wanted to go home and climb into a hot tub and soak away the traumas of the day. Instead, dutiful employee that I was, I drove to the Community Center.

I was over an hour late, and I hadn't had time or opportunity to do anything about cleaning myself up. I raced into the AAC-FOP meeting room, hoping the blood on my coat didn't show and that no one noticed my fingernails and knees. At least the blood on my shoes was long dried or worn off.

I found the committee huddled around a table, faces focused in concentration, papers strewn in organized chaos. A barrel-chested man with a mane of white hair and a slight limp was prowling the floor, talking and gesticulating, but I hardly noticed him.

All I could see was Curt whom I hadn't realized would be here. He looked so strong and sane and normal. All I wanted was his embrace to wash away the past few hours.

When he saw me, he lost his polite, I-wish-I-were-somewhere-else expression and smiled broadly.

"We can do it, folks!" the white-haired man was saying, and I pulled my attention reluctantly from Curt. "I know we can do it. We can feed not only the needy of Amhearst but of the surrounding communities, too. Why, we're almost past last year's total, and we have another week to go. And the local grocers have yet to make their contributions. With the coverage *The News* is going to give us, the Amhearst Annual Christmas Food Project will make history!"

He was so good at pep talks that even I, weary as I was, felt a slight urge to cheer with the other wildly clapping people around the table. Instead I concentrated on dragging my camera out of my purse.

"And here, I presume, is our photographer now!" The white-haired man said and everyone turned.

I smiled weakly in apology for being so late.

"Come on, everyone," the man said. "It's free PR time. Let's get ourselves set for our picture." And he began telling everyone where to stand. He finished with, "Curt, stand right there in the middle. You're our celebrity and honorary chairman, and we want to take advantage of that."

I felt Curt's eyes on me and became unexpectedly shy. I studied my camera intently, adjusting this and manipulating that. My problem was that I could never quite figure out how to react to him in public.

Back when I'd gone with Jack, he ignored me most of the time, sort of expecting I'd follow along, which like an idiot I did, so public response wasn't an issue. Now I worried about Curt. I couldn't rush to his side because we weren't really going together or anything—though I suspected that was more my fault than his. I also couldn't ignore him. Basic manners aside, I didn't want to. I mean, maybe someday he and I would be going together. I hope, I hope. I think. Maybe.

So I stood there flat-footed and thought about how gorgeous he looked and how worn I must look and how shallow I was not to be thinking of the tragedy of Arnie.

Curt ignored his orders to stand in the middle and walked over to me. "Hi."

Sudden tears sprang to my eyes. "Hi." It came out as a whisper. I realized for the first time how close I was to losing control.

Curt took my arm, concern leaping to his face. "Are you all right?"

"Barely."

He began to lead me to a chair. "Sit down."

I pulled my arm free and shook my head. "If I sit, I'll start to cry and ruin my professional image. If I have one left after my lateness."

He started to protest, but I cut in. "I'll tell you all about it later." I saw over Curt's shoulder that the white-haired man was bearing down on us. "And you'd better go stand in the middle before you're dragged there."

He went to stand where he'd been told as the white-haired man came up to me.

"Hello, there, darlin'," he said, smiling with great charm. "I'm Harry Allen Bushay."

I looked at him with interest. Was this the Bushay of Bushay Environmental where Jack was working on his audit?

"How do you do, Mr. Bushay." I extended my hand, blood encrusted nails and all. He took it and held it a moment or two too long. He leaned close.

"Just call me Harry Allen, darlin'."

"Thank you," I said noncommittally.

With a cozy, just-between-you-and-me grin, Harry Allen turned and took his place next to Curt. I snapped several pictures, hoping that everyone looked decent in at least one of them. I had pulled out my spiral tablet to get everyone's name when Harry Allen handed me a sheet of paper.

"Here are our names," he said helpfully. "They are in order and all spelled correctly."

"Thank you," I said as I flipped my tablet closed. "How thoughtful of you."

"I'm a thoughtful kind of guy, darlin'."

I smiled weakly. The last thing I felt like dealing with tonight was a flirt with white hair, no matter how premature the white or how charming the manner.

I needn't have worried. Harry Allen turned and with a clap of his hands called the AAC-FOP meeting back to order. "Only fifteen more minutes, people. Only fifteen more minutes."

Everyone took their places at the table except Curt.

"I don't have to stay," he said as he helped me into my coat. "I'm only the honorary chairman."

"It must be tough being a celebrity," I teased. "Why, I even saw an original Carlyle hanging in a mansion tonight."

He grinned. "I hope you were properly impressed."

We walked out of the meeting room and into the front hall, shoulders rubbing companionably. I still had trouble comprehending that this man said he was falling in love with me. Me!

I was slim enough and not too tall, but I had this spiky hair that insisted on drooping, a striped nose, and a prickly side to my nature that had been asserting itself with a vengeance since I'd moved to Amhearst. I kept waiting for him to realize his mistake and fall for someone like, say, Airy. Someone beautiful and lovely and all those other wondrous, feminine things. Why, I bite my nails, for goodness sake!

Curt stopped in the hall and checked over his shoulder. When he was certain we were alone, he turned me to face him. "What's wrong, Merry?"

"Oh, Curt," I sobbed, burying my face in his chest. "We found him shot, and then she tried to move him and the police questioned us and her mom fainted and they ignored her and—"

"Whoa." He patted me gently on the back. "Just cry and then tell me. Both at once don't work too well."

Of course, as soon as he told me I could cry, the tears dried up, sort of like a toothache disappearing as soon as you entered the dentist's office. I huddled against him a few minutes longer, then stepped reluctantly back.

"Poor Arnie," I said.

"Arnie?"

"Meister, Jolene's ex or almost ex. Though now I guess he'll never get to full ex status, will he?" Somehow that seemed very sad. Not that ex status was a good thing, but never to achieve it or anything else ever again, that was sad.

Curt took hold of my shoulders. "If I follow you correctly, you're saying that Jolene's husband has been shot?"

I lifted shaking hands and brushed my hair out of my eyes. "Killed. Murdered. We found him."

He looked at me with such concern that the tears sprang to my eyes again. This man could do extraordinary things to me.

Suddenly the phone on the receptionist's desk in the darkened office to our right began to ring. I jumped at the noise.

"Should we answer it? Maybe it's for someone here." I took a step toward the office.

He put a hand on my arm. "The answering machine will get it. That's what it's for."

Sure enough, the machine kicked in after the second ring.

"If anyone can hear this," a voice boomed loudly, "and Harry Allen Bushay is still there, please get him to the phone. This is the police."

Curt and I looked at each other. Then I lunged for the phone, and he took off for the meeting room.

"We're getting Mr. Bushay," I told the person on the other end. "He'll be right here."

"Thank you," said a familiar voice.

"William, is that you?"

"Who's this?" he countered suspiciously.

"Merrileigh Kramer."

There was a short pause. Then William asked, "What are you doing at the Community Center with Mr. Bushay?"

"Taking his picture."

"What?"

"For the paper. He chairs the Amhearst Annual Christmas Food Project, and my assignment is to take a committee picture. I'm just fortunate they were still here because I was very late." I minded my manners; I didn't say it was his fault.

"Interesting that you have been with two people closely associated with Mr. Meister this evening, isn't it, Merry?"

Harry Allen was associated with Arnie? "Coincidence, Sergeant."

"So you say," he answered, but I could hear a smile in his voice.

Before I had time to respond, Harry Allen came hurrying down the hall, worry and apprehension written all over his face. He grabbed the phone from me.

"Yes?" he barked. "What is it?"

Whatever William Poole said, it seemed to alleviate Harry Allen's fear. His shoulders eased and his brow cleared. Then, abruptly, he jerked upright.

"What? You can't be serious!"

As Harry Allen listened some more, I looked at Curt. Should we leave or should we wait and see if he needed assistance of any kind—though the idea of Harry Allen Bushay needing assistance seemed ludicrous to me.

"Yes," he finally said. "I'll come right away. No, I do not wish to wait until tomorrow. I want to get it over with. I'll be there in a few minutes."

He hung up the phone and stood still a minute, lost in thought, appearing almost disoriented.

"Can we do anything for you, Harry Allen?" Curt asked. "Help in any way?"

He looked up. "Yes," he said. "You can tell the committee that the meeting's over for tonight."

Curt nodded.

"Oh, never mind," Harry Allen said in disgust. "I'll do

it. I have to go back in anyway to get my coat. I have to go to the police station."

I looked at him with great interest. "Arnie Meister?"

He focused all his intensity on me. "How did you know that call was about Arnie Meister?"

"I talked to Sergeant Poole tonight at Arnie's house. I was with Arnie's wife when she found his body."

One bushy eyebrow rose. "Bad?" he asked.

I nodded, tearing up yet again. Curt put his arm around me and pulled me close.

Harry Allen snorted, half in distress, half in disbelief. "Arnie Meister's dead. Murdered. Absolutely unbelievable. Wait till they find out that he and I had a big fight yesterday. I mean a *big* fight. And wait until they try to get me to tell them what it was about." He looked at us, his lips clamped together. "I'm not talking to anyone."

FIVE

Curt and I sat in a booth at McDonald's where I stared unenthusiastically at my cheeseburger.

"Come on, Merry," Curt urged. "You'll feel better if you get some food in you."

I pulled a French fry out of the red cardboard holder and nibbled. "It feels like everything's sticking in my throat."

"Take a drink."

I obediently sipped, and the moisture helped the dryness. Maybe the Coke's bubbles would settle my stomach.

"There was so much blood, Curt. It's hard not to keep seeing it." I shivered as I looked at the little cup of catsup he had placed next to his fries.

He took my hand in his. "Merry, you'll be okay. Just give yourself time. But for now, eat." He put my cheeseburger in my other hand. "Bite. Chew." I did. Satisfied, he took a huge bite of his Big Mac.

The door behind me flew open, and I glanced over my shoulder. Anything to stop staring at the cheeseburger. Airy Bennett and a strange man entered, followed by my old Pittsburgh flame and current Amhearst pursuer, Jack Hamilton.

Ack! Just the perfect ending to a perfect day. Jack and Curt and me, a jolly threesome at McDonald's. Rub-a-dub-dub, three men in a tub. I could feel an ulcer developing as I sat there. I shrank as low in my seat as I could.

But Jack didn't see us. He was too busy talking to his companions. He paused in his story only long enough to order his meal and follow Airy and the man to a table across the room where he sat with his back toward me. Risk diminished.

But not alleviated. He might glance around at some point and see me. Surely even self-absorbed Jack got curious about the people around him, didn't he?

All unaware of potential disaster, Curt continued eating. When his eyes slued from his food to someone approaching our table, I knew the worst was about to happen.

"It is you, isn't it?"

That wasn't Jack's voice. Giddy with relief, I smiled at Airy Bennet.

She looked anxiously at me. "You're the woman who was with Jolene Meister earlier today, aren't you? I recognize the red coat."

I nodded.

"Well," she said, "I've got to apologize. I am very embarrassed by the way I acted."

I waved my hand in a dismissive gesture. "Don't worry. It's okay."

"No, it's not, though it's kind of you to say so." She smiled, and I thought she was probably a nice person when away from Jolene. At least she didn't deny her complicity in the fight.

She continued. "Jolene has brought out the worst in me for years. I'm always dumb enough to get sucked in, no matter how many times I promise myself I won't let her push my buttons. I see her again and boom! I explode." She sighed. "Maybe someday I'll grow up." She said it without much hope.

"Don't worry," I repeated. "As far as the traumas of the day go, it's at the bottom of the list, believe me."

Since she didn't know about the traumas at the top of

the list, Airy thought I was just being polite. "Believe it or not," she said, "it's not like me to be so nasty."

I nodded. Standing here with her coffee in her hand, she looked like a regular person, reasonably polite and intelligent. Besides, I knew Jolene.

"When I told Sean how I made a fool of myself, he couldn't believe it." She glanced back toward Jack and the other man. "That's Sean," she said. "The blond guy."

Sean looked up at that moment and smiled widely at Airy. I noticed the mustache Jolene had referred to. It wasn't very obvious at this distance, his being blond and all, but it looked nice as far as I could tell. He saw me looking at him and dipped his head in acknowledgment. Jack started to turn to see who Sean was looking at, and I spun around so fast I made myself dizzy.

"By the way, I'm Airy Bennett," she said, holding out her hand. "We never did get introduced earlier." She grinned ruefully.

"Merrileigh Kramer," I said. "And this is Curt Carlyle."

Airy looked again at Curt. "Of course," she said, and I grinned proudly at him. Big-time artist. Name recognition. "Mr. Carlyle. I thought you looked familiar. You teach phys ed and coach—what? Soccer or something?"

So much for being a famous artist. I was disappointed, though he didn't seem to mind.

"I coach soccer and tennis," he said, "but I don't teach anymore."

"I was a senior the first year you taught." Airy grinned. "We girls were all so impressed to have a single male teacher who was good-looking and all. I bet they miss you now."

"I doubt it," Curt said with his charming smile.

Airy suddenly waved her arm toward Sean. "Come here, honey," she called. "I'd like you to meet some people."

Double ack! I wondered if I could slide under the table before Jack saw me, but Curt and Airy'd probably notice.

The blond man walked to our table, soda cup in his hand. Introductions were once again made. I smiled weakly.

"So you like to eat late, elegant dinners just like we do." Sean raised his cardboard cup.

"Class all the way," agreed Curt.

Everyone smiled and wondered what to say next. Into our little silence my social bomb detonated.

"Merry? Merry! Is that you, sweetheart?" Jack had approached when I wasn't looking. "What are you doing here?" He slid into the seat beside me and kissed me on the cheek. His breath smelled like French fries. He looked absolutely delighted to see me.

I sat turned to stone. I wanted to look at Curt and see his reaction, but I couldn't make myself lift my eyes from the stupid cheeseburger.

"This is the girl I was telling you about," he said to Airy and Sean, no doubt beaming as he took one of my fries and dunked it in Curt's catsup. "She's the reason I took the job at Bushay. Isn't she wonderful?"

Help me, Lord! Help me get out of this mess! I'll never shirk from saying what needs to be said again. I promise! Just please don't let it get any worse!

Jack looked at me. "Sean here works at Bushay. He's their comptroller, and he's helping me get acclimated as I begin the audit."

I found I could look at Sean. "That's nice," I managed.

"I'm Jack Hamilton, by the way." He stretched his arm across the table to shake hands with Curt. "Merry's boyfriend."

Oh, Lord, I asked that it wouldn't get worse!

I still couldn't look at Curt, who no doubt was wondering how he could have fallen for someone cowardly enough to keep Jack's presence in town a secret. Or maybe—and I almost gasped audibly at the thought—maybe he thought I was trying to be coy and play him against Jack!

"Her boyfriend?" Curt said. "Really?" I shivered as I heard the acid in his voice.

"Really," Jack said happily, complacently. "She's my best girl, my only girl." With a proprietary air, he slid his arm across my shoulders.

I jerked as the weight of his arm fell on me. When I did, my left elbow snapped forward, bumping hard into my Coke. It toppled, the lid popped off and the dark liquid ran unerringly and with great speed across the table and into Curt's lap.

I groaned and squeezed my eyes shut.

Curt sputtered as the cold Coke drenched him. He jumped to his feet as much as he could in the booth and grabbed for a cluster of napkins. He built a paper dam to hold back the surging flood, but it breached the dam at the sides and made new caramel-colored spatters on his khakis.

Such was the state of my nerves that I started to giggle. I slapped a hand over my mouth, but I couldn't stop.

"I'm sorry," I said or tried to say. I think I got as far as I before the giggles got me again. I may not be good at a lot, but at making a fool of myself, I'm first-rate.

"Are you okay, old man?" Jack asked Curt with a complete lack of genuine interest. If I wanted to think bad thoughts, I'd think Jack was enjoying the whole mess.

"Here." Airy thrust a handful of napkins at Curt. She slapped others down on the soda on the table, sopping it up. She at least had been practical and run to the condiment stand where she'd grabbed as many napkins as were available.

"We need a cleanup over here," Sean called to a girl behind the counter. She nodded and disappeared into the back, never to return.

"Thanks," Curt took the proffered napkins from Airy and brushed at his soaked pants. He tried to slide out of the booth without getting splattered anymore and ended up sitting on a couple of ice cubes that had flown straight and true to where they could do the most damage.

"You'd better go home and get changed," said Jack blandly. "We wouldn't want you to catch a cold or anything. I'll take care of Merry."

He sounded so proprietary that I almost gagged. That's what happens, I told myself, when you neglect to tell someone that things have moved beyond his knowledge of the situation.

Curt looked at me and I looked sadly back. I had stopped giggling, but now all I wanted to do was cry. He probably hated me for not being open with him.

Well, no. I caught myself. Not hate. That was too nasty a word for Curt. Maybe he just disliked me, thought I had deceived him, duped him, played him false, hoodwinked him, defrauded him, taken him for a ride.

I took a deep breath. When I started reeling off synonyms, I was in way over my emotional head.

Too much for one day, Lord. Way too much.

"Merry, are you all right?" Curt asked quietly as he stood beside the booth.

I saw that he understood how confused, distressed and embarrassed I felt. Maybe he even understood what a rotten person I was sometimes. Tears began to slide down my cheeks. I didn't deserve someone as nice as him to fall for me. I deserved someone insensitive and unfeeling like Jack. Not that I wanted him, but I deserved him.

Airy looked at me in surprise. "It's okay, Merry," she said kindly. "His slacks will clean."

Jack looked at me and stiffened when he saw the tears. "Come on, Merry. What's the big deal? It's only spilled soda."

"She's had a very bad night," Curt explained. "I need to get her home."

Everybody looked at me, and all I could do was nod and

sniff. I smiled a wobbly smile in Curt's direction and grabbed my scarf and purse. Not only did I need to get out of here before I made a greater fool of myself; I also had to get Curt away before he mentioned the cause for my bad night. It appeared that Airy didn't yet know that Arnie was dead, and I didn't want to be there when she found out. Curt, of course, didn't realize the danger.

Poor Curt. It was hard to be a principal player in a story when you didn't know all the plotlines.

Airy reached into her purse and pulled out her tissue packet and handed it to me. I took it with shaking hands and decided she definitely was nice.

"I'll be okay," I managed shakily. "Curt's right. I just need to get home."

Jack sat like a lump, blocking my exit. I nudged him pointedly. He looked at me and smiled. He didn't move.

"We all have bad days, Merry," he said with what he considered to be sympathy. "You just can't let it get to you."

"This was a bit more than your average bad day," Curt said as he reached over and wiped a tear from my cheek.

My heart swelled with delight. He was defending me in spite of what a dodo I'd been!

I shoved Jack. "Let me out. Now."

Jack buckled under the gaze of the entire group and slid slowly to the edge of the bench. I prodded him along. When I got free, I planned to grab Curt and pull him out of here before he talked too much.

I heard Curt take a deep breath and saw Airy, Sean and Jack look in his direction. Jack even stopped sliding to listen.

No, Lord! Please, no!

I socked Jack in the shoulder. "Move!" I hissed desperately but to no avail.

Curt the Kind, Defender of Distressed Damsels, said the inevitable. "Merry and a coworker found the coworker's husband murdered this evening."

Everybody blinked in surprise and turned to me. I smiled weakly and watched Airy for her reaction.

She saw me looking at her. "Who?" she asked with real fear.

"I'm sorry, Airy," I said sadly. "Arnie's dead."

"Arnie." She staggered and her face lost its color. Sean grabbed her and lowered her to the chair across the aisle from us.

Curt looked at her, consternation on his face. "I'm sorry. I didn't know."

I gave Jack a final shove and freed myself from the booth.

"They were old friends from school," I said, squeezing Curt's hand. "You couldn't have known." I knelt in front of Airy.

"Why? How?" she mumbled, eyes bright with tears. "Who? Who would do a terrible thing like that to poor Arnie?"

"He was shot at his house sometime late this afternoon," I said. "Jolene and I found him." That warm, yellow room appeared in my mind, Arnie lying on the floor, and I felt sick all over again. "I have no idea who's responsible."

Airy shook her head. "I can't believe it! Why would anyone do that? Arnie was such a great guy." She looked at Sean, her great, gray eyes shimmering with tears.

Sean had his arm around his wife's shoulder. "You mean Arnie Meister, right?"

I nodded.

"Is that the guy from Bushay?" Jack asked Sean. "The guy I met yesterday?"

"Yeah." Sean's shoulders slumped. "The guy in marketing. Airy's known him for years. They actually went together for several years before she met me." He patted her shoulder awkwardly but tenderly.

"Wow." Jack shook his head in amazement. "I never knew anyone who got murdered before."

We all chose to ignore his comment.

"I'm sorry, Airy," I said again, taking her hands in mine. They were ice.

She nodded dumbly.

Sean left her side, went to their table and came back with her coat. He pulled her to her feet and helped her into it. He reached into her pockets and pulled out her gloves, holding them out to her one at a time. She stuck her hands in without being aware of what she did.

"Come on." He handed Airy her purse. "We're going home."

She blinked, looked at the purse in her gloved hands, then reached for her neck. "My scarf," she said.

We all looked at the table, but it wasn't there.

"It must be in the car, honey." Sean pulled her collar up and kissed her. He took her elbow and led her outside. As soon as the door swung shut, Curt touched my arm and indicated the other door. I nodded and we turned to go.

"Merry, wait," Jack called as he grabbed his coat.

"Another time, Hamilton." Curt let the door fall shut on Jack's protests.

I got into my car and drove home with Curt following in his car. I turned down the lane that led to the converted carriage house where I had an apartment and pulled into the little parking area. We walked down the sidewalk to my first-floor apartment, passing the great lilac tree, creaking in the cold.

Curt took my key from me, inserted it in the lock, and opened the door for me.

"Thanks," I said. "I'm sorry."

He looked down at me, his eyebrow arched above his glasses, his lips in a wry smile. He shook his head. "You are amazing."

"In a good sense like, 'Wow, you're amazing!' or in a bad sense as in, 'Ack, you're amazing'?"

"Both," he said.

I nodded. "I was afraid of that."

"But we'll talk about it another time. Right now you just need to get in there and go to bed."

"After I write my story."

For the first time he noticed that I had my laptop slung over my shoulder.

"Merry!" he protested, ever my protector. "You've been through enough for one evening!"

I put my hand over his mouth. "Curt, we've had this discussion before. I have a job I love, and I'm going to do it, even when it's difficult."

He just looked at me and shook his head. "Amazing." Then he bent to kiss me good-night, his arms wrapping tightly about me. I hung on, drawing strength from his strength. His love and understanding scared me because they seemed too good to be true, but there was no doubt about it: He was a great hugger and kisser.

He finally pulled back and said huskily, "Good night, Merry."

He walked back to his car whistling, "Merrily we roll along, roll along, roll along."

He liked to whistle it, he said, because I was the only person he knew who had her own song. Funny how something that used to drive me wild when others did it, especially Jack, now seemed endearing.

I was smiling as I shut the door behind me. I was still smiling as I walked to answer the ringing phone.

"And just who was that big oaf kissing you on your front doorstep?" an angry voice demanded.

SIX

"Where are you, Jack?" I was sputtering with anger.

"Look out your window, sweetheart, and I'll wave to you."

"You followed me home!"

"Somebody's got to take care of you, baby, because you're sure not picking your company very well."

The nerve of the man! "Who I come home with is my business, not yours."

"What you do has been my business for more than six years, sweetheart."

"Well, not anymore! And get out of my parking lot!" I slapped the receiver firmly back in its cradle.

When the phone rang again, I lifted the receiver, heard, "Merry!" in Jack's most critical tone, and dropped it back in the cradle without saying a word.

Almost immediately my purse began to play *Finlandia*. I pulled out my cell and punched Off, a move sure to frost Jack. I padded to the kitchen and pulled the jack out of the kitchen phone midring.

I gathered Whiskers in my arms and, lugging him and my laptop, went to the bedroom. I put the cat on the bed and got into my warmest pajamas. I listened to the phone ring four more times, silenced each time only when I lifted the receiver to break the connection. When the doorbell rang, I refused to answer. In no time, the phone rang again. I reached behind the bedside table and unplugged the wire from the jack.

I hoped nothing really important happened overnight because I certainly wasn't going to know about it if it did.

"It's my fault, Whiskers." I stared bleakly at the cat curled at the foot of the bed. "I'm a coward. I never told him how different things were now." Whiskers ignored me in favor of kneading the comforter. "But I've barely heard a word for several months. How was I supposed to know he'd decided what he decided?"

A thought crystalized and I became furious all over again.

"And why would he think that I'd just be sitting around mooning over him anyway?" I glared at the cat who was now grooming himself with total disinterest in my monologue. "Because I was stupid enough to live that way for six years! That's why!"

The adrenaline from my anger at both Jack and myself fueled me. An hour later I e-mailed two fifteen-inch stories on Arnie's murder to the paper, one straight news, the other a human interest piece including the innocuous statement Harry Allen Bushay had given me about Arnie's death.

"Arnold Meister was a reliable and able employee," Harry Allen had said for attribution as he and Curt and I left the Community Center earlier in the evening. "Bushay Environmental will certainly miss his contributions to our workforce."

Though the words hadn't sounded complimentary but critical when spoken, they read nicely. It was the lack of any character qualities in the statement that I found fascinating even though I had no idea what that absence meant, if anything.

Tomorrow morning I needed to call Harry Allen and probe. Tonight, though, I was shot. Wasted. Wrung out. Drained. Fatigued. Bone weary.

Still I picked up my Bible from my nightstand and read for a bit. I was reading the Christmas story from Matthew's gospel this week. Then I planned to do the same in Luke. I had decided the comfort of the familiar story might help me feel less lonely. Certainly Mary and Joseph had found themselves alone in more unique circumstances than I could ever imagine. If they could do it, so could I. Of course, God was directly involved in their story; it is, after all, his story, too.

But I was a Christian. That meant he was also engaged in my story. "I will never leave you nor forsake you," he had said.

Lord, you know how alone I'm feeling. You know that everything that's ever been Christmas to me—except you, of course—is in Pittsburgh. Mom, Dad, Sam, Grandmom Kramer, Aunt Sissy and Uncle Arch. What am I supposed to do on Christmas this year? Watch Whiskers open his rubber mouse?

Maybe you could encourage Maddie and Doug to ask me over? What are best friends for if not to make Christmas less lonely? Or maybe Curt would ask me over or out to dinner or something? I don't mean to complain, Lord. I really don't. Well, maybe I do, just a bit. But please, Lord, don't let me be alone.

Suddenly Arnie swept across my mind. Poor Arnie. No more Christmas worries for him. And poor Jolene and Mr. and Mrs. Luray.

Okay, Lord. So my situation isn't as bad as lots of people's. But that doesn't mean it's good either, you know.

I sighed so loudly that Whiskers raised his head and blinked at me.

I lay down, certain I wouldn't sleep. I was too keyed up about Christmas and Arnie and about Jack and Curt. To my surprise my alarm wakened me Wednesday morning before I even realized I had slept.

As soon as I thought the dry cleaners would be open, I

slipped out of the newsroom and dropped off the plastic bag, my coat, scarf and gloves now stashed inside with Jolene's things.

"How's next Friday for pickup?" the woman behind the counter asked.

I blinked. "Next Friday? The sign in the window says twenty-four-hour service."

"That's only if you ask."

"Well, I'm asking. We need these things back right away. That's my new coat in there." Like she actually cared.

The lady hummed "Silent Night" as she wrote out the slips. I checked them when she handed them to me and almost swallowed my tongue.

"These prices are unbelievable!"

She shrugged. "Twenty-four-hour service is expensive. And that coat's leather and fur."

"Fake fur."

"Real fur. And blood's hard to get out. Were you guys in an accident or something?" She looked me over, searching for injuries.

I didn't want to discuss Arnie with her, so I said, "Sort of."

My coat wasn't all that expensive, and I figured Jolene could handle her costs since she was, as she had said, rich.

Which brought an ugly thought to my mind. If Arnie had had enough money for all that electricity and the glorious house to shine it in, who inherited? Surely that wasn't why Jolene declared she was rich, was it? Talk about a motive!

And where had that money come from to begin with? I distinctly remembered Jo telling me that Arnie's family was poor and he went to college on scholarships. Though a job in "marketing" undoubtedly paid well, it didn't pay on the scale I'd witnessed.

At least it didn't pay legally.

Immediately my mind began spinning. Bushay Environmental. I'd heard about illegal dumping in the waste management business almost all my life. There were vast tracts of open land, thousands of rushing streams, and huge stands of deciduous and evergreen forests in sparsely populated central Pennsylvania where you could dump stuff. Was Arnie facilitating or organizing such activity? For Harry Allen? Was activity like that still possible with the tight laws we now had on the books?

Did Jolene know where Arnie got his money? Did she care?

Was I going crazy, or was I on the trail of a big story?

When I got back to the office, I immediately made a phone call.

"Bushay Environmental, Caroline speaking," said a lilting voice. "How may I help you?"

She must be Caroline-recently-returned-from-Hollywood. Bless little Amhearst.

"Hi, Caroline. Welcome back!" I was her new best friend.

"Thanks," she said. "It's good to be back."

"You don't miss the bright lights?"

She laughed. "Well, sort of. But I decided I liked eating regularly better than being blinded by bright lights."

I laughed, too, and decided Caroline was probably going to be all right back home. "Look, I'm calling about any publications I might read to learn more about the waste management business."

"Well." She hesitated. She was, after all, still fairly new to the job and I imagined not many called about such reading matter. "I know we get an industry newsletter called *Waste News* around here. You can also subscribe to the online version."

"Great," I said, jotting the title down. "Just what I needed to know. Thanks." Then, as if it were an afterthought, I asked, "Could you connect me with Elsa?"

I hoped she didn't say "Elsa who?" because I hadn't the vaguest idea.

"Sure. Just a minute."

In no time I was talking with Elsa.

"Hi, Elsa. I saw Astrid the other day." I wanted to es-
tablish a connection before she realized she hadn't the
vaguest idea who she was talking to.

"Ah. You must have eaten at Ferretti's."

"I did," I agreed. "Great food."

"Well, she and Dom pour their whole lives into that place.
I keep telling her she works too hard, but does she listen?"

"You know what sisters are like," I who did not have one
said sympathetically. "But I didn't call to talk about Astrid.
I really called about Arnie Meister."

She tsked. "I tell you, I can't believe it. I went to school
with Arnie."

"I know. That's why I called you. Do you know anything
about arrangements? You know, the funeral or a memorial?"

"I haven't heard a thing."

I sighed. "He was such a great guy."

Elsa sighed back. "Rich, handsome and nice. I never
understood why Jolene left him. Of course I never understood why he married her to begin with. Not after sweet
Airy all those years!"

"I bet everyone at work liked him, didn't they?"

"Oh, yeah. What's not to like?"

"Even Mr. Bushay?"

"Mr. Bushay likes everybody," she said, though I
thought I detected a bit of hesitation.

"Oh, I guess I misunderstood. I thought Arnie and Mr.
Bushay were having some problems."

"What do you mean?" She was suddenly cautious.

"I heard they had a fight just the other day. I mean,
wasn't that a shocker?" I tried to sound scandalized. "Here
are these two great people, and suddenly they're fighting!"

"I know." She was clearly upset by the memory. "I heard
their voices through the door. It was awful."

"You heard the whole thing?" I didn't have to pretend to be stunned. I was.

"Well, yes and no. I heard their voices roaring at each other, but the words were muffled by that big door of his."

"So you couldn't understand any of it?"

"I know it seems weird, but it sounded like they were arguing about the Communists."

"The Communists? Who argues about the Communists these days?"

"I know. It doesn't make any sense, does it? But I think I heard Commies this and Communists that."

"Amazing, Elsa." Disappointing was what it was. "Well, let me know if you hear anything about plans for Arnie, okay? And may I speak to Mr. Bushay, please? He's such a hard guy to get hold of, you know."

"Oh, not really." She almost giggled. "It's not golf season."

"But where was he yesterday afternoon? Answer me that."

"Well, he did take a really long lunch, but he was here from three on. You must have called early in the afternoon."

"Where does he go for these long lunches, Elsa? Ferretti's isn't exactly high-roller territory."

She actually laughed. "He hates Ferretti's, though of course I'd never tell Astrid. I think it was the red cabbage in the Caesar salad that finally got to him. He always goes to the Country Club."

"Even in the off season?"

"Sure. They've got a great cook."

I smiled to myself. I could easily check out this lead. I made my voice brisk and businesslike again. "Well, he's in now, isn't he?"

"Oh. Yes." She had forgotten that I hadn't called to speak with her. "Of course. Who may I say is calling?"

"Merry Kramer."

There was a pause during which she must have realized she didn't know any Merry Kramer. Then I heard the silence of being on hold. Finally Harry Allen's voice boomed in my ear. "Merry Kramer! What a wonderful pleasure!" He made it sound as if my call had made his day. "When will the article and picture about the Amhearst Annual Food Project be in *The News?*"

"Actually, sir, I'm—"

"Sir? My dear Merry, you make me sound like an old man! It's Harry Allen to you."

"Thank you, ah, Harry Allen. I wanted to ask you—"

"Are you all ready for Christmas, Merry? Do you have your shopping done? Will you be spending the holiday with your family?"

"I'm afraid I won't be able to get home this year," I said. "Christmas will be somewhat solitary." Somewhat? Totally!

"I know what you mean." His voice dripped sympathy. "My wife and I are separated, and Christmas is always a lonely time." He sighed. Then abruptly he said, "I must go, Merry. A very important call has just come in. Any questions about the food project can be handled by my secretary. Thank you for calling." And he was gone.

I hung up thoughtfully. Harry Allen Bushay wasn't a stupid man. He knew exactly what I wanted to talk about. He just didn't want to talk about it with me.

Communists, Elsa had said. Was there such a thing as selling waste management secrets to—who? Who were the Communists these days? Anyone besides Fidel Castro or the Chinese? So assumption number one had to be that Elsa had misunderstood. Whatever they had argued about, it wasn't political philosophy.

Had Harry Allen caught Arnie in some illegality? Did he hope to protect his company's reputation by keeping such actions by one of his employees quiet?

Or was he protecting himself? Maybe it was the other way around, and Arnie had caught Harry Allen out, and Harry Allen felt he had no option but to kill his accuser.

I turned to my computer and went on the Internet. When Google asked me for an address, I typed in *Waste News*. In no time I was on the Web site for the *Waste News* e-zine. I sighed. To get most of the news here, I'd have to subscribe. I glanced toward Mac and decided that he wouldn't want to explain to whoever bought the paper about a line item reading: subscription: *Waste News*.

I Googled *waste management* and ended up at the web page of the Solid Waste Association of North America and learned about WASTECON, the big annual convention. I found I could attend the 35th Annual Land Fill Gas Symposium or get information on FEMA Debris Management as well as order my own personal Have You Hugged Your Garbageman Today T-shirt.

Following Google links I found a waste site that informed me that "death begins in the colon." Definitely not what I was looking for. Wrong kind of waste.

I was satisfied that I could find out some basic industry information without too much difficulty, so I clicked on Bushay Environmental. I learned that they were "your one-source stop for all your waste disposal needs, both home and industrial." But the most fascinating thing, at least to me, was that Harry Allen no longer owned Bushay. He ran it as part of a huge waste management corporation. Whether that fact meant anything or not I'd have to learn.

For the next little bit I scrambled like crazy trying to get both Jolene's work and mine done. She, of course, had not come in today. I realized quite quickly that I'd underrated Jolene's contribution to *The News*. Her dumb blonde act covered a very organized mind, and she did a lot more than make the newsroom resemble the Philadelphia Flower Show. As the day wore on, I began to feel more and more like the proverbial sluggard to Jolene's ant.

"Go to the ant, thou sluggard," I muttered in King James. "Consider her ways and be wise."

When I got a minute, I worked on the list of all the times
I'd seen Jolene in *The News* office yesterday afternoon, just
as Sergeant Poole had requested. To my surprise, the list
was very short.

I'd seen her return to the newsroom after lunch.

I'd seen her when she saved the life of the grape ivy.

I'd seen her when she wanted to leave at five.

For the almost four hours in between I hadn't con-
sciously noticed her—which of course meant absolutely
nothing, right? I slid the list in my top drawer.

I laid out prints of my murder scene pictures on my desk.
As I studied them, Jolene's shock and distress were evident.
Certainly when Sergeant Poole saw the copies I'd emailed
to him, he'd realize her innocence. The traditional suspect,
the spouse, would fade from the list of possible perps, and
her unaccounted-for afternoon would be immaterial.

I studied the kitchen shots I'd snapped while Jolene and
I waited for the police. They seemed utterly innocuous to
me. No matter how I studied them, I always ended up with
the same things: trash, dirty glasses, a bullet in the cabinet
and notes on the refrigerator.

I studied the trash. I'd read enough mysteries and seen
Audrey Hepburn and Cary Grant in *Charade* enough times
to know that collections of things always held hidden clues.
In books and movies. In real life orange juice containers were
orange juice containers. Frozen dinner wrappers were frozen
dinner wrappers. Clear plastic was clear plastic, and if it had
wrapped something significant, I sure couldn't tell what.

It was the same with the drinking glasses. Dirty glasses
were dirty glasses. There was no poison in the dregs as far
as I knew, and even if there was, it was immaterial. Arnie
had been shot. If there were fingerprints on surfaces, I
couldn't identify them. That was a police matter, and I
could only hope they'd be kind enough to share what they
learned with me. I made a note to check.

I studied the picture of the bullet in the cabinet. I knew the police would be able to find out a lot of information about the bullet if it wasn't too badly damaged, but unless someone found the gun that the bullet came from, the value of that information was limited.

I was intrigued, though, by the certificate that read $50,000. What did it mean? Salary? His, hers or theirs? Considering that house, the figure was more likely the amount owed on the mortgage each month. Or maybe it was the amount paid or demanded for an illegal dumping activity? Just the sort of thing everyone posted on their fridge.

When I finally had time to talk to Mac after lunch, I wasn't willing to reveal my detectival inclinations just yet lest his caustic humor have a field day at my expense. I needed to have something besides questions before I suggested anything to him.

"Nice articles on the murder," he said. "Anything new on who killed Arnie?"

I shook my head. "I've been on the phone several times with Sergeant Poole. They're waiting for autopsy reports, crime scene reports, stuff like that. I thought I'd go out to His House while we wait. I'll interview Dawn Trauber and see how that story develops."

He nodded approval. "You'll like her. She's really pretty." His voice was strangely wistful. "A class act."

I thought of Dawn's picture with her warm smile, her kind eyes. "I didn't realize you knew her."

"I don't. Not really. I've just met her at civic events or at brief interviews. Stuff like that. Nothing substantive. She probably doesn't even remember me."

I started to turn away.

"Think she'd go out with me?"

I blinked. When he asked me out, there was never that longing note in his voice. I could see he regretted speaking, so I decided to treat the question as a joke. I leaned over and whispered conspiratorially, "I bet she'd go to church with you Christmas Eve."

He looked startled. "Yeah, right. Forget it."

I gave him a friendly grin and walked to my desk.

"Welcome to His House," Dawn Trauber said a short time later. Her smile was wide, her brown eyes alight with goodwill. She stood back for me to walk into the large front hall of the great Victorian that housed the ministry she managed.

I looked around with undisguised interest. In offices that opened off the foyer I could see a woman busy at a computer, a man reading reports and a woman in a glass-enclosed area talking earnestly with a girl.

"Betty here works full-time in the office, and her husband Ken is our maintenance guy. They have an apartment over the garage and live on site." Betty glanced up from her computer and smiled.

Dawn indicated the woman in the glass cubicle with the girl. "Julie is our counselor. She has an apartment on the third floor. Roger here is a lawyer and board member who comes in at least weekly to be certain we're in compliance with the all state and federal law."

Julie, behind her soundproof glass and deep in conversation, was unaware of my presence, but Roger looked up and nodded.

Dawn led me to the great room that stretched across the middle of the house.

"There's a lot of Christmas glitz here," she said. "The girls love decorations, and their idea of beauty is often—" She shook her head in mock horror.

While the carpeting was a tasteful mossy green and the sofas and chairs were muted cream, forest and crimson plaids and stripes, the decorations were another story. A large artificial tree sparkled in one corner. It held the gaudiest of baubles, and on the top bough perched an immense angel in a violent violet robe and sparkly golden wings. String after string of twinkle lights blinked off and on in oddly unsyncopated patterns.

Someone had plastered the bulletin board over the hall table with a mix of Christmas cards and pictures of babies in cute and overly cute Christmas outfits. Gold tinsel outlined the collection and paper chains sprinkled with glitter hung everywhere imaginable. More gold tinsel outlined all the doorways and windows.

"Very cheery," I said, trying to put a positive spin on what looked a decorator's nightmare.

Dawn grinned. "Yeah. They're working to keep their Christmas spirits in spite of their situations."

I nodded. I understood all too well the fragility of seasonal emotions.

The unknowing object of Mac's interest sat across from me on a hunter sofa piped in crimson. She looked friendly and charming and very competent. Maybe there was more to Mac than I thought if he was attracted to someone like Dawn. Maybe he wasn't suffering just a Christmas guilt trip but a compelling need to analyze his life. Maybe he wanted to change. Maybe he felt the need for God and was searching.

Maybe I was reading too much into one short question.

Behind Dawn the tree lights blinked madly, enough to give anyone with brain wave difficulties a major seizure and me a splitting headache.

"Can you stand the blinking?" Dawn asked with sympathy. "Let me unplug it." She got up and did so. She was wearing jeans and a bright red sweater with a huge Frosty the Snowman pinned on her right shoulder. Frosty's big red eyes blinked maniacally. She saw me looking at it. "Lonni gave it to me. I've got to wear it."

"How old's Lonni?" I asked.

"Seventeen. She's one of the older ones. At the other end

of the spectrum there's Karyn with a *Y.* She's thirteen. The boy's sixteen."

"Thirteen!" I knew babies were having babies, but thirteen!

"Her mother brings her in each day for counseling. Julie's talking with her now."

"Do you counsel many girls who don't live here?"

Dawn nodded. "We have an extensive outpatient counseling program, though no one else is Karyn's age, thank goodness! She's such a sweet girl, young for her age. She brings a different stuffed animal with her every day." Her eyes got a sad, faraway look. "She didn't even know what was happening to her."

At that moment a bright-eyed, well-groomed, healthy child appeared in the doorway, her pregnancy far advanced, a Pooh Bear cradled in her arm.

"Hey, Karyn," Dawn said, rising, the sad look banished. "How are you feeling today?"

"I'm getting kicked to death, Miss Trauber."

Dawn laughed. "I just bet you are. It won't be long now."

"Mom and I have our bags packed," Karyn said. "Maybe I'll have a Christmas baby, just like Mary." Her face shone at the idea.

"Maybe," Dawn said.

"Then every year everyone will think of my baby when they sing about Jesus." She hugged Pooh. "Wouldn't that be great?" Her face grew pensive. "But he'll always get cheated on birthday gifts, won't he? That'll be really sad. But—" the smile reappeared "—it'll be worth it to share Jesus' birthday."

Dear God, I asked, *how can such innocence and naiveté be having a baby?*

The front door opened and a woman came in.

"Hey, Mom," Karyn said. "Let me get my coat." She put Pooh down and grabbed a Land's End Squall from the clothes tree in the corner. It zipped over her amplitude, and I realized it was probably her father's coat, borrowed for the duration. She gathered Pooh and walked smiling to the door. Her mother, haggard and in obvious emotional pain, followed.

"Her mother says that every time she looks at Karyn, it's a knife in the heart," Dawn said.

I looked at the closed door. "I can't even imagine."

Suddenly the door flew open and several girls in various stages of pregnancy fell in. Instantly the air crackled with energy.

"Hey, Miss Trauber," called a tall, skinny girl with a ponytail and a tummy of magnificent proportions.

"Hey, Pam. How are you feeling today?"

"Let me tell you, sitting in school is getting harder and harder every day! I want this baby to come now! I got to be able to breathe again, you know?"

The other girls all laughed with understanding as they thundered toward the stairs and their rooms above. One of the girls grabbed *The News* on her way past. The sports pages were on top, and I thought Larry Schimmer, our sports guy, would be glad to know he'd been read.

"Was that Karyn leaving?" Pam asked, pausing with one foot on the stairs.

Dawn nodded.

"Poor kid." Pam shook her head. "We pray for her all the time."

The other girls nodded agreement.

"It's bad enough for us," the girl with the paper said. "But she's a baby!"

And they were gone.

Dawn smiled as she resumed her seat beside me. "You can see why I'm very hesitant to have the girls themselves featured in the paper. Legal and privacy issues aside, they don't need the publicity. Nor do their parents."

I thought of Karyn's mother and had to agree.

"We have eight girls currently in residence," Dawn said, "and half of them are here with the full support of their parents. The others have been banished to us. Of the eight, seven are having trouble of one kind or another with the babies' fathers or the father's family. They've come to us at various points in their pregnancies, and we keep them through delivery and, if they give their babies up for adoption, for a month or more after they deliver."

I looked at her in surprise. "Even those who are getting along well with their families?"

Dawn nodded. "We keep them beyond delivery to help them through the grieving process. Giving up a baby is like a death, you know. Everyone tells them to forget what happened and get on with their lives. They mean to be kind, but they aren't. We let the girls cry and talk about their babies. We listen to their dreams and prayers for the little one they gave up, their worries about the people who have taken him or her. We look at the newborn pictures over and over and over because they need someone to do that with them."

I didn't know many people who had given up their babies. Most of my friends or acquaintances kept them and began the complicated dance of survival that goes with single motherhood, educational needs, jobs, social stagnation and loneliness. Still adoption had always fascinated me. "Do many of your girls give their babies up for adoption?"

"A lot more than the national average," Dawn said.

Pressure, I immediately thought. Oh, I hope they don't put pressure on these girls.

Dawn knew what I was thinking. "We're careful not to apply any pressure. We present all the options with their difficulties and benefits. To adopt or keep is one of the most difficult and far-reaching decisions these girls will ever make, and they have to make it with solid information balancing their emotions."

I knew from my research that about ninety-five percent

of the unmarried mothers kept their babies. "Why are your numbers different from the general norm?"

"Two reasons, I think."

But I didn't learn those reasons. A scream caused us both to turn abruptly toward the steps. The girl who had retrieved *The News* sat there, her hand pressed over her mouth, a look of horror on her face. I thought she had gone upstairs with the rest, but obviously she hadn't.

"Lonni!" Dawn ran to her. "What's wrong? Where do you hurt?"

Lonni looked at Dawn, shook her head, and hand still pressed to her lips, raced outside, *The News* scattering across the floor in her wake. Dawn raced after her.

I watched them go and thought that it wasn't a physical problem that had made Lonni cry out. No one in the throes of pain could move so quickly. So something else had distressed her.

I gathered the paper thoughtfully and folded it into a neat pile. Had something in *The News* caused that flight? On the sheet facing me was a headline that read Youth Held In Hit And Run. Another said Underage Drunk Driver Goes To Trial In Deaths. Did she know these boys? Was one of them her baby's father?

As I pondered that interesting and appalling idea, another scream cut the air. This one came from upstairs. Immediately voices called and feet ran and an excited young face peered over the railing from upstairs.

"Miss Trauber! Miss Trauber! It's Pam! Her water just broke! I think she's in labor!"

My heart stopped momentarily. Then I rushed to the door where Dawn had disappeared. I looked madly to the right and left and saw Dawn and Lonni huddled under a bare beech tree in the backyard, deep in conversation. I hesitated.

Another scream sounded from upstairs and my decision was made.

"Dawn," I yelled. "Dawn! Pam's in labor!"

Dawn and Lonni looked at me, at each other and ran for the house. On the step, Dawn paused.

"Lonni, we'll talk again. We're not finished."

Lonni said nothing, but she looked angry and balky and incredibly sad.

Suddenly the whole complement of girls rushed down the stairs, Pam in their middle. One held her hand, another had her suitcase and a third had a big red Bible. I felt like I should boil water or tear sheets or something.

Pam looked both shocked and elated. "This is it, Miss Trauber," she whispered, holding her belly.

Dawn grinned and grabbed Pam in a bear hug. "Dear Jesus, be with Pam! Take care of her and this wonderful baby. Give them safety. Give Pam joy."

All the girls shouted, "Amen!" as Pam groaned again with pain.

"Blow!" Lonni yelled. "Come on, Pam. Out your mouth! Wush, wush, wush!"

"She doesn't want to breathe," one of the girls said with a scared half smile. "She wants drugs."

Everyone laughed as Pam nodded vigorously.

"Car's ready." It was Julie, the counselor. "Here's your bag, Dawn. You guys have a wonderful time. We'll be fine until you get back."

Dawn helped Pam into the backseat and a reclining position. As we all waved good-bye, Lonni yelled, "Call us, okay? Call us as soon as anything happens!"

We walked inside with a mix of contained excitement and anticlimax. There was still a lot to happen, but we were no longer directly involved.

I asked Julie, "Will Dawn stay the whole time?"

Julie nodded. "She's Pam's coach. She's there for as long as it takes."

"That's nice," I said.

"No, it's not," Julie said. "It's necessary. Pam has no one else."

"No one?" I thought of the tall, outgoing girl.

"No one. Her father she never knew, and her mother left town three weeks ago with her latest boyfriend, heading for parts unknown. Her brother's in jail. She absolutely needs Dawn and me and the other girls." She gestured at the others as all but Lonni straggled back upstairs. Lonni stood in the corner hugging *The News*.

I couldn't begin to imagine the magnitude of Pam's need, but I was beginning to get a small understanding of what His House was all about.

"Besides that," Julie said, clearly in lecture mode, "a first pregnancy is a first pregnancy and a first baby is a first baby. It should always be treated as the miracle it is, regardless of the situation. Dawn's there to hold Pam's hand and rub her back, to count between contractions and give her a drink whenever she needs it. She'll encourage her when she wants to give up. She'll push her hair from her forehead and mop her sweat and hug her and get giddy when the baby finally comes. And she'll weep with her when she kisses her baby good-bye." Julie looked at me to see if I understood. "Dawn'll give Pam positive, godly memories of an otherwise terrible, terrible time."

I walked slowly to the door, thinking of what Julie had said. And I'd thought Karyn naive.

I was so lost in thought that I jumped when Lonni said in my ear, "Excuse me. Did I hear you and Miss Trauber talking about interviewing one of us?"

I smiled at her and nodded.

"Well, I'd like to give an interview." Her voice was hard enough to cut glass. "I've got lots to say."

"That would be wonderful. When do you want to talk?"

"Now?" she said. "I want to tell you all about the person who has made my life a living hell."

I looked at the girl with concern. It seemed obvious that whether she had information for my story or not, she needed to talk. Dawn had left with Pam, so I was now to be her listener.

"Come on." I headed for the sofa where I'd recently sat with Dawn. She followed me and flopped awkwardly down. As I watched her try to get comfortable, I guessed her to be about six months pregnant.

"You know," she said, "you think there's someone you can really trust, and then all of a sudden you find out how wrong you were!" Her whole countenance screamed rage.

"A guy?" I asked. Given her situation, it seemed a likely guess.

"Oh, yeah." She looked oddly vulnerable for someone so angry. "I can't believe how he turned on me!"

As I opened my mouth to say, "Tell me," five girls came running down the stairs and flopped in the various chairs and sofas about the room. One grabbed the TV remote and what I imagined to be the first of several programs that ran for the rest of the evening flashed onto the screen.

"We were talking here!" Lonni yelled.

The girls looked at her and shrugged. "So who's stopping you?" one asked.

I looked at Lonni and patted her hand. "We can talk later."

She scowled furiously at me, but I knew she wasn't angry at me. The rest of the world maybe, and some guy in particular definitely, but not me. "Saturday," she said. "I'll meet you at Ferretti's at noon. Then no one will interrupt us." And she stalked upstairs to brood.

SEVEN

First thing Thursday morning I called Sergeant Poole.

"Ah, Merry. Always a delight to hear your voice." He was so good at PR that I almost believed him.

"Has the autopsy report come back yet?"

"I have it on my desk in front of me as we speak."

"And?"

"Patience, patience. I'm opening the folder, not stone-walling you. Here we go. Arnold James Meister, age twenty-seven, was shot with a .38 caliber handgun, probably a Smith and Wesson. The bullet recovered from a cabinet in the Meister kitchen has been sent to the state police lab for further analysis. The shot entered Mr. Meister's lower left chest, traveled on a slightly upward angle, emerging just below his left shoulder blade. There was great internal trauma in spite of the through-and-through wound, but the cause of death was basically ex-sanguination and shock. We're just lucky that the bullet didn't distort inside the body."

"Tell me more about the gun."

"If it's an S&W .38 Special like we think, it's double action. That means it doesn't need cocking and has no safety. You pull the trigger and bam! It's a good gun for quick action, but you have no room for error with it."

"And do you know who used this gun yet?"

"The investigation is moving apace. We are doing everything in our power to bring to justice the person responsible."

"Right. What about fingerprints on the glasses in the sink?"

"The FBI has them and will run them through AFIS." AFIS—Automated Fingerprint Identification System—is a great aid in law enforcement with its millions of prints on file for comparison. But it only works if there is an exemplar fingerprint to match the questioned print against. Even as sophisticated as the system is, the final match has to be made visually by a fingerprint expert. "But don't hold your breath on this one."

"What," I asked before he hung up on me, "did Harry Allen Bushay and Arnie Meister fight about the day before Arnie died?"

There was a short silence. "I'll call you when we have anything new." And he was gone.

I hadn't really expected an answer to that last question, just hoped.

I told Mac what William had told me. He was less than happy.

"Apace? Apace? Who in the world says *apace*?" He scowled at me like it was my fault the sergeant used archaic words.

I ignored his pique and checked over my shoulder to be certain no one was close enough to hear me. "You don't think Jolene had anything to do with this, do you?"

Mac looked flabbergasted. "Jolene, the Queen of Confusion? The Mistress of Melodrama? The High Priestess of Hypochondria?"

If that were me talking, all that alliteration would have meant real concern about Jolene, but I think all it meant in Mac was overkill. "I don't really think she did it, either," I said. "I just don't know where she was Tuesday afternoon."

"Don't worry. She was out running errands for me. I've

talked to the police several times, and they've got a copy of the places she went. I can only assume they're checking with the stores and such for verification."

He handed me another copy of the list. "Check yourself if it'll make you feel better. But don't bother to check Staples. I have the receipt and the office supplies. Or the MAC machine. She gave me the receipt and the cash she withdrew for me. Or the grocery store. I got the orange juice and bread I asked for. Or the drugstore. I got the prescription and the athlete's foot stuff. Or Bob's Books. Or the Hallmark store. She brought me the books and the Christmas cards. But you can check the other places."

I glanced at the list he'd handed me. Hennessey's Pharmacy. Bob's Books. Staples. A MAC machine. Grocery store. Hannah's Hallmark Center. "There are no places left to check."

"Sort of puts a hole in your Jolene as murderer theory, doesn't it."

"Um." I thought for a minute. "Ah-hah! When did you send her on the errands? When did she come back?"

He looked at me and shook his head. "You're hopeless. Are you sure you weren't Nancy Drew in a previous life?"

"I never had a previous life. This is my one and only. Now come on. When did she leave?"

"Well, after you and she made that ghastly public spectacle of yourselves in the ladies' room at Ferretti's—"

"How'd you hear about that? And it wasn't me!"

"I have my sources, and so you say."

"Astrid." I thought dark thoughts about the brassy blonde. "And I most definitely say."

He merely smiled. "After Ferretti's Jo came back here. So did you, and we talked about His House. Then the plant attacked you. Then I sent her out. Must have been about one thirty-ish."

I nodded. "And when did she come back?"

Mac thought. "About 4:45. At least that's when she gave me the things."

"It took her more than three hours? But everything except Staples is right here in Amhearst. And Staples is only fifteen minutes away by the bypass."

"So she got stuck in traffic."

But speculation danced in the air between us.

"Do you have the receipts?" I asked. "They'll have the time on them. At least Staples and the MAC machine will. And probably the grocery store."

Mac rifled papers for a minute, then pulled out a Staples receipt. I leaned across his desk to read. In the upper right-hand section of the receipt, just below the name, address and phone number of the store, was the date, 12/18. Immediately following was 02:38 p.m.

"How about your withdrawal slip for the MAC machine?" I asked.

He fished out his wallet. A little storm of white MAC receipts fluttered to the desk.

"You're supposed to enter them in your checkbook, you know, not save them for the next ticker tape parade."

He ignored me as he searched for the pertinent one. "Here." He spread it on his desk for us to read. Right at the top of the receipt was a row that read Date, Time, Location. Under Date was 12/18 and under Time was 02:05 p.m.

"She stopped to get your money on the way to Staples," I said. "How about the grocery receipt?"

He shook his head. "Long gone along with the bag."

"A minor glitch, no more. I'll just check the times she visited the other places. But, Mac, I don't really believe she did it. Look." I laid the pictures I'd taken at Arnie's house on his desk.

They drew him like they did me—Jo's imperious, impatient beauty giving way to disbelief and absolute horror.

He shook his head, momentarily at a loss for words.

Finally he said, "After the cops see these pictures, they'll never doubt her innocence, that's for sure. Or else," and his habitual cynicism surfaced, "I've got Meryl Streep's long-lost sister working for me."

Feeling something akin to desperation, I said, "That's the trouble with murder. It makes everyone suspect everyone!"

Mac tsk-tsked like an old maid aunt. "Merry, Merry, do you mean you suspect me?"

I frowned at him. "I've got another question for you. A totally different area. What, if anything, do you think Arnie's job might have to do with his death?"

"What?"

"Bushay Environmental. Illegal dumping. The mob."

I waited for his mocking laugh. Instead he surprised me by saying, "Interesting thought. Why don't you find out if there's a connection? Wouldn't it be something if Harry Allen Bushay, outstanding, upstanding citizen, was bent?"

I didn't tell him I'd already begun my preliminary digging. Instead I nodded and changed the subject. "Have you ever been to His House?" I asked.

"Whose house? Harry Allen's?"

"Mac," I said in exasperation.

"Oh, that House. No, I've never been there."

"It's marvelous. Impressive. Interesting. I met a sixteen-year-old named Pam who Dawn had to rush to the hospital to have her baby while I was there." I still smiled at the memory of the excitement. "And a thirteen-year-old who's due at any minute."

"A thirteen-year-old?" Mac looked horrified.

"Cutest little thing you ever saw."

"Didn't anyone ever take time to tell her the facts of life?"

"I don't know. It's just very, very sad."

We were quiet a minute, thinking about Karyn. Then I said, "Your Dawn is a neat lady. I liked her a lot. We didn't get a chance to talk too much because Pam chose that moment to go into labor, but we're going to get together another time."

"She's not my Dawn." Was that regret I heard? "And how'd you make out in terms of interviews with the girls?"

"It's a touchy situation," I said. "Dawn doesn't like the idea much, and if you'd seen the mother of the thirteen-year-old, you'd know why. But one of the girls did offer to talk with me."

"Yes!" Mac was clearly pleased. "Was she a good interview?"

"I haven't met with her yet. We're scheduled to have lunch Saturday. She's meeting me at Ferretti's."

"Wow! Working on your day off! I'm impressed."

"Enough to give me Christmas as a comp day?"

"No."

"Enough to give me a raise?"

He snorted. "I haven't even gotten a raise yet, and I'm the new editor. Take your place in line."

My quick smile faded, and I said slowly. "About this interview with Lonni. Something doesn't feel right to me."

"She approached you, didn't she? You didn't pressure her or anything."

"That's not what I mean." But I didn't know how to articulate what I did mean. It was too nebulous, amorphous, indistinct, unclear, cloudy, vague, without form. But my mental litany of synonyms told me how unsettled I was. "Let me do the interview and then maybe I'll know what's bothering me."

Mac nodded. "And talk to the mother of the thirteen-year-old. And the father. I suppose it's too much to ask, but if you could talk to the baby's father…"

I walked back to my desk berating myself for not having thought of the parent angle myself. It was a touchstone perspective since so many mothers and fathers feared finding themselves in Karyn's parents' position. "The best pieces have three points of view," an old journalist back in Pittsburgh had told me when I began my career. And I hadn't remembered that wisdom.

I called His House and was pleased to connect with Dawn. "What's the news on Pam?"

"Baby boy, born at 12:01 a.m. Pam and the baby are doing well. I'm wiped out. This coaching is hard work! Too little sleep."

"Does the baby have a name?"

"David. Pam says—" Dawn's voice thickened with emotion "—she says she hopes and prays he'll become a man after God's own heart like the original David."

I found myself swallowing hard, too. "So what happens next?"

"She has another day to enjoy David before she comes back here and he goes to his new family."

"Don't they take the baby right after he's born and the mother never sees him again?" I'd heard more than enough adoption horror stories on TV talk shows.

"No, they don't grab the babies and run these days. Pam will get to feed David and change him and talk to him and cuddle him and do all those other wonderful mommy things."

"For two days." What a dreadfully short piece of both his life and hers.

"For the duration of her hospital stay, which in Pennsylvania happens to be mandated to be at least forty-eight hours."

"And she'll still be able to say good-bye after having him that long?"

"Not easily. But she's got to make this decision from strength, not weakness. And she's got to have memories to help stem the flood of regrets that will crop up later. This caring for the baby in the hospital isn't just a His House policy. It's in keeping with the latest sociological findings as well as being about as humane as a closed adoption can be."

"A closed adoption?"

"The birth mother and the adoptive parents don't know any identifying information about each other. There are also open adoptions where the birth mom gets to choose the adoptive parents, sometimes even meets them, sometimes visits in their home after the adoption to keep contact with the baby. We let our girls decide what format they want to follow."

"And Pam chose a closed adoption?"

"Yep. She says she doesn't want to know where David goes because she wants his new parents to be free from worrying about her trying to reclaim him. She says God will put him in a better home than she ever could anyway."

"Wow." I was impressed. "What other things do you do with the girls to make the separation easier?"

"We suggest they send something with the baby, something that shows they loved the child."

"Like what?"

"Like a letter or something made expressly for the baby. It's important for both the mother and the child. She knows she has a chance to convey her love and the child knows he was loved, not abandoned."

"Can you tell me what Pam has done?"

"She knit a sweater. She'd never knit before in her life, and Pam's definitely not the domestic type, but she persisted through countless dropped stitches and rip outs. She ended up with a little yellow sweater she's so proud of. And she's written David a note. Again, she's not a great student, but it'd make your heart break if you read it. She loves that little boy fiercely."

One of my friends back home had kept her baby, mainly because she couldn't stand the idea of giving her up.

"I didn't get an abortion," she'd said, "because I believe those incredibly tiny feet and those tiny hands and that little beating heart belong to a real baby. But I'll keep the baby because they're my baby's feet and hands and heart. No one else will get to care for her. Only me."

I knew she was stating the feelings of most girls and young women who are pregnant outside marriage and who choose not to terminate their pregnancies.

"If Pam loves David so much," I asked, "how can she let him go?"

"That's why she can let him go," Dawn said softly. "We try to teach our girls to make choices for their babies based on the same kind of love God showed when he sent Jesus. God made his choices based on our need, not his. Pam needs to choose based on David's needs, not hers."

"But there's so much heartbreak in giving up a child!"

"That there is," Dawn agreed. "There's heartbreak all over an unwed pregnancy, no matter what you do. But remember, Pam has no one to help her, and I mean that literally. Her family's nonexistent. She's only finished ninth grade, so she has no education, no training, no skills, no job prospects. If she keeps David, what does she do? Flip burgers all her life? Who can raise a family on that kind of money? Go on welfare? Okay, say she does go on welfare for a time so that she can go back to school. Who keeps the baby while she goes to school? The baby's father? He disappeared even before he knew Pam was pregnant. Day care? Day care costs money. A friend? All her friends are either in school or not trustworthy. And there's the issue of a dad. Pam says her baby deserves a dad. Not a father, mind you. He's got that, just like all the rest of us. A dad."

Abruptly Dawn stopped. I waited.

"I'm sorry," she finally said. "I tend to climb on a soapbox."

"Don't apologize. Aside from the fact that this information is fascinating all on its own, I need it for my article."

"Oops," she said. "I've got to go. Karyn's here. She and I are talking the realities of life again today."

"She wants to keep her baby?"

"She does."

"Her mother?"

"She's torn. This is her first grandchild, but this is also her daughter who is barely past childhood herself. What's best for the baby? What's best for Karyn? And can they possibly be the same? Terrible choices no matter how you look at it."

"I'd like to interview Karyn's mom. Can you give me her name and number so I can contact her?"

After a short, considering silence, Dawn said, "Why don't I ask if she's interested, and if she is, she'll call you."

That wasn't the way I'd prefer, but I also knew that's the way it was going to be.

"Okay," I said. "And when can you and I get together?"

Dawn thought a minute. "I have to go into Amhearst on Saturday to take Lonni. She's already asked me about three times. I could meet you while I wait for her to accomplish her secret project."

"Ah, I'm afraid I'm her secret project. She and I are having lunch together."

"Oh." There was a definite unhappy tone to the single syllable.

"She approached me, Dawn. I didn't go to her."

"It's okay," Dawn said. "If she wants to speak to you, it's her choice. I'll have to trust you to handle her honestly and kindly."

I had to laugh. "You're good," I said. "Concrete instructions about my expected behavior disguised as confidence in my character."

Dawn laughed back. "You're on to me. How about if you and I meet for something to eat Sunday after church?" We set a time to meet and I hung up. I had just closed my His House file when the phone rang.

"Hi, Merry." It was Curt.

"Curt." I blinked as I heard myself. My voice was soft and almost sexy, quite a feat coming from someone I consider about as sexy as cold spaghetti. I became brisk to counter my inadvertent slip. "What can I do for you?"

"Are we still going to Longwood Gardens this afternoon?"

"Absolutely," I said. I knew from my research that Longwood Gardens was originally the private estate and gardens developed in the early part of the twentieth century by Pierre duPont of the world famous family and chemical company. He had endowed the Gardens so that they might remain and be open to the public. "Somehow going there doesn't sound all that much fun alone."

"You sure you wouldn't rather go with Jack?"

Did he sort of spit out the word *Jack,* an eminently spitable word now that I thought about it? Smiling at his (maybe) little show of jealousy, I said, "I can't go with him. He's at work."

"Umph," Curt grunted, and I had to smile even more.

"Besides, I look forward to spending the day with you."

This time his grunt sounded pleased.

"I'll expect you about 12:30," I said. "We just have to be back by 7:30 for the final bell choir practice before Christmas."

When I walked out to the parking lot at 12:30, I felt sort of tingly with anticipation. Easy, girl, I told myself as I climbed into Curt's passenger seat. This is strictly a business endeavor. This is not a date. There are no romantic overtones.

Right.

I was also a bit nervous because Curt was probably waiting to hear all about Jack and why I hadn't mentioned the little fact of his presence, and what did I think I was doing, trying to play both ends against the middle, and was I just stringing him along for the fun of it, and did I plan to dump him now that Jack was here, and what was so great about Jack anyway and…

I sighed.

"What's wrong?" Curt asked as we drove south on

Route 82 through open, rolling fields that were beautiful even in the starkness of winter.

"I'm a mess."

"Oh." Curt nodded with understanding.

"You don't have to agree."

"I don't."

"Well, you just nodded like you did."

"Only trying to be amenable."

"Which is more than you can say for me, right?"

He glanced at me as I huddled against my door. "I'm not touching that comment for anything in the world."

I stared out the front window and berated myself. Why was I being sharp with him? It was Jack I was mad at. Or me. But not him. Definitely not handsome, huggable him. I sighed again.

"What's wrong this time?" he asked.

"I'm a mess. I am. I'm a mess."

He reached over and ran the back of his fingers softly over my cheek. "You look pretty good to me."

I caught his hand and held it to my face. "I didn't ask him to come here, you know," I said with something like desperation. "He just showed up." I was afraid he wouldn't believe me.

"I know."

"You do?"

"You couldn't be that devious if you tried."

"I bet I could. If I tried."

"Do you want to be devious?"

"Well, no."

"Then why are you being defensive? I think I just paid you a compliment."

"That was a compliment?"

He nodded. "I happen to think it's good to be open and honest instead of devious."

I thought about that for a moment and smiled. "Thanks."

"Do you have to sit against the far door?" he asked.

"Well, no."

"Then move closer."

I grinned as I slid over, and we drove the rest of the way with our hands clasped companionably over the gear console.

Longwood Gardens in Kennett Square, Pennsylvania, was bigger and more wonderful than I expected. Of course I wasn't sure what I expected, but I knew it wasn't this magnificent place.

"Wait until dark," Curt said as we strolled along the walkway from the visitor's center to the conservatory. "It's a fairyland with thousands of lights. These days when I think of Christmas, I think of Longwood."

"Not Jesus?" I teased.

"Of course I think of Jesus," he said. "There wouldn't be Christmas without him. I mean as far as celebration is concerned. The lights and the beauty."

"I think of home, and I get teary," I said. "I can't believe I'm going to be alone." And I got teary. Curt squeezed my shoulders with understanding, and we walked in silence for a few minutes.

On the pavement outside the conservatory was a great Christmas tree adorned with seedpods and pinecones and all manner of bird food. I pulled out my camera and took a shot or two. A pair of twins about five years old were eyeing the tree.

"What do you think of it?" I asked them.

"Where's the tinsel?" the boy asked.

"And the lights?" his sister asked.

"It's got fat on it," the boy said, pointing to lumps of suet.

"I want lights," repeated his sister.

I didn't bother asking for their names. I didn't think their quotes went with the tone of the article I had to produce.

"Come on," Curt said, laughing at the kids. "Time for lunch." He grabbed my hand and led me away from the conservatory and across a walking bridge to The Terrace restaurant, which offered sit-down dining or a cafeteria.

"The restaurant looks great," I said as I read the menu. "But we're in a time bind. We'd better go to the cafeteria."

We took our places in line and I was immediately overwhelmed by all the choices and specialty areas. I hate cafeterias. There's too much available, and it all looks good, and I always pick more than I need, and I never know where to find the butter or the beverages, and then I never know where to sit, and I stand there like an idiot with my loaded tray in my hands, and the junior high lunchroom flashes in front of me like a slow-motion nightmare. Then when I finally sit down, whoever I'm with has a meal I like better than the one I've got, and I never even saw their stuff!

But I was now the new Amhearst Merry; confident, secure, pressing on to a new life. I could deal with cafeterias. I took a deep breath and grabbed a tray. I wandered among the different food areas with what I hoped was a sophisticated insouciance. I took vegetable soup, Caesar salad (without red cabbage), a ham and swiss on rye and a very tall Coke. Unfortunately they didn't have any Oreos, not even any pulverized ones to put on soft ice cream. I settled for a piece of lemon meringue pie.

Now all I had to do was find Curt so we could pay for all this stuff and find seats. Then maybe I could relax and enjoy my food.

I spun around to look for him and found to our mutual regret that he was immediately behind me, tray laden with food, a tall ice water and a cup of coffee. My tray crashed into his as I spun, and we watched in horror as his tray skidded over mine and upended my Coke, which crashed into his ice water, which took out his coffee.

The resultant tidal wave, ice floating on its breaking swell, swamped his lunch—a hot beef dish that looked much tastier than my choices—and rushed over the little lip of the tray onto his front. It cascaded down his open tan suede jacket, his yellow sweater and his jeans to form a sickly brown pool around his feet.

I froze, mortified. All I could do was stand there in the ebbing flood and stare at the floor and the ice cubes skittering madly in all directions. And I wondered which was more painful coursing down your leg, ice cold water and Coke or steaming hot coffee.

I thought that if I was ever going to faint, this would be a good time.

"Clean up by desserts," yelled a woman.

"Watchit, watchit," shouted a man.

"Gimmee that, lady." A young man brusquely took my tray. "You, too, mister. And get outta the way so Hector can do the floor."

I stepped aside for Hector and his mop and bucket. "I'm so sorry," I said, finally making myself look at Curt. I'd drenched him twice in two days!

He shook his head. "Don't worry about it." He sounded resigned. "It was just one of those things. Why don't you take a seat while I go to the men's room and try to clean up a bit. Then—" he sighed "—we'll start all over again."

"You're a very nice man," I said to his back as he stalked off. "A very nice man."

I didn't think he'd heard me, but he paused and glanced over his shoulder with a smile.

Eventually we purchased our lunch and I inflicted no more calamities upon us. As we ate, we managed to talk intelligently in spite of my obvious limitations. I even laughed at a few lame jokes Curt told to cheer me up. I downed my Coke in little gulps because my beef stew—I decided he had found a tastier dish than I and opted for his on my second chance—tasted dry in spite of the gravy drenching it. When Curt said, "Umm, good," I realized it wasn't the kitchen's fault that the stew tasted so wooden. Embarrassment deadens your taste buds. It's a known fact.

Finally, when it was time to leave and I knew I could put it off no longer, I clasped my hands in my lap and looked him straight in the eye.

Curt watched me muster my courage, and I could almost hear his mental uh-oh. He braced himself.

"Why do you like me?" I asked urgently.

He blinked and I waited. Then he carefully stacked all the meal's debris from both our trays onto his. I still waited. He slid his tray over my empty one.

"If you were anyone else, Merry, I'd say you were fishing for compliments. But as I said earlier, you can't be devious."

"I could be. If I wanted."

"Merry, I'm not impugning your intelligence here. I'm complimenting your character. And the answer to your question is that sometimes I wonder why myself."

We looked at each other, measuring the stability of this fledgling relationship. Then suddenly, for no reason that I could see beyond the fact that there was a relationship at all, we started to laugh.

"That's one reason," he said as he stood. "You make me laugh. And every time I'm with you, it's an adventure. And I mean that in the nicest way." He draped his arm over my shoulder as we walked outside.

It was time for me to get to work. We met with a staff gardener who explained how the conservatory displays were designed and mounted. An arborist told us how the lights were draped on the outside trees over a three-month schedule and then carefully removed over a one-month span. A Longwood spokesperson told us about the problems of squirrels chewing through wires and power outages from overloaded systems.

But no matter what anyone told me, I was unprepared for the glorious displays we saw. In the conservatory orangery marvelous banks of scarlet poinsettias edged squares of the most perfect lawn I'd ever seen. The rich scarlet was broken by clusters of creamy white narcissus and pink candelabra primrose. Giant baskets of crimson poinsettias hung suspended over the lawns, and creeping fig wound itself up the grand pillars that supported the great glass roof.

At the far end of the conservatory, the music room and its great Christmas tree were decorated in antiques, the pièce de résistance a large and wonderful music box that played Christmas carols in the distinctive plinky sound reminiscent of harpsichords and chimes.

In the east conservatory, bunnies fashioned from sea lavender skated on a small pond and people filed into the ballroom to hear a concert on the largest residence organ in the world. We sat next to the wall that hid the pipes, and as the organist played, I could see the fabric that formed the wall tremble under the sound waves.

When the concert finished, I reached to Curt to tell him how wonderful it had been. My hand brushed his thigh, stopped, and rested there a minute.

"Curt! Your jeans! They're still soaking wet!"

"Um," he responded. "Don't worry. They'll dry."

And he didn't even add "eventually."

By the time we emerged from the conservatory, it was both dark and cold with a nasty little wind blowing. I pulled on my gloves and wrapped my scarf about my neck, wishing for my new, warmer coat. Curt zipped his jacket and pulled up his collar.

Then I looked around and gasped. The grounds, lovely by day, had been transformed. "You're right! It's a fairyland."

Giant evergreens were outlined with cones of lights running in straight lines from point to ground. Others had lights shining randomly from their needles much like trees at home. Deciduous trees from slight dogwoods to broad, towering beeches had lights wrapped about their branches, reaching in rainbow hues into the dark sky.

"The trees look like they're strung with Skittles," I said.

"Not M&Ms or Reese's Pieces?" Curt asked.

I shook my head. "Skittles."

We wandered toward the entrance slowly, hand in hand, enjoying the wonder and beauty of more than 400,000 lights. Snow started to fall, touching everything with magic.

We came to the open-air theater where dancing fountains played under colored spotlights in time to music. We walked to the far side and stood waiting in the snow for the few minutes until the next performance began.

Suddenly music burst into the air and the fountains erupted, now splashing softly, now soaring majestically. The spotlights turned the surging water red and green and blue and white in time with the music. A gust of wind swept across the grass where we stood and I shivered. As "O Tannenbaum" began, Curt reached out and pulled me against him, my back to his front.

"I'll warm you up," he said into my hair.

Smiling, I leaned my cheek on his jacket. I straightened immediately. It was wet.

I looked up at him at the same time he glanced down. He knew why I had moved so quickly and he smiled. I shifted slightly and found a dry spot to lean on.

As I turned back toward the dancing waters, the lights flashed a brilliant white, illuminating the audience as my eyes swept past. And stopped. And stared.

Standing at the other end of the grassy area were a man and a woman. Actually there were many men and women and lots of children, but one particular couple caught my eye. She was leaning back against him and he had his arms wrapped around her. They were the picture of a couple in love taking advantage of the opportunity to be close and keep warm. He leaned down and kissed the top of her head.

She turned to say something and the reflection of the white lights bouncing off the fountains illuminated her face.

"Curt," I said in a strangled voice. "It's Jolene."

EIGHT

As I spoke, the world turned black. After a disorienting second, I realized nothing sinister had occurred. Rather, the water show had abruptly ended.

Curt looked at me. "What'd you say?"

"Jolene!" I hissed. "Over there! With some man!"

Curt looked where I pointed, but the crowd was streaming out between the evergreens that marked the edge of the theater, and all we could see was a collection of bundled-up backs.

"Come on!" I grabbed his hand and pulled.

"Easy, girl." But he let me lead him toward the entrance.

"She's with some guy!"

"So?"

I spun around to face him. "So she's a new widow! She should be home mourning!"

"Merry," Curt said with some exasperation. "She's hardly in deep mourning. She's been separated from Arnie for how long?"

"But you should have seen her. She was positively distraught when we found him. She cried and cried."

"Well, you were distraught, too, as I recall. And I seem to remember you shed a few tears of your own."

"It wasn't the same thing."

"How do you know? Anyone gets upset when they find someone they've loved dead, especially by suspicious means."

I heard the pain in his voice and remembered his sister Joan. Her death had been under unusual circumstances and quite soon after his parents' deaths in an auto accident.

"Why," Curt continued blandly, "I bet I'd even feel funny if I found Jack dead." Again he sort of spit the name.

"Curt! What a terrible thing to say!" But I giggled.

He nodded. "But I make my point. Finding anyone dead is distressing, and finding someone you once loved is horrendous. But it doesn't guarantee deep mourning. As for the guy with her, maybe Arnie wasn't the only one with fidelity issues."

I stopped, shocked at the idea, but he kept herding me toward the exit.

"You've got five minutes before we have to leave if you want to make bell practice on time," he said. "You can go to the ladies' room or the gift shop."

"It was the long line at the cashier," I explained to the bell choir as I rushed to my place along the row of padded tables. "I'm sorry."

Ned Winslow, the director and church minister of music, grunted noncommittally. "All right, people, bells up."

I loved bell choir, absolutely loved it. I was a marginal musician, and every week it took every ounce of my limited skill to perform adequately. That evening I did quite well for the most part. When I did foul up, which was only once, as usual I did it royally.

All I know is that when we practiced the song for Christmas Sunday, I got off count by two full measures, something a real musician would never do and could never understand. As a result I arrived at my run of notes way before anyone else in the whole room.

With fierce concentration I moved from my C bell to C

sharp to B, then B flat, feeling clever and ambidextrous. I was a musician, I was. I was ringing the B flat with satisfaction and pride when I finally heard the cacophony I had created. I also heard Ned yelling, "No, no, no!"

"Yes, Merry!" cheered my best friend Maddie Reeder, pumping her hands in the air. Maddie stood to my right, playing D and E. The rest of the bell choir all clapped and grinned at me. I know they say it means you're a part of the group when they tease you, but…

Fortunately Curt, who had dropped me off because there was no time to get my car from *The News* lot, wasn't there to see me be so wonderful.

"All right," Ned said with an unbelieving shake of the head. I wasn't certain whether he couldn't believe me or the rousing support of my fellow choir members. "Let's try again. Take it from the top, people."

I did fine this time, and I think I would have done so even if Ned hadn't so kindly helped me along with, "One, two, three, four, one, ready, Merry, play, now, two, three, four!"

I knew I'd have moments of cold terror between tonight and Sunday morning over the possibility of the same mistake happening in the middle of the Christmas worship service.

"Maddie," I said as she drove me to my car, "pray for me that I don't ruin Sunday. I know I'm going to do it again!"

"No, you won't." She patted me on the back like I was a frightened kid. She was a high school teacher and knew about frightened kids.

"And that's only one of today's faux pas. I managed to spill half my lunch all over Curt."

"You didn't!"

"And last night I spilled my Coke all over him."

"You're not trying to get rid of him, are you? Because if you are, there are drier ways."

"I'm afraid he's going to get rid of me. He was wearing a tan suede jacket."

"Ah, that jacket." Maddie nodded. "Maybe he will dump you. Joan gave it to him the last Christmas she was alive."

I looked at her in distress.

"I'm only teasing," she said hastily. "I don't think you need to worry. I've seen him look at you. Believe me, he likes what he sees."

I cleared my throat. "Jack's in town."

She turned to stare at me. "*The* Jack? Pittsburgh Jack? The one you moved here to escape?"

I nodded. "He's doing an audit on Bushay Environmental, so he'll be here for several weeks, maybe even months. He says he's here for me."

"I hear a definite hesitancy there. You don't believe him?"

"I think I'm afraid I do."

"Ah, the difference a few months makes!" Maddie grinned at me. "If he'd showed back in September when you first came here, you'd have run right back home with him."

"I know. And the big change in me sort of scares me. How did I change so much in such a short time?" I looked at her like she could give me the answer. "And then there's Curt. He scares me, too. He wants to fix things for me, sort of protect me from myself."

"He has a savior complex," Maddie agreed. "He developed it trying to help Joan with her problems."

"And since it didn't work there, he's trying it again with me?"

She nodded. "It's because he cares."

"I know, but I'm learning that I'd rather fix things myself, even if I make a mess of them."

"He's trying to be supportive without strangling you, you know. He told me so."

I stared at her, her long hair falling in a brown velvet cascade down her back. "You talk about me with him?" Was I pleased or horrified?

"Only once, I think. And I brought it up. Curt's too con-

tained to gossip, especially about you. I was just suggesting how he could have a better chance to win your heart."

"Maddie! Please! No more! Promise me!"

We drove a couple of blocks in silence as I thought
about the people in my life, especially Maddie, Curt and
Jack. "You know, I feel sort of sorry for Jack."

"You do?"

I nodded. "He's not really that bad a guy. He's just got
a commitment problem. Or he did. Poor guy. He came
here thinking I felt the same way about him I'd always felt.
Now he finds out I don't."

"You've told him then? Good."

I thought back over Jack's and my conversations. Had
I ever told him? "I haven't spelled things out clearly. He
probably just thinks I'm angry."

"Not good," Maddie said. She reached over and squeezed
my hand. "You can tell him and still be kind. I know you can."

I grinned at her. "You're good, girlfriend. You make me
almost believe that."

She grinned. "It comes from talking to high schoolers
all the time. The girls are always telling me their troubles,
and I'm always giving my opinions and advice. One of the
main things I always say—aside from, 'Trust in God' any
time I think it's appropriate—is, 'Be certain you choose
from strength.' Your choice for Jack all those years was
from habit and desperation."

When I started to protest, she shushed me. "Yes, and you
know it. Distance and Curt have allowed you to see more
clearly, and now you're choosing about Jack with wisdom
and perspective."

"Is that what it is? Sometimes it feels like animosity."

"You're resenting those six years. You've got to let them
go. After all, if you hadn't waited all that time, you'd never
have become desperate enough to come here and you'd
never have met Curt."

"And you." I smiled at my friend.

She smiled back and nodded. "Take your time over choices about Curt. You aren't under any time constraints there. No pressure except from yourself. Just enjoy him and see where God leads you. And make your choices from strength."

I nodded. She seemed to me to be speaking the truth in love if ever I'd heard someone do so.

"But let me tell you as your dear friend," she added with a grin, "if you let Curt get away, you're nuts!"

"Oh, I'm so glad there's no pressure here." I thought that I just might agree with her. Probably did. Most likely. There was just so much fear, so many memories of six long, painful years with another who said, "I think I love you, but let's wait a while before we make any commitments. We'll talk again in six months."

As we pulled into *The News* parking lot, the car radio began playing "There's No Place Like Home for the Holidays." I sighed, homesickness washing over me.

"What are you doing for Christmas Day?" I asked.

"We're going to my parents' for Christmas morning, and then we'll go to Doug's for Christmas dinner."

"Sounds wonderful," I said wistfully.

"It's not going to be wonderful," Maddie said in a tight voice as she stopped beside my car. "It's one of the hardest days of the year for me. The only one harder is Mother's Day."

I looked at her. "I thought you liked Doug's and your families."

Maddie nodded. "I love them. All of them. They're great people."

"Are they all tall?" I thought of Doug Reeder who, at six and a half feet, strode with his head in the stratosphere. "And skinny like Doug, too?"

"The Reeder men like *lean* better than *skinny* and the sisters like *slim*. And everybody but Doug married tall." Maddie was a little over five feet and comfortably rounded.

"I always come home from a Reeder gathering with a crink in my neck. Fortunately my family is more reasonable about height."

"Well, if you like everybody and can live with the crinky neck, what's the problem?"

Maddie was quiet for so long that I knew I had stepped into a very sensitive area. I reached out to her. "Hey, I'm sorry. You don't need to tell me anything here."

"It's okay." When she turned to me, I could see tears glistening on her cheeks. "And I know I'm much too sensitive." She sniffed. "It's just—" She sniffed again.

I dug in my purse and pulled out what was left of Airy's little pack of Kleenex from the other night at McDonald's. Her hand was shaking as she took it. She blew her nose and dabbed at her cheeks. The tears continued.

"It's the kids, all those dear little kids," she said, pain in every word. "All the nieces and nephews. They're so precious and so cute and so huggable, and I want one so badly I could die!"

"Oh, Maddie!" I bit down my surprise. She always looked so much the competent career woman that I'd assumed she and Doug had chosen not to have kids or not to have them yet. I hugged her, and she held on tightly for a minute before pulling back.

"I had no idea." In many ways it was the fact that Maddie and Doug had no children that made my friendship with her so easy. If she and I wanted to do something, no mothering responsibilities held her back.

"All I've ever wanted was to be a mom," she said. "I know it isn't chic or stylish to be so elemental, but that's been my heart's desire ever since I can remember. I always did well in school, not so I could have a career but because I liked learning stuff. I do well as a teacher because I like teaching stuff. But I want to be a mom!"

"Isn't it still early in the game for getting too upset?" I

asked hesitantly. Thirty-one hardly heralded the hour of midnight on her biological clock.

"In one way, yeah, but—" She took a deep shaky breath. "We've been trying for six years without success. Other teachers go to graduate school in the summer. I enroll in fertility programs. And nothing!" It was a cry from the heart, desolate and full of sorrow. "There's no concrete reason we can't have a baby—but we can't. 'Relax,' they all say, all the sisters and sisters-in-law who have conceived so easily. Or— and this one really makes me feel good— 'God must have something special planned for you.' Sure he does. Sterility."

Oh, God, I was busy praying as she talked. *What do I say here? I've never thought much one way or the other about having children. I guess I just always figured it would happen eventually, but I don't feel a Maddie-type yearning. Toward marriage, yes. Toward kids, no. Maybe if I ever figure out the husband thing—*

"Do you want to come to my house for Christmas instead?" I asked. "No kids there. You could teach me how to make a turkey. Then I might have the nerve to ask Curt to come."

Maddie gave a hiccuppy laugh. "Thanks, Merry. You have such a kind heart. But I want to be with our families. I really do. I just hope no one announces another pregnancy!"

I patted her hand. "It'll be all right," I said. "You'll see." Now there was a useful comment.

She shrugged. "I just have to watch that I don't get resentful about the joy they all take in their pregnancies and babies. They should be happy about them. They should laugh and brag a bit and be filled with satisfaction. After all, that's the way it's supposed to be."

"I'm going to pray for you," I said. "I'm going to pray for you every day between now and Christmas that you enjoy the day, that you enjoy your family. And I'm going to pray that you have a baby real soon."

Maddie sniffed one last time and stuffed damp Kleenex in her coat pocket. "From your lips to God's ear."

I gave my friend a final hug and climbed into my car. Maddie backed out and drove away, but I sat for a few minutes, thinking. I tried to imagine what it was like to be Maddie and yearn for a baby so desperately. Then I tried to imagine what it was like to be Pam or Karyn and be having a baby so easily and inconveniently. I failed completely on both accounts.

God, I have enough trouble being me on days like today, let alone figuring out what or how someone else thinks. Just help me be a good friend.

As I pulled out of *The News* lot, I decided that all this thinking and heavy conversation had made me hungry. I needed a hoagie. Dr. Merry's prescription for dealing with emotional trauma, whether my own or someone else's, was food, especially a mouthwatering sandwich that excluded only the kitchen sink.

I drove one exit west of town on the bypass to the strip mall where the best hoagie shop was located. I bought my sandwich and carried my tightly wrapped treasure to the car. The marvelous fragrances of onions and garlic and salami and other wonderful Italian spices filled its interior.

I was traveling through the wooded area between the mall and the bypass entrance when bright beads of reflected light on the left side of the road caught my eye. I looked just in time to see a deer and her sparkling eyes disappear into the thicket at the road's edge.

My breath caught in my throat at the beauty of her leap, and I was thankful she wasn't one of the deer carcasses I saw lying on the shoulders of the roads all the time. I'd seen red stains on the Route 30 bypass from more than one deer who'd bought the farm, and I'd heard countless stories from people about their run-ins or near misses.

In fact I'd even pitched a story to Mac about an interview with one of the county game wardens whose job was collecting the carcasses when and if he had the spare time from his other duties. As I understood it, there was even a special dump where he disposed of the bodies. Mac hadn't bought the idea.

Thankful that the deer I'd sighted was safe in the woods, I glanced back to the highway, and there she was, a second deer, directly in front of me, blinded by my headlights. I'd forgotten the adage that where there is one deer, there are usually more.

She looked at me, startled rather than afraid, her ears and tail at attention. I didn't even have time to slam on my brakes.

NINE

It happened in slow motion even though I hit her at full speed. She smashed my headlights and the fragments of glass flew up over the hood, peppering the windshield, making me flinch. She flew up over the grill, too, her huge body and frail legs landing with a terrible thud on the hood. I was sure she was going to come through the windshield and land in my lap. I imagined the hoofs kicking and slashing and the blood and guts. My guts.

Instead she kept sliding and sliding to the right across the slick hood until she fell off and disappeared into the darkness.

I stamped on the brakes and pulled to the side of the road. I was shaking all over. I forced myself to walk on my wobbly legs to the front of the car and inspect the damage. I had no glass across the front. Headlights, turning signals—all were gone.

I looked back up the road toward the accident site. I couldn't see anything in the dark. I made myself walk back to where I thought I'd struck her. I couldn't let her lie in the street in agony if she wasn't dead.

Not that I knew what I'd do if I found her thrashing and moaning. Except be sick. Thank goodness I hadn't already eaten my hoagie.

I knew I was there when my feet crunched on broken

glass. But there was no deer in the road. I walked along the shoulder, but all I saw were wisps of my own frosted breath.

I climbed back in the car, and because I had no headlights, drove myself slowly and cautiously home. As soon as I got home, I called the state police and reported the accident.

"Don't worry about it," the officer told me. "We'll take it from here."

Feeling very relieved and slightly hungry again, I sat down in front of the TV with my hoagie, some chips, a decaf diet Coke and a couple of Oreos for dessert. Whiskers sat on the back of my overstuffed chair like a furry vulture, a feline Snoopy.

"Not for you, baby," I said.

He stalked away, tail straight up in the air.

Well, I guess I'm sleeping alone tonight.

But the boy loved a soft mattress and shared body heat more than the hard floor.

The next morning, Friday, only four days to Christmas, I called Mr. Hamish, the car rental man.

All I had to say was, "Mr. Hamish, this is Merrileigh Kramer."

"Miss Kramer! I been waiting for your call."

"You have?" How did he know about my deer?

"Sure. I read in *The News* about you being involved in another murder. I knew it was just a matter of time." He was very taken with what he called my exploits. "What happened this time? They shoot out all your tires? Your windshield? They run you off the road? They force you over an embankment? They cut all your hoses so you couldn't follow them and get the goods?"

Mr. Hamish obviously watched way too much TV. "I hit a deer."

"Ah," he said. "Too bad. Them deer practically beg to get hit. This one foiled your chance to get the crooks, I bet. What a shame. Well, come on down. I have just the car for you."

"Thanks. I appreciate your quick help."

Now all I needed was a ride to Mr. Hamish's from Taggart's Garage where I wanted to drop my car to get it fixed. I didn't feel right asking Jolene given the circumstances, and Maddie would be going to school. That left Jack or Curt. No contest.

"Why do you need to get your car fixed?" Curt asked when I called. "What happened, Merry? You're all right, aren't you?" I could hear the stress in his voice.

"I'm fine. And I think the deer is, too. She disappeared into the woods."

"You're sure you're all right? I mean really sure?"

"I'm fine."

"You're hard on my heart in more ways than one, lady. I never knew anyone who got herself into so many scrapes!"

"Are you saying I'm careless or incapable or something?"

"Adventurous is the kindest way to say it. And a tad defensive."

"I am not!"

"Hah!" And he hung up.

Mr. Taggart promised quick repairs on my car, and I don't think it was just because Curt stood towering silently over both of us, looking unhappily at my damaged front end. When he drove me to Mr. Hamish's, he was so quiet it made me nervous. I started to bite my nails. Absently he reached over and pulled my hand from my mouth and held it, but he wasn't present in the car.

"What's the matter?" For once I couldn't think of anything I'd done wrong.

He pulled into Mr. Hamish's, ignoring my question. "I'll give you a call tonight to see how the rental works out and to hear what Mr. Taggart says."

"Uh-uh," I said. "I'm not getting out until you tell me what's wrong."

He smiled, but he still wasn't present. "Go on. I'll talk to you tonight."

I sat with my arms folded, staring at him.

"You're going to be late for work."

"So I'm late. I have an excuse. Now what's wrong?"

He stared at the steering wheel, his hands gripping it at ten and two.

"Curt, talk to me. What have I done wrong?"

He looked surprised. "You haven't done anything wrong."

"Then what's the problem?"

His knuckles were white where they gripped the wheel. "I need to think. I'll tell you when I know."

"When you know what?"

"Go on." He leaned over and pecked me on the cheek. "You need to get to work. So do I."

I watched forlornly as he drove away. Why couldn't he discuss whatever was bothering him with me? Unless it was me.

On that happy thought, I drove to work in a brand-new white Sable. I called my insurance agent first thing and started the claims process. He promised to go to Mr. Taggart's that very afternoon to check on the damage and issue a check.

After the day's paper went to press, I putzed around the newsroom doing things like answering my mail and reading about waste management and efforts to protect the environment on the Internet. When my mind was swimming with codes and penalties and uncertainty about how it all applied to Bushay Environmental and Arnie, I decided a trip to the dry cleaners would be just the thing to clear my mind. I took Mac's list of Jolene's Tuesday afternoon errands with me when I went.

Our coats were each packaged in its own plastic bag. All the other things—scarves, gloves—were sealed in a single small plastic bag. I pulled my red coat out of its bag before I left the store and looked it over carefully. They'd done a good job, and I put it on with pleasure. I hung my old coat on the hanger and slid the protective plastic down over it. I traded my old scarf for the new red paisley, its silky side against the collar, its warm wool side against my neck. My gloves had cleaned up well, too, and I pulled them on. I laid everything on the backseat, taking care to spread the coats neatly so they wouldn't wrinkle.

My first stop on my investigative journeys was to Hennessey's, the drugstore down the street from the paper. I went to the back of the store to the prescription area.

"Can I help you?" a woman about my age asked.

"I hope so. My boss, Mac Carnuccio at *The News*, was supposed to get a prescription from here on Tuesday—"

"Oh, yeah! Jolene already picked it up."

"You know Jolene?" Small town Amhearst strikes again.

"Sure. And Arnie, too." She shook her head. "You never think someone you know will get murdered, do you?" She looked at me wide-eyed. "And just think! She was here mere hours before she found him."

"Do you remember what time Jolene came in?"

"I do. I just got back from my lunch break, about 1:30."

"Thanks." I turned to go.

"Oh, and if you see Jo," she called after me, "tell her I'm real sorry about Arnie. Even stuck-up people probably feel sad, don't they?"

My second stop was at Bob's Book Bin across the street from *The News*.

"Sure, Jolene was in here the other day," Bob told me as he rearranged a shelf. "She picked up an order for Mac. Don't tell him I said so, but the man has no taste in reading whatsoever."

I grinned. "Can you remember what time Jo was in here?"

Bob frowned. "That was Tuesday and I was reading a Dick Francis. I finished it before three, Tuesday being a slow day. She got me just before the big race where the hero figures everything out. Must have been about 1:30 to 1:45. Somewhere in there."

Hannah's Hallmark was in the minimall east of Amhearst with the Giant food store, Fashion Bug and Payless Shoes. Hannah's was crawling with people buying last-minute holiday cards and wrapping paper. I grabbed a couple of little gift bags I didn't need and took my place in line so I could talk to the cashier. I was sure no one would remember Jolene, with all the people rushing about these aisles.

Finally it was my turn, and I handed the cashier my two little bags, feeling quite the piker. Her hair was disarranged, and her lipstick long gone.

"A friend of mine was in here on Tuesday buying Christmas cards. Jolene Meister. I don't suppose you remember?"

She just looked at me.

"They were for her boss, Mac Carnuccio, editor of *The News*."

She shrugged. "That'll be $7.96."

Sighing, I paid and carried my purchases to the car. So I didn't have the times Jolene visited the grocery store or Hannah's, but all the other times were early afternoon. Hennessey's—1:30. Bob's—1:45. MAC—2:05. Staples—2:38. I was willing to bet that Giant was the grocery store she visited when she stopped here at Hannah's. Even if she stopped here after Staples, by my calculations that left at least an hour and a half—from 3:15 to 4:45—unaccounted for.

So where was Jolene in the late afternoon? She definitely had time to go to the house. But did she?

The last thing on my list before returning to work was a visit to the Country Club out by the reservoir outside Coatesville. The attractive new gray stone clubhouse fronted on the water, and the windows of both the formal dining room and the 19th hole offered a charming vista of Canada geese skimming across the water or standing on one leg on the rime about the edges. I was fascinated to notice that they all faced into the wind.

I looked into the 19th hole and smiled at an attractive waitress.

"Want a seat?" she asked.

"No, thanks." Standing in a private club without a membership made me feel like an underage drinker waiting to be carded, not that I'd ever been one, of course. I smiled pleasantly. "I was wondering if Harry Allen Bushay left his briefcase here earlier in the week? I think it was Tuesday."

She thought for a minute. "I don't know," she said. "But why don't you ask him?" She pointed across the room. "He's right over there."

Harry Allen chose that moment to look up from his menu. When he saw me, he smiled broadly, his pearly teeth nearly as white as his shock of hair.

I smiled weakly back and waved. I don't think I ran from the place, but it may merely be an issue of semantics.

I returned to the newsroom where I'd barely sat down before the phone rang.

"Merry, you've got to help me."

"Jolene?"

"Of course Jolene. Who else?"

I could think of lots of possibilities, but I said, "What can I do for you?"

"I need to go out to my condo, but I don't want to drive out there alone. I'm a bit gun-shy about walking into places these days."

I could understand that. I glanced at my watch. 3:30.

"Let me check with Mac. Are you at your mom and dad's?"

"Yeah, I've been staying here. I don't want to be alone."

I thought of the guy who had held her close and kissed the top of her head last night. That didn't seem too alone to me.

"And if you're good," she said, "Mom'll feed you."

I recalled the tantalizing fragrances of the other night. "That sounds wonderful. And I've got your coat and stuff. Wait until you see the price!"

Mac was preoccupied when I finally tracked him down, but he waved me off to Jolene's. "She needs you more than I do."

"Mac, you're a softie under your wiseguy front," I teased.

"Don't start that rumor, whatever you do. I have a reputation to uphold."

Jolene was dressed in jeans and a plaid flannel shirt of her father's, and she had her hair pulled back in a ponytail. I'd never seen her in casual clothes before, and she was even more beautiful than when she was all gussied up. Real hair instead of big hair made her seem fragile, and I couldn't imagine why someone who looked like she did would hide all that beauty under the layers of makeup she usually affected.

Her mother waved as we left. "Bye-bye, Jolene, dear. Goodbye, June."

I waved and smiled sweetly at Mrs. Luray, then looked directly at the split in the curtains next door and waved to it. The slit disappeared fast.

"Jo, has the lady next door always been so nosy?"

"Mrs. Samson? Yep. She's got no life of her own, so she lives through other people."

"What happened to Mr. Samson?"

"He was killed in Korea."

"As in the war? But that's over fifty years ago."

"She's been a widow ever since. Could never find another man stupid enough to marry her."

"But she had kids, right? Wasn't that guy the other night her grandson?"

"That's Reilly. His father is Mrs. Samson's son, and there's a daughter, but she was smart enough to move to Wyoming."

"Why do you dislike Mrs. Samson so?"

"Because she's nasty and pushes her nose where it doesn't belong. And she hates me."

"Your mom seems to like her."

"And you consider that a character reference, June?"

We pulled into Jolene's cul de sac, and she directed me to a beautiful gray stone-fronted condominium with shining white doors and shutters, a fascinating and varied roofline and perfectly groomed shrubs. A gorgeous wreath of greens, ribbons, silk poinsettias, pinecones and a brass English hunting horn hung on the front door.

"Oh, Jolene, it's lovely."

She grunted. "You're so easy." She led the way up the walk.

We were almost at the front door when the door to the neighboring unit opened and a white-haired lady of comfortable girth and a good-natured smile walked out. She led a Scottie dog on a leash. The animal gave a shout of joy when he saw Jolene. He rushed across the lawn and sat directly in front of her. Even sitting, his hind quarters twitched with excitement.

"Well, Jolene, honey," the woman said, her smile broadening. "MacDuff's so glad to see you. Aren't you, sweetie?"

MacDuff wagged his stubby tail harder. He continued to stare lovingly at Jolene, who continued to ignore him.

"Mrs. Forester," Jolene said with a noticeable lack of enthusiasm. "How nice to see you." She finally glanced down at the little black dog. "MacDuff."

MacDuff went nuts, whining, wiggling, wetting the pavement.

"Hi, MacDuff," I said, kneeling and holding out my hand. He didn't even glance at me. His eyes never left Jolene.

"Oops, I left something in the car," Jo said. "Be right back." And she almost ran back down the walk. MacDuff tried to follow, but his lead brought him up short after five steps. He sat and stared soulfully.

"That girl," Mrs. Forester said with a strange mixture

of approval and disapproval. "She's something, she is. Her husband may have just been killed, but she doesn't let that stop her. Not that I like to gossip."

Yeah, right. Tell me another one.

"But last night he was here again. Spent the night. They think nobody notices if he leaves at dawn. Naive, don't you think? Them, I mean. Not me. They're not considering old people's bladders at all."

"What?" was all I could think to say.

She grinned her contagious smile and with a wave of her hand she was gone, MacDuff waddling beside her.

So someone was here with Jo last night. Logic said it was the guy from Longwood. The question was: Who was he? Not Airy's Sean. Oh, please! Surely not him.

Jolene came up the walk with her leather and fur coat slung over her arm. She had her freshly cleaned gloves and scarf in her hand. "Almost forgot them. What are you standing here for? Go on in where it's warm."

"I'm waiting for you to unlock the door."

"Oh. Silly me," she said and tried the knob once, twice, a third time. "It's locked."

"I should hope so. You've been away."

I held her fancy coat while she fished in her bag for her keys. She unlocked the door, and we walked into the entry. And stopped abruptly.

"Oh, Jolene!" My hand went to my mouth as I stood, appalled.

The potted plant that sat on the table in the entry hall was spilled on the floor, dirt making an ugly scar across scattered newspapers. The drawer in the front of the table was ajar and its contents hung out or lay on the floor. The mail from the past couple of days was strewn across the thick, white carpet. The coat closet was open and a number of coats lay in colorful puddles on the white floor, their pockets turned inside out, their arms bent at weird angles. Long scarves, short scarves, plaid scarves, plain scarves, leather gloves, knit gloves, mittens, berets, Indiana Jones hats and ski caps festooned the entry like large chunks of confetti.

"Merry!" Jolene screamed, finally finding her voice. "I've been robbed!"

TEN

She rushed into the living room with me right behind her. Her sofa and chair cushions were askew or on the floor, silk flowers lay on their sides, magazines were strewn across more white carpet. Volumes of leather-bound classics sat in neat piles on the floor rather than on their shelves on either side of the fireplace. I was too busy taking in all the chaos to wonder at Jolene and leather-bound classics. That came later.

In the kitchen, drawers and cabinets were open, and sugar was spilled across the countertop. Pots and pans sat about on the floor, some upended, some with their lids neatly on.

"Don't touch anything!" I said as I stepped over a Crock-Pot and dialed 911. Not that Jolene was touching things. She seemed frozen in place, unable to believe what she saw.

When I hung up, she looked at me, eyes huge with distress. "Who would do this? And why? Do you think it has something to do with Arnie?"

I shook my head. *Lord, how much can she take? Comfort her, please. She's been through more than enough these last few days.*

While we waited for the police, we went upstairs to see what, if any, damage had been done there.

In the master bedroom we found the closet open.

Dresses, slacks, blouses and jackets littered the floor. The white comforter, strewn with huge pink and scarlet cabbage roses, was thrown back, the bedding jumbled and trailing on the floor, the pillows scattered about the room. Dresser drawers hung open, some pulled off their tracks and lying upside down on the floor. Expensive silk scarves, slips, panties, bras and incredibly feminine and lacy nightgowns—a sharp contrast to the oversized T-shirts I slept in—spilled in a pastel rainbow about the room. It was as if some desperate person had grabbed handfuls of the delicate garments and thrown them.

"Someone's been in my most private stuff!" Jolene shouted. "Someone has been running his slimy hands through my underwear!" She shivered with revulsion. "And did you see my coats downstairs? Did you see them? Dumped on the floor and the pockets and sleeves all turned inside out! And up here it's my personal stuff! And my closet!"

She grabbed at some of her underwear like she wanted to put it back in the drawers, and I grabbed at her. "Don't touch, Jo. Don't touch."

"But I don't want the cops to see all this!"

"Don't worry. They've seen it all before." I dragged her from the bedroom, but not until we'd seen that the medicine chest in the adjoining bath was open. Pill bottles as well as the innards of a tube of toothpaste filled the sink. Towels were pulled off their racks and from the linen closet and spread all over the floor.

"How did someone get in?" I asked as we sat on the edge of our chairs at the kitchen table, waiting once again for the police.

"How do I know?" Jolene snapped, then recovered enough to throw, "Sorry," in my direction.

"The front door was locked when you last left, wasn't it?" I asked.

"What are you suggesting, Merry? That it was my fault some lowlife broke in and robbed me?"

"Easy." I put my hand up in a pacifying movement. "You've had a very difficult few days. Maybe you forgot to lock up when you last left. That's all."

"But I haven't been here since before Arnie was killed, and that was three days ago. All I know is that I usually lock up very carefully. What woman who lives alone doesn't?"

I understood what she meant. I was sort of paranoid about locks, too. Still, according to MacDuff's mom...

"Did the burglar actually rob you, Jo?"

"How do I know? How can I tell if something's missing with a mess like this?"

"Point taken. But what did you do for clothes if you weren't here?"

"I've got things at Mom and Dad's. Not much as you can see." She indicated her jeans and flannel shirt. She sniffed dramatically. "I couldn't bring myself to come here alone. I just couldn't."

"So ever since Arnie's death you've been at your parents'? You haven't been here? You haven't gone anywhere?"

"I haven't been here. I haven't gone anywhere. I've just been crying and holding their hands and picking Mom up off the floor as necessary." She raised shaking hands to her face. "It hasn't been a pretty time."

I stared at her bowed head and thought about the lies. Why did she tell them, especially since they'd be so easy to disprove?

"I can't believe it, Merry." Her distraught voice slid out between her fingers. "Someone's been in my house!"

The doorbell rang and I answered it. Sergeant Poole's craggy face brightened when he saw me.

"Merry, a mere robbery? No corpse?"

"Mere robbery nothing," Jolene yelled from the kitchen.

"It's my house and there's nothing mere about it!" She stormed into the entry, the fire of righteous indignation blazing in her eyes.

William held up a hand. "I'm very sorry. My joke may have seemed inappropriate. I certainly didn't mean to make light of your situation." He held out his clipboard and incident report sheet. "Tell me what you've found in as much detail as you can. Tell me from the time you walked in the front door."

Jolene sniffed, somewhat placated. "Well, we came in and found this mess." She flung her arms wide. "Why would someone dump coats and stuff all over the floor? And upstairs my personal things are scattered everywhere!" She shivered. "That's sick. It really is."

She led William from room to room, pointing out the destruction. Finally we stood in the bedroom once again. Jolene sputtered and spit and finally exploded. "Somebody's got to pay for this, and if I find out who…"

She let the threat trail off, but I was glad I wasn't the culprit. Having Jolene that mad at you seemed a very bad thing, like having the Wicked Witch of the West on your tail, murderous monkeys and all.

"Look around the room carefully, Mrs. Meister," William said. "Are you sure nothing's missing? Nothing's gone from your jewelry box?"

"I don't see anything missing," she said with a weary shake of her head, then looked at William, her great brown eyes lustrous with unshed tears. "I feel so vulnerable."

"I'm sure you do," William told her. "After you've had time to make a thorough search, please call me if you discover anything missing after all."

Jolene nodded, but somehow I knew she wasn't going to search and so did William. Finally he left with bland and meaningless assurances that the police would do their best to get the bad guys.

"Thank you," she whispered. "You're so kind."

As soon as he was gone, she became brisk, picking the plant up off the floor and hanging up the coats.

I stuck a navy blue windbreaker back on its hanger. "You were very impressive. Have you considered a career in theater? Of course you couldn't have dinner with your parents every night if you worked in New York, but you'd soon be rich enough to move them to the city with you. But then you're already rich, aren't you? And you haven't moved them yet."

Jolene stared at me through slitted eyes. "What are you talking about?"

"I'm not quite sure, Jo." I swallowed my pounding heart, hoping that it would once again take its proper place in my chest. Maybe then I'd be able to hear myself think over its tattoo. "Still, I think I've got you pegged."

"What?" She was livid.

I took a deep breath. "Someone really, truly broke in here, didn't he? That's why you're so all-fired mad, right? What did the thief get into, Jo? Your coat closet and your bureau? Is that why you're so angry about those things being tossed about? You set up your little charade, and then someone made it the real thing?"

Her eyes were wide and innocent. "What are you talking about, Merry?"

"You were really surprised at the locked front door, weren't you? What did you do, go back to the car so I'd be the one to find the door ajar? But it wasn't ajar. It was locked. That must have been a nasty shock."

"Really, Merry." Jolene gave a brisk shake of her ponytail. "I can't believe you're implying such awful things about me. I thought we were friends." She actually worked up a tear in one eye.

"Can it, Jo. I'm not Alvin or Eloise. I know a setup when I see one, and I suspect that Sergeant Poole does, too.

The questions are, why did you do it, and who beat you at your own game?"

"You know, you're not a very nice person sometimes." She stalked to the kitchen.

Maybe not, but certain things had to be said. She couldn't be allowed to set her own rules forever. I trailed her to the kitchen and stood leaning against the doorjamb, watching her clean up the spilled sugar by hand-sweeping it into the sink and washing it down the drain.

"You could always help, you know," she said.

"Not a chance. You mess it, you clean it."

"You're a hard woman, Merry. I never saw it before, but you are. I pity poor Curt."

I didn't even bother to respond to that. "You messed things up too nicely," I said instead. "If someone had really ransacked the place, things would have been a bit more chaotic. Vandals like to ruin, and nothing's ruined here. The sugar would be ground into the floor along with lots of other kitchen things like oil and syrup and soap—things that damage. The plant in the entry wouldn't have conveniently fallen on a piece of newspaper. The books would have been tossed helter-skelter, their spines broken, their covers damaged, their pages bent. And that toothpaste in the upstairs sink—I bet it's an Arnie leftover, and you can't stand the brand."

She went absolutely still for a second, and I knew I'd scored.

"Why'd you do it, Jo? So the police wouldn't think you had anything to do with Arnie's death?"

"I told you. I haven't been anywhere since Arnie died. How could I do it?"

"I repeat. I'm not Alvin and Eloise. And you could have done it with your lover's help before the two of you left at the crack of dawn this morning. The question is why?"

"My parents will tell you I was at home all night!"

"I don't doubt they will. I get the feeling that they do pretty much anything you tell them. But Mrs. Forester isn't so docile and easily led. And neither am I, though you obviously thought I was when you asked me to bring you here."

Jolene's eyes welled with tears once again. "I thought you liked me. I thought we were friends. I want us to be friends." Sniff, sniff. "But obviously I read you wrong."

"Jo, hasn't anyone ever told you that friends aren't for manipulating?"

"I know what friends are for," she blazed, pain and sorrow forgotten. "Friends are for supporting and helping. You should be supporting me!" She was indignant and self-righteous, as lethal a combination as bleach and ammonia.

"Why aren't you answering me?" I asked my question quietly.

"A friend shouldn't have to answer for her actions to a friend. Friends trust each other. They don't accuse." She picked up what appeared to be never-used dish towels and threw them angrily into a drawer.

"Where were you Tuesday afternoon, Jo? After you ran Mac's errands, I mean. Did you go to the house?"

She pointed one of her long, lethal nails at me. "Accusing, accusing. You're conveniently forgetting that I suffered the trauma of finding his body."

I looked at her. "I guess that's why you were at Longwood last night, to find relief from the trauma."

She blinked, startled, and it took her a moment to regroup. "Whoever told you I was at Longwood was lying."

I shook my head. "I'm the one who saw you, Jo."

When she took a deep breath to argue more, I turned toward the door. "I'm leaving now, and if you want a ride to your parents, you are, too."

I walked out the front door, strode to the car, and climbed in. I sat there for a couple of minutes to give Jo a chance to come out and to give my stomach a chance to cease its heaving and tossing. I had no idea whether she would be willing to get in the car with me or not. I just knew I wasn't willing to be as easily baited as Airy or as easily manipulated as Eloise and Alvin.

When the winter chill began to seep into my feet, I glanced at the house. The lights still blazed upstairs and down. I sighed and reached for the ignition just as the bedroom lights went out. I waited a couple more minutes, and lights blinked off room by room. Finally Jolene appeared on the front porch, pulling the door shut and checking to see that it was locked.

She climbed into the passenger side and sat silently huddled against the far door. I wondered if she thought she was punishing me by withdrawing her presence. If so, it wasn't working. I didn't care enough to be anything more than slightly annoyed at her petty attitude—and greatly relieved at the quiet.

When we reached her parents', she turned to me. "Mom's cooked a ham for you." She smiled warmly. "And she's made her world-famous pineapple casserole and melt-in-your-mouth scalloped potatoes."

I stared. I was her new best friend again? "I'm still coming to dinner?"

"Of course." She laughed a sweet, little I'm-delighted-at-your-wit laugh. "You won't regret it. Nobody beats Eloise Luray in the kitchen. She's even made you a from-scratch apple crumb pie."

I was impressed in spite of my pique, and my stomach rumbled.

"Just don't mention the break-in, okay? I don't want to pick Mom up off the floor this evening. And don't mention the murder. It's still a sensitive area."

I waved politely to Mrs. Samson, Master Spy, as we went up the steps and into Wonderland. Alvin Luray grabbed my coat before the door was even closed, a congenial Mad Hatter. "We've been looking forward to your company all day, Merry. Haven't we, Mother?"

Mrs. Luray came rushing from the kitchen, the flustered White Rabbit. "Hello, June! I'm so glad you came. I've been cooking for you all day. Oh, aren't we glad Jolene Marie has a nice friend like June, Daddy?"

The meal was everything Jo had promised it would be and more. Jo herself was sweet and charming and slightly ditzy, all traces of the shrew and manipulator carefully wiped away. But eating with the Lurays was definitely a down-the-rabbit-hole experience of non sequiturs and nonsense. The third time Eloise Luray asked me if I thought we'd have a white Christmas, I said, "Only if Bing Crosby or Rosemary Clooney comes to sing for us."

"But Bing's dead, June," Mrs. Luray said seriously. "And Rosemary doesn't live in Amhearst. I don't think anyone famous lives in Amhearst, do you?"

I shook my head, to clear it as much as to indicate a negative, and took another bite of the pineapple.

"That's right, June, dear. Eat up. I don't like leftovers. Did I ever tell you about the flowers Arnie brought me the first time he came to take Jolene on a date?" Only about four times. "Daisies and mums. Yellow and white. So pretty. He's such a delightful boy. I'm so glad Jolene married him instead of—"

"Mom!" cut in Jolene quite loudly. I jumped, surprised at her volume. "Mom, I think Merry wants some of your delicious apple pie."

"Do you, dear?" Mrs. Luray looked pleased.

"We all do, Eloise," Mr. Luray said as he began collecting dirty dishes. "May I help you cut it?"

We were just finishing the wonderful pie when the doorbell rang, and the Red Queen entered.

"Mrs. Samson," Eloise Luray fluttered. "How nice to see you. Come have a piece of pie with us."

"I can't stay," she said, eyeing Jolene with loathing. Off with her head! "But I'll take a piece with me."

"Wonderful!" Mrs. Luray clapped her hands. "Let me go get it for you."

Mrs. Samson turned to Mr. Luray and smiled. "Alvin, dear," she all but purred, "I need a ride to the grocery store tomorrow. Can you take me?"

Mr. Luray nodded. "Still don't have your car back?"

"No. That deer did me in, let me tell you. Did my car in, too. Totaled it."

"Did you hit a deer?" I asked. "Me, too!"

"First time," Mrs. Samson said.

"First time for me, too." Good grief. I had something in common with the Red Queen. "I was on a back road west of town last night, not too far from the mall."

"At my age I was beginning to hope I would die without hitting one. Then, boom!" She looked at me proudly. "I killed it. The police came. I had to go to the hospital. I had to be towed."

"Wow." I tried to look properly impressed. "I just needed to get my car repaired."

She turned to Mr. Luray. "This is probably the last time I'll need to bother you, Alvin. I get my new car on Monday."

"Wonderful," he said.

"Reilly went with me this afternoon to buy it. He's such a wonderful boy." And she glared at Jolene.

Ah, I thought as I watched her depart, piece of pie in hand. The light dawns.

When I finally left at about 7:30, my stomach was purring with pleasure and my head was about to explode. I rubbed the throbbing vein in my forehead as I walked to the car. Jolene walked with me, her arms wrapped around herself in a vain attempt to keep warm without a coat.

We were halfway down the stairs when Mrs. Samson's door flew open, and Reilly Samson dashed out. "Hey, Jolene."

"Go away, Reilly," she snapped.

"Ever thought about being polite?" he asked sarcastically and disappeared up the street.

"His grandmother thinks you like him," I said.

"His grandmother's an idiot."

I opened the Sable's door and slid in. Jolene stood beside me, looking down. I could feel her hesitation.

"I was trying to protect myself," she said suddenly. "I know they look at the wife first, and I don't want to be looked at. I know they think I did it for the money. It screams motive! But half of the money's always been mine anyway. But they'll say I wanted it all." She shrugged. "I just wanted to look like a victim, too."

"Just tell the police the truth." I smiled encouragement. "The truth is always the best course."

She smiled sourly. "How did you get to be so naive?"

I clenched my teeth and thought nasty thoughts.

When I braked for the stop sign at the end of the block, I glanced in my rearview mirror. I wasn't all that surprised to see Jo come rushing out of the house, this time with her leather and fur coat on. I watched over my shoulder as she hurried up the street after Reilly Samson. When they met, they kissed quickly, then climbed in a car and drove off in the general direction of Jolene's condominium.

My mind was still whirling as I walked past the lilac to my front door. I straightened the wreath hanging there. Mom had made it for me of the realest-looking artificial evergreens, and the red bow kept lurching to the left, causing the fabric angel with the Spanish moss hair to list drunkenly, too.

Beautiful but imperfect, I thought, just like my family. Though since meeting the Lurays, they look a lot more perfect than ever before!

Oh, dear God, I'm going to miss them! Help me survive, okay?

I pulled my key from my purse and slid it into the lock. I turned the key and prepared to push the door open when it suddenly registered that not only were lights on inside, but through the sheer curtain that covered the glass-paned upper half of the door, I could also see someone moving.

ELEVEN

Someone was in my house!

Through the sheer curtain, I watched, frozen, as the giant inside turned and stalked toward the door. He paused just the other side of the glass panes and stared through the curtain at me. Then he pulled the door open and reached for me.

Suddenly I could move again.

"Jack!" I stepped up and in and he was reduced to his normal size, a mere five eleven.

I pushed him out of my way as I strode into the living room. "You scared me to death!"

Scowling fiercely and muttering about fear-induced heart attacks, I hugged the dry-cleaning bag to me like it would soothe my racing pulse. Whiskers watched me with great interest from the back of the sofa.

Jack was studying me as if he'd never seen me before, and his attitude made me angry all over again. "I think it would be a good idea if you went home."

Of course he ignored my suggestion. What else is new?

"Easy, Merry." He reached for me, but I ducked his embrace.

"Don't you touch me," I snarled.

He put his hands up placatingly. I could see him trying to control his anger, though why he was angry was beyond me. I was the one who had been scared out of the few wits I possessed.

"You know, Merry, this move to Amhearst hasn't done much for your disposition."

That stopped me in my tracks. "What?"

"You used to be this nice, pleasant person who was a joy to be with. You laughed and smiled. Now you're this— this termagant." He hurled the word at me like a pitcher aiming for a brushback.

"I'm a what?" I could picture him with his box of a thousand vocabulary flash cards, looking for one that applied to me. He'd found a doozy.

"You're a shrew," he said. "A fury. A harridan. A nasty—"

"I know what termagant means," I said stiffly.

"So what are you going to do about it?" he challenged.

I stared, astonished at his gall. If anyone was being shrewish, it was not me.

"You quarrel and pick at me all the time," he said. "You hold me at arm's length. You won't even talk to me on the phone."

"After the way you spoke to me the other night? I should say not."

"Here I am, waiting for you because Friday nights have always been our nights, and you're not even here!" He said the last with such incredulity that I could only stare.

"Of course I'm not here! You haven't been here. As usual, you just assumed. In fact, for six years you assumed, and I was stupid enough to meet all your expectations. I was pliable, acquiescent and stupid. Well, no more, buddy!"

"See what I mean?" He pointed an accusatory finger. "See?"

I took a deep, steadying breath. "Jack, over the last four months things have changed."

Did I see a flash of fear race across his face before he grabbed on to his anger again?

"It's not *things* that have changed, Merry," he said, his eyes hot.

I don't know what I would have said, but I was saved by the bell. I stalked to the phone and grabbed the receiver. I took a deep breath and spoke as calmly as I could.

"Hi, it's me."

"Hi, me." What was it about Curt's voice that made my bones turn to water?

"How was your day?"

"Straight out of Alice in Wonderland. I'll tell you tomorrow."

"That's what I called about. I'll pick you up at 6:20 and we'll go get Maddie and Doug. Dress up."

"I look forward to it," I said softly.

"Hey, Merry, honey," Jack called loudly. "Isn't dinner ready yet? I'm famished!"

I spun and glared at him. He glared back.

"Who's that?" Curt asked, his voice suddenly taut. "Jack?"

"He's just leaving."

"No, I'm not," Jack all but shouted. "The evening's still young. I can't leave my favorite girl yet."

"Want me to come over?" Curt asked, ever the White Knight.

"Why?" I asked, my anger at Jack, at Jolene, at my lack of a Christmas spilling over to scald poor Curt. "To protect me or to see that I behave correctly? I can take care of myself, thank you!"

In the stunned silence that echoed down the phone line, I watched Jack smirk with satisfaction.

I shut my eyes to block him out as I sagged against the wall. My face flamed with mortification. I can take care of myself, thank you!

Suddenly I realized I had been yelling that last line

directly at Jack, but how could I explain that to Curt? All he knew was that I had screamed at him when he tried to be kind, pouring vituperation—now there was a word to keep *termagant* company—all over him instead of my usual Cokes.

I needed to apologize. I needed to ask forgiveness. I needed to throw myself across my bed and weep at my ineptitude.

But I certainly wasn't going to do any of it in front of Jack.

"Can I call you back in a half hour?" I asked in a small voice. "I think I need some time."

"Please," came the terse answer. "You do."

I hung up and walked into my bedroom, shutting the door behind me. I stood in the darkness and wondered if maybe I *had* become a termagant. My face flamed anew.

Lord, when did I get so nasty?

There was a tentative knock on the door. "Merry?" It was Jack.

"Go away," I said wearily.

"Come on, sweetheart. Talk to me."

Now that was exactly what I wanted, more conversation with Jack. I slumped to the floor, my back against the wall, and stared at the bar of light beneath the door.

"Merry! Are you all right?"

"I'm fine."

"You don't sound it."

"No?" I was too drained to say more.

After a minute he spoke again, genuine concern in his voice. "I'm sorry, Merry. I didn't mean to upset you."

I snorted, sounding just like Jolene. Just like a termagant.

"I didn't," he insisted. "You know I'd never want to hurt you." But he had, he had, so many times.

"Come on out, Merry. Please."

I wanted nothing more than to be alone, to mourn who I had become, but I knew he wasn't going to suddenly become sensitive and go away. Jack was Jack, and I had no one but myself to blame for his thinking he still belonged in my life. I sighed, pulled myself to my feet, and opened the door. The light was so bright that I recoiled.

Jack came to me immediately, wrapped his arms around me, and kissed my forehead. "It'll be okay," he said gently.

I stood in his embrace and felt all the delight a wooden statue might. "What'll be okay, Jack?"

"Uh-life, I guess. You and me. Us." He lifted my chin and kissed me.

The wooden Indian became a block of ice. Even Jack finally had to acknowledge that I wasn't responding.

He dropped his arms and stepped back. He was genuinely confused. "Merry, what have I done? Surely you're not mad because I teased you a bit when what's-his-name called, are you? Come on, sweetheart." He took my limp hands in his. "Tell me. What's really wrong?"

"What's wrong?" Tears filled my eyes. How about his being here in Amhearst? Or maybe murder? Theft? Accidents? Snippy coworkers? Collapsing mothers? Pregnant teens? Sharp tongues? And a heart that was so bent on independence that it had just damaged the best thing in my life?

I opened my mouth to explain, then snapped it closed again, overwhelmed. What could I say that he could possibly understand?

After several minutes of heavy, uncomfortable silence, he finally said, "I guess I'd better go, huh?"

I nodded. "I think that would be best."

As he pulled his coat on, a thought percolated up through my melancholia.

"Wait a minute." I stood. "I need to ask you something."

His face lit up, and he threw his coat in the direction of the chair. He looked very nervous. "Is this about us?"

"Us? No, no." I didn't begin to have the energy needed for a conversation about "us." "It's about Bushay Environmental."

"Bushay?" I couldn't have surprised him more.

"Yeah. I keep thinking that there might be some kind of a connection between Bushay and Arnie Meister's murder. What if Arnie knew something sinister about the business or maybe even about Harry Allen himself? What if he knew about or was involved in racketeering or taking kickbacks or something? What if he learned Harry Allen was dumping illegally?"

Jack looked at me incredulously. "You can't be serious."

"Come on, Jack. Play along here. Would any indication of illegal dealings show when you did your audit? Could you tell if there had been financial hanky-panky of some kind?"

"Merry, people don't leave evidence like that lying around—if there is such evidence, which I strongly doubt."

"But what if someone was really clever?"

"I've only been at Bushay for a week, but the company seems exemplary to me. Everyone I've met has been very cooperative and welcoming."

"Do they have a choice?"

He shrugged. "Well, no, but still—"

"Just do me one favor, Jack. Let me know if you find anything at all odd, okay? Even if you don't know why it's odd, I still want to know. Arnie's money has to come from somewhere."

"But not from Bushay." He spoke with conviction.

"How do we know that? He knew whoever shot him well enough to have in the kitchen of his house. Maybe it was someone from work, maybe even Harry Allen."

"Merry, don't. The police will take care of it." He stretched his long arm across my shoulders.

"Don't yourself," I snapped as I stepped away. "I want you to take me seriously here, Jack."

"Take you seriously?" He laughed harshly. "Give me a break."

"Give me a break, Jack." The air between us vibrated

with hostility. "I solved a murder once before. I can do it again—if people give me the help I need."

"I suppose what's-his-name has bought this fearless girl reporter act?"

"You know something? He has." At least most of the time.

We glared at each other, and Jack blinked first.

"I made a mistake coming to Amhearst, didn't I?" he asked with disbelief. "You didn't wait." He grabbed his coat from the floor, stuffed his arms inside, and stamped out.

He finally knows it's over! Maddie, he knows!

Just before he shut/slammed the door, he paused. "You'd better get that pane of glass replaced or you're going to have someone besides me in here."

He was gone. I sagged onto the sofa, pulled Whiskers into my arms, and buried my face in his comforting fur. I still had the problem of Curt to deal with, but Jack was gone, gone!

Then his words penetrated my euphoria. I jumped up, unceremoniously dumping poor Whiskers in the process. Replace what pane of glass? When I left this morning, all the panes were present and accounted for.

I felt the draft even before I pulled the curtain aside. I stared in consternation at the small rectangle in the lower right corner beside the lock. I reached out and thrust my hand through the opening. I looked down. No glass on the floor.

I went to the wastebasket in the living room. No glass. I found the shards dumped neatly in the kitchen wastebasket, and my dustpan and brush back in the cabinet.

So who? Why? I scanned the living room, dining room and kitchen and saw nothing out of place, nothing missing. I went to the bedroom, and this time I turned the light on when I entered.

My top bureau drawers were open, and my slips, scarves, nightgowns and panties were tumbled all over the floor and the bed. I noted with passing regret how utilitarian my things were compared to Jolene's silky, feminine collection.

On a hunch, I went to my bedroom closet. I wasn't surprised when I found all my jackets, blazers and coats lying on the floor, their sleeves half inside out, their pockets hanging out like little tongues in need of water. All the detritus on the closet shelf had also been pulled off and scattered, a strange collection of ski caps, gloves and scarves. A collection of used tissues, scraps of paper, loose change and pen caps cluttered the floor, too, residue from countless pockets.

I was staring at the mess, trying to conjure a connection between my break-in and Jolene's when I heard a click in the other room. Then I heard a step and a creak.

Whiskers, I thought, being noisier than usual.

At exactly the time that it occurred to me that Whiskers couldn't click, I felt something brush against my ankle. I looked down to see his great eyes staring back. Something had spooked him and sent him scurrying for protection.

Suddenly I couldn't breathe. I grabbed Whiskers and held him to my chest, a furry shield against any impending attack. I waited without moving, straining to hear. Apparently so did the creaker.

I peeked out of the closet, Whiskers still in my arms. I saw no one, but I hadn't expected to because the noise came from the front of the apartment, which is why I was brave enough to peer out. I was tiptoeing across the bedroom toward the bedside phone when I heard the front door yanked open. Apparently I wasn't the only one tiptoeing around. Before I could move, I heard running, footfalls slapping across the porch and into the yard.

I felt the cold draft from the open door as I, too, ran. I braked in the front yard and looked right and left. Down the alley, almost to the street, ran a figure in black, visible only because of the distant streetlight. The runner veered around the corner onto Oak Lane. I started to run again. I was barely out of the yard when I heard a car start. When I reached Oak Lane, I was just in time to see two taillights disappear around the corner of Oak Lane and Albany Street.

"I have no idea what kind of a car it was," I told William Poole when he came in response to my 911 call. "It was dark, it was too far away, and I don't know makes of cars anyway."

We stood in my bedroom staring at the shambles.

"Could you tell if it was a man or a woman?"

I shook my head. "But it was someone who was slim."

"Is there anything missing?"

"Not that I can tell. I checked while I was waiting for you. Without touching anything," I hastened to add as I saw his face.

We walked back to the living room, and I looked again at the missing pane—or the place where the missing pane should be.

"Do you think this person will be back tonight?" I asked as I imagined a hand, more a green, misshapen claw with long, ugly nails, reaching in to unlock the door.

"I don't think he'll be back," William said, his craggy face thoughtful. "Getting trapped in the house was probably more than enough for one night. If you tack some cardboard over the opening until you can get hold of a glazier tomorrow, you should be fine."

Nodding, I looked around my place. It was a very comfortable size for one person, for a couple even, but it had few hiding places, not even a living room closet. "Where was he all that time?"

We launched a search. I knew he hadn't been lurking in the bedroom because I was there when he ran off. And there was that click. Nothing in the bedroom clicked like that.

I tried all the doors in the apartment, listening to the noise they made. Since there were only three doors besides the front one, it didn't take long. The bedroom door moved without any noises and shut with a sound more like an umph than a click. My bathroom has two doors, one leading to the bedroom like any normal bathroom, and one leading to the living room. Neither had a lock, unnerving when there was company. The bathroom door leading to the bedroom also made no unusual noises. However the bathroom door leading to the living room clicked distinctly when the knob was released.

"That's it," I said. "That's definitely what I heard."

We looked around the little room and were drawn immediately to the most obvious place—behind the shower curtain. Bingo. There in the tub, lying on the blue no-skid mat, was a dusting of dirt, the outside type, not the I-don't-clean-my-tub type and a couple of dried leaf pieces.

As I stared at the debris, I thought of the fact that I had sat in the dark in the bedroom, mere inches away. It was a very spooky feeling, that invasion of my private space. Would I have been in grave danger if I'd discovered the hider? Had Jack's presence saved my life? Ack! Did I owe him big-time?

"William, do you think there's a connection with Jolene's break-in?"

"Good question." But he had no answer.

After he left, I tacked a piece of cardboard over the missing pane. Then I sat down and thought about Curt. How can I tell him I was sorry over the phone? It was so impersonal. I'd rather look him in the face so I can see his reaction.

I glanced at my watch. It was only ten in spite of all that had happened. A little late maybe, but not prohibitive. I ran out to the car.

I'd only been to Curt's home once, when I first met him as a reporter doing an interview about his upcoming art show at Amhearst's City Hall. I found his place again with only one false turn. Then I sat in the car at the curb, trying to get up my nerve to go to the door.

What if he doesn't want to talk with me, Lord? What if my snippiness tonight was the final straw? What if I've fallen in love with him just when he's probably fallen out with me.

My breath caught in my throat as I listened to what I'd just thought. *I've fallen in love with him.* And I knew it was true. Somehow when I'd been searching for myself, I'd found him.

I pulled myself out of the car and walked sadly to his door, musing on the irony of it all.

When he opened the door, he just stared.

"Hi." I waved at him like an idiot. His curly hair was rumpled, his sweatshirt and jeans had paint on them, and he looked tired. In other words, he was gorgeous.

He pushed the storm door open. "Come in."

I slid past him into the living room, so conscious of him I could barely look at him. I started talking immediately, before I lost my nerve. "I'm sorry! I was so rude. You were being kind, and I was abominable."

He opened his mouth, but I kept right on going. "I wasn't mad at you. Never at you. It was Jack. I was furious at him. I came home, and there he was in my house! And I yelled at you. I'm sorry." And I started to blubber.

This time the arms that embraced me were more than welcome, and I responded by breaking down entirely. I sobbed and sobbed, saturating yet another shirt in the whole unlovely process.

"Shh, sweetheart, shh." He ran his hand gently over my head. "It's okay." His fingers caught in my moussed spikes.

"You're just saying that because you're nice." I sniffled as we struggled to separate my hair from his hand. It didn't pull too much.

"No, I'm not."

"Yes, you are." I finally got loose and pulled away. "But it's okay. Really, it is. I like that you're nice."

"Merry, I'm not being nice." His voice was most emphatic.

"Sure you are. Just listen to yourself. You're not criticizing me or anything. Nice. Kind."

"Merry." He took me firmly by the shoulders. "Look at me."

I raised my swollen eyes to his and wished he weren't wearing his glasses. Then he wouldn't be able to see how terrible I must look.

"Stop telling me what I mean," he said. "It drives me crazy! I'm not being nice. I mean it when I say it's okay."

I stared at him.

"Do you understand me?" His voice sort of kited up at the end.

His nose was practically against mine. All I wanted to do was kiss it, so I said, "Can I have a drink of cold water?"

He sighed, straightened and dropped his hands. He looked at the ceiling and said, "Dear God, why her?" I've rarely heard a more ardent prayer.

He went to the kitchen, and I could hear water running and ice cubes popping. I wanted to follow him because I never wanted to let him out of my sight ever again. I decided to try and be mature instead.

I sat in a rocking chair and looked around because you can learn a lot about a person by his house. But as I looked, I knew I wasn't seeing Curt but his mother. This had been his parents' house before their deaths, and at Joan's encouraging, he had quit teaching, moved in here and become a full-time artist. I was willing to bet he'd left things just as they were when he got here. He had other, more important things on his mind. Even this rocker, large, pine, with gold decals patterning its back, wasn't him. He would have a sleek cherry or maybe a leather recliner to lie back in and think up new pictures.

I was willing to bet that the empty picture hangers all over the walls were his, though.

"What's with the empty hangers?" I asked when he handed me my water.

He glanced at them. "When I have pictures to offer, I hang them up here so people can get a feel for how they would look in a home. Between the show early this month and Christmas all my reserves have gone. Right now I don't have any extras to hang." He smiled. "It's a wonderful problem to have."

"You know what else you don't have?" I asked. "You don't have a single Christmas anything. No decorations, no tree, no wreath, no candles, no greens. Nothing."

"Yeah, I know." He looked absently around the room. "I'm not much into celebrating Christmas." And he left the room.

TWELVE

I watched Curt's retreating figure thoughtfully. Why did he say he wasn't interested in celebrating Christmas? Everyone was interested, even nonChristians. Everyone liked the music and the lights, the trees and the presents, the angels and, of course, the Babe, even if they only acknowledged his birth and ignored the ramifications of his death and resurrection.

Then it hit me, in a small flash of insight that was as close to an epiphany as I'll probably ever get. This wasn't about celebrating or not celebrating Christmas. It was about being alone. Curt was alone. Was there a more painful time to be alone than Christmas? Maybe if you ignored the holiday, pretended it didn't exist except in its deepest spiritual sense, maybe the aloneness won't hurt so much.

"These days when I think of Christmas, I think of Longwood."

That was what he had said when we were walking toward the conservatory. Not people, not joy, not fun. Longwood. Remembrance with no emotional involvement. And the key words were *these days*. These alone days.

Tears rose as the world suddenly looked gray, not a classy, luminescent pearl gray but a dirty, gritty, grimy gray, the color of exclusion. Sure, I was alone for Christmas, too, at least geographically, but I knew there were people back in Pittsburgh who wanted me there as much as I wanted to be there. Curt had no family anywhere waiting to be with him.

And I'd been too dumb, too self-absorbed to see his hurt. I had been waiting, even praying, for him to make my Christmas happy when it should have been the other way around. I should have been trying to make his Christmas joyous, trying to fill up the unfillable gaps.

By the time he returned with his own glass of water, I had reached a decision. I was going to make his Christmas a blessed and happy day whether he liked it or not.

"Curt, I want to get a Christmas tree tomorrow. I haven't gotten one so far because I didn't feel tall enough or strong enough to handle getting it inside and into a stand and all that stuff. My father made such a big deal of getting the tree just right that I'm paranoid."

In my memory, I could see Dad lying flat on his stomach under the tree, muttering to himself as he tightened the stand screws while Mom, Sam and I stood around the tree telling him which way it was leaning.

I looked at Curt. With his broad shoulders and strong arms, lugging a Christmas tree would be nothing. "Will you come with me to help me out?"

"Why not get an artificial one? It'd be so much easier to deal with."

"Did you have an artificial one growing up?" I asked with dread. Could a live tree person and an artificial tree person have an enduring relationship?

He shook his head. "Nope. We'd always go cut our own."

"Really?" I was enchanted. We'd never done that. We just went to the Boy Scouts in the Tasty Freeze parking lot.

"Don't get too starry-eyed about it," he said. "It always managed to rain or sleet or something the Saturday we went. It's cold, messy work getting a tree."

"Take me wherever it is that you go, please?" I could see us now, walking hand in hand through snowdrifts, cheeks rosy, breath spurting out in little foggy puffs. Curt would have an ax swung over his shoulder, and after we found the perfect tree, he'd fell it with a few well-placed chops. Then we'd drag it down the hill to a house which had the smoke from a cozy fire coming out the chimney. We would sit and sip hot chocolate before the fire while the tree, filled with a myriad little lights, shining balls and scarlet ribbons, gleamed in the background.

Who cared that our last snow had melted and that my apartment wasn't at the bottom of a hill and that it lacked a fireplace? I could at least get some hot chocolate, the Nestlé's instant kind with the little marshmallows. And we could sip it on the sofa while Whiskers purred beside us.

"It's supposed to rain tomorrow," Curt said.

"Please."

"Don't bat your eyes like that at me," he said, but it worked. He sighed. "I'll pick you up at nine. Just be sure you wear your warmest long johns. I'm afraid you're going to need them."

I hugged him in thanks. "After my adventures tonight, I look forward to a sweet Saturday."

"What happened tonight?" Was that dread in his voice?

After I regaled him with a long, lurid and detailed rendition of the thefts, the Lurays, the break-in and Jack, he shook his head in disbelief. "I can't leave you alone for a minute."

He followed me home and nailed a piece of plywood over the cardboard insert I'd put on the window. "I think you have some sort of magnetic field that shimmers about you, attracting the most bizarre occurrences." He studied me over the raised hammer. "You look normal. You talk normally. You act—" Pause. Swallow. "—almost normally. I just don't understand it."

* * *

Then he kissed me goodbye and left.

I was ready at nine the next morning, though I wasn't wearing long johns. I didn't own any. I did put on a pair of heavy opaque hose under my jeans, and I bundled up with scarves and gloves and my Indiana Jones hat. I also wore my raincoat and my L.L. Bean duck shoes.

When we climbed out of the car at the tree farm, I squinted through the downpour as Curt opened the trunk. He drew out a small bow saw.

"What, no ax?"

"Trust me," he said, looking superior.

We began walking between rows of evergreens, comparing them as if it really mattered whether my tree was five feet tall or six feet tall, whether it was fat or skinny, whether it sat in the corner and could therefore have a large bald spot.

Finally I peered through the drips falling from the brim of my hat and pronounced, "This is the one."

"You're sure? You can't change your mind, you know."

I was sure. It wasn't as fat as some we'd seen or as thick. But it was healthy and it had a straight back and a top spear of branch just right for my angel to sit on. Of course, I didn't have the angel yet, but I would before the day was over.

Curt got down on one knee, lifted the lowest branches and began to saw. A few healthy swipes and our tree toppled. That was when I realized that we had to drag it uphill to get back to the car.

By the time we reached the crest of the hill, had the tree bound and tied to the roof and grabbed a couple of free fistfuls of greens, I was shivering. My jeans were soaked from the knees down. I could no longer feel my feet, though I assumed they were still there. My hair was one giant droop, and Curt's glasses needed wipers.

"What fun!" I said as I collapsed into the front seat.

Curt shook his head. "I believe you mean that."

But he was smiling softly and I knew he'd had fun, too. He was still smiling after the tree stood straight in its stand.

"We'll decorate it tonight after dinner," I said. "Maddie and Doug can help, too, if they want."

Whiskers loved the tree, batting delicately at the lower branches. He disappeared under the boughs, and the tree began shaking and threatened to topple. Just my luck, a tree-climbing cat.

Curt laughed. "A word of advice—don't buy expensive baubles. They won't live into the New Year."

When I rushed into Ferretti's for my appointment with Lonni, I was only ten minutes late. She was waiting for me in a booth against the far wall. As I slid in across from her, I looked at her long blonde hair, combed straight and shining, her wonderful dark eyes and her slim graceful hands. She was a beautiful girl except for the unhappy set of her mouth and the shadow in her eyes.

The first few minutes were spent placing our orders and getting organized. I set my little tape recorder on the table where she could see it but enough to the side that hopefully she'd forget it.

"So, tell me about yourself, Lonni," I began. "How old are you? What year at school?"

"I'm seventeen and I'm a junior at Amhearst High. And I can't wait until I'm eighteen!"

"Freedom?"

"Freedom," she agreed. "I can finally do whatever I want whenever I want with whoever I want."

Not really, I thought, looking at her protruding belly, but I didn't comment. Instead I asked, "How about your family?"

She took a deep breath. "I'm an only child. My mother went away when I was four. I see her sometimes in the summer, but she doesn't care much for me, and I don't care much for her. She lives on a ranch in the middle of absolutely nowhere. Talk about boring!"

Our sandwiches arrived, a hamburger with everything for her and a BLT on wheat toast for me. She took a huge bite before she continued. I was pleased to note that she chewed with her mouth closed.

"But I want to tell you about my father." She practically choked on the last word. "Everyone thinks he's this wonderful guy. They think he's fun and handsome and charming. 'You're so lucky to have him as your dad,' is what people say all the time. If they only knew the truth, they wouldn't think he was so wonderful. They just don't know what he's like behind closed doors! He's—he's—" She couldn't get the word out.

I listened with my blood turning to ice. Had I inadvertently stumbled into the taping Girls Who Were Ravished by Their Fathers, today, twelve noon, live from Ferretti's.

She tried again. "He's strict!"

I almost wilted in relief. Strict I could deal with.

"It's always, 'Where are you going? What are you doing? When are you coming home? Who's going to be there?' It's like he doesn't trust me or something," she wailed, seeing no irony between her pregnancy and his lack of trust.

I made sympathetic noises, though I knew that if she were my parents' daughter, they'd have been asking the same questions. They'd certainly asked them of Sam and me, and they'd expected answers.

"He keeps giving me curfews," she said, disbelief heavy in her voice. "Like I'm his to order around."

Suddenly she grinned mischievously. "I just ignore him. And I'm real good at climbing out my bedroom window onto the limb of the big beech tree. I don't think he ever knew."

She grabbed her final French fry, bit it savagely in half, and looked at me seriously. "Don't you agree that the restrictions he set for me were abusive? He even wanted me to clean the house and do the dishes! What does he think Lucinda's for? Like I'm supposed to do her job? I told him I'd set the authorities on him if he didn't leave me alone. I even quoted the Child Abuse Hotline number at him."

"Did he ever hit you?" I asked. "Did he ever try to harm you in a sexual context?"

"He wouldn't dare," she said scathingly.

Her poor father, I thought, my sympathies entirely with him. How in the world could he exert any normal parental control over someone as rebellious as Lonni? And she looked so innocent and angelic.

"And my boyfriend," Lonni said, waving the remains of the fry at me. "You should hear the terrible way he talks about him."

"What's your boyfriend's name?"

She smiled. "I call him Hunk."

Too cute.

"And he calls me Beautiful."

"His real name?"

She shook her head. "I don't tell anyone. Not even my father."

"You mean even after you knew you were pregnant, you still wouldn't tell?"

"Nope. I didn't want to cost him his job. I knew my father would go after him and try to ruin him. He's got an awful lot of power, you know. But he learned Hunk's identity about a week ago. I think he hired a private detective. Can you believe that? Where's the trust?"

I quickly filled my mouth with the last bite of my BLT just in case Lonni's question wasn't rhetorical.

"Then my father went nuts." Lonni turned white as she recalled the scene. "He screamed. He shouted. He threatened to blow Hunk's head off or run a knife through his heart or hang him by the neck until dead."

"I'm sure that was just because he was angry."

"It hurts to sit there and hear all sorts of terrible things said about someone you love. Your heart sort of bleeds."

"I'm sure it does. But I wonder if it wasn't exaggerated speech on your father's part. It's like a mom saying to her kid, 'You do that one more time and you're grounded for life!' It's overstatement."

"It was more," she said darkly and with absolute conviction.

I was appalled at the certainty with which she spoke. Who was her father? A would-be Mafia enforcer out to make his bones on her boyfriend?

She washed the last half of her fry down with a swallow of Coke. She smiled brightly and brittlely. "So what else do you want to know?"

"What doesn't your father like about Hunk?"

"I don't know." She seemed honestly confounded by this. "Maybe that he's older and married?"

I almost lost my mouthful of Coke. "You're dating an older married man?"

"Not an old one. He's just older than me."

"By how much?"

"Only ten years." My mind boggled. "And he hates his wife. She's a shrew. He told me so."

"And you believe him?"

She sat up straight and looked down her nose at me. "Hunk would never lie."

No, just sleep with an underage girl while married to someone else. "Maybe your father thinks that Hunk is robbing the cradle?"

"That's only because he still treats me like a kid. Hunk knows I'm a woman. He tells me so all the time. 'You're mature far beyond your years,' he says." She glowed with pride.

She must have seen the skepticism in my face. "What's our age difference to you or my father anyway? If Hunk and I are happy, why should either of you care? It's none of your business!"

"You don't think sleeping with married men is wrong?" I asked.

She shook her head. "Not if you love each other. The guys in *People* and on TV do it all the time."

Unfortunately that was true. "But what about the Bible?"

She looked confused. "What's the Bible got to do with anything?"

"It says sex outside marriage is wrong."

"It does?"

I nodded.

"And you agree?"

I nodded again.

"Are you married?" she asked.

"No."

"Ever been married?"

"No."

"Ever had sex?"

"No."

She stared. "Never?" She clearly couldn't imagine such a thing as reaching my advanced age as a virgin.

"Never."

"Is something wrong with you?"

I had to smile. "I'm fine, believe me. I just believe in sex in marriage."

"So you think having this baby is wrong?" She was defensive.

I shook my head. "I think having the baby once it's conceived is fine and good. It's the conceiving it outside marriage that I think was wrong."

Lonni stared at me a minute, her eyes narrowed and hard. "And just who are you to tell me what's right and wrong?" she demanded. As she stared at me with her sneering, unrepentant face, I thought that if she looked this way at her father, no wonder he hated Hunk.

"It's not me who says it's wrong," I said, trying to smile to break the judgmental sound of my position. "It's God."

She reached out and grabbed my tape recorder and slapped it on the table. Several people at nearby tables jumped and looked our way. One man even started to get out of his seat. In the back of my mind I found it interesting that Reilly Samson was having lunch at Ferretti's, too. Small world. He settled back to finish his coffee when he saw Lonni and I were okay.

"Is this supposed to be my interview," Lonni hissed, "or your sermon?"

I knew I'd said enough, so I changed the topic. "Tell me how you came to be living at His House." It seemed a safe and neutral question. Wrong.

"He made me go." She spit it out.

"Your father?"

"Who else? But I'll be eighteen in another month. Then I leave. Hunk's proud of me for doing things legally rather than making my father angrier and risking him getting the police involved."

I bet Hunk preferred it that way. We weren't talking statutory rape, but we were talking public opinion at the very least. An adult getting a high school junior pregnant. Nasty.

"What do you like best about His House?" I asked, hoping this was an okay question. For all I knew, she had a vendetta against her housemates, too. I wouldn't have been surprised at all. But I'd finally asked a question that got a positive answer.

She half-smiled, and the seventeen-year-old who might have been was visible. "It's going to sound corny," she said, "but what I like best is that the people there care. I like that a lot. Dawn and Julie are wonderful to us. They're not easy on us, but they like us. They put in long hours and will sit and talk anytime we want. They eat meals with us and they watch TV with us. They play games with us and teach us all kinds of stuff because they want to help us."

I smiled. She was confirming my initial response to His House.

"Of course most of what they say is sh—" She caught herself and looked at me. "It's garbage. I was going to use a more descriptive term, but I won't say it because you and God won't like it. But I don't agree with what they say and I won't believe." She spoke slowly and deliberately, daring me to make an issue. I declined.

"How about the other girls there?" I asked. "Do you like them?"

"The others are nice," she said. "Some of them have terrible stories, poverty and beatings and stuff. And their boyfriends! It's enough to curl your hair. Pam's one like that. She says no one ever loved her before. She says no one ever cared what she thought or felt. She says Dawn just loved her to Jesus." Lonni shrugged. "Whatever that means. I just know she's a lot nicer now than she was when I first came. She was a real toughie then. And that baby Karyn. Have you met her? I feel so bad for her. And her mom. She looks like she's dying a little bit more every day." Lonni shook her head in sympathy.

"Don't you think your dad feels that sad about you?"

A derisive puff of air burst from her lips. "Are you kidding? No way. You know what he said to me? 'Since you've got the morals of an alley cat, let's put you somewhere where you can get religion! That'll teach you.' Hah! Like he's some good guy himself."

I had to agree with Lonni that sending her to His House to get religion wasn't a great idea. Talk about waving a red flag in front of an already enraged individual.

Lonni leaned across the table and said in a low voice, "Do you know that he wanted me to get an abortion?"

"Hunk did?"

"No! He was excited. My father did. Can you imagine that?"

Unfortunately I could. "Why did you refuse? To get back at him?"

She flipped her hand through the air like such an idea wasn't worth the time it took to state. "I didn't want an abortion because I want to have Hunk's baby. I love him and I love the baby."

"When will you be getting married?"

Her face was suddenly full of sorrow. "We won't."

"But I thought you said—?"

"Circumstances have changed." That was all she would say. She was too busy trying to keep herself from breaking down in front of me. She kept swallowing and blinking and making abrupt little shakes of her head. "I've got to go," she managed to whisper. She grabbed her coat and stood up. She stared at me, her eyes alive with pain. "Just make sure you let everyone know what a terrible man my father really is. That's all I ask."

She turned away and started for the door. I noted Reilly Samson leaving his seat at the same time.

"Lonni," I called. "I forgot to ask. What's your full name? And do you want me to use a pseudonym when I write about you?"

"Bushay," she said. "Lonni Allen Bushay. And use my real name. Please."

I watched Lonni stride outside, and I watched through the big front windows as Reilly Samson caught up with her on the sidewalk. He put his arm around her shoulders and she leaned into him. He talked gently with her for a few minutes as she cried. His face was full of concern.

Lonni Allen Bushay! Harry Allen's daughter. One of

Amhearst's outstanding do-gooders had a daughter who wanted to hang him out to dry. The question was: Did he deserve it? Trying to keep tabs on a rebellious daughter wasn't wrong. Yelling threats in a fit of anger wasn't necessarily wrong. Acting on those threats would be wrong indeed.

Threats to his daughter and a vicious fight about Communists somehow didn't go with the man-about-town image Harry Allen had cultivated. Which was the real Harry Allen?

And how did Reilly Samson fit into things? I thought he was Jolene's current flame. Was he also Hunk? But then he'd have to be married, and I didn't think he was. Or maybe he just told Lonni he was so she could be kept in her place, wherever he perceived that to be.

My head buzzing with ideas, I walked slowly back to *The News* and sat at my desk, staring at my blank terminal. Mac was the only other person in the newsroom.

"Yo, Kramer!" he bellowed, and I jumped.

"You don't have to scare me," I said in mild rebuke. "A polite 'Merry, my dear,' will do."

"I called you politely three times with no response, so I yelled."

I wandered to his desk. "I just had my interview with Lonni Bushay, one of the girls at His House."

"Harry Allen's kid?"

I nodded.

"And?"

"And something's not ringing true. She wants to hurt her father because he's strict—"

"You're kidding."

"Nope."

"You're not talking abuse."

"No. To quote her, 'He wouldn't dare.' She also thinks he'll hurt her married boyfriend."

"She has a married boyfriend? How old is she?"

"Seventeen." I grinned. "She doesn't know why Harry Allen doesn't like him."

"I must be getting old. These kids scare me."

We both laughed at the idea of Mac, the perennial playboy, getting old or being scared.

"By the way I'm meeting Dawn for lunch at one tomorrow at Ferretti's."

"Like I care," he said, but I could see him storing the information.

"They have the Eagles on TV," I said as an added incentive—or more correctly, as an excuse should he feel the need for one.

I went to my desk and checked my voice mail and found a message.

"This is Sandy Rasmussen, Karyn's mom," it said. "Dawn said you wanted to talk with me. I think that would be a good idea. Call me whenever you can. Karyn and I are renting a small apartment until all this is over. I have nothing to do but sit and wait. At least your phone call will be something positive to wait for." And she left a number.

I glanced at my watch. 2:30. I dialed the number but there was no answer. Apparently Sandy Rasmussen had something to do after all. I hoped it was Christmas shopping and not rushing Karyn to the hospital.

"Don't worry about missing me," I told the answering machine. "I'll call again."

I hung up, dialed the Amhearst police number, and asked for William Poole.

"Hey, Merry," he said. "What can I do for you?"

"Do you ever go home?" I asked.

He laughed but didn't answer. For the first time I wondered if he was married or had children or liked pizza or went to church. It was easy to forget that there was a private life behind the uniform.

"So what's the latest on the fingerprints? Have you heard back from AFIS?"

"I assume you mean on Arnie Meister. Nothing. No match. Also no surprise."

"Were the fingerprints on the two iced tea glasses the same or different on each?"

"The same and the deceased's thumb, second and third finger, right hand, pretty clear."

"So what do you do next?"

"More of the same. Asking questions, listening, analyzing. By the way, Harry Allen Bushay said I should tell you that he found his briefcase, whatever that means."

I was just glad William couldn't see my red face.

I left shortly after that to go shopping for things to hang on my Christmas tree. I drove my white Sable through the last-minute shopping traffic to Waterloo Gardens in Exton and bought a glorious angel in a white gown with gold trim, gold wings and a gold halo on his/her head. Undoubtedly the girls at His House would think it bland, but it said "keeper" to me. I also bought two scarlet poinsettias, real ones, one for me and one for Curt. It was the quickest way I could think of to get some Christmas into our places. Then I returned to Kmart to shop where my budget was more comfortable.

I was pushing my shopping cart toward the checkout when I saw a familiar mustache over in small appliances. Sean Bennett was Christmas shopping, and I was afraid he was going to give something with a plug. Poor Airy.

I started to push my cart toward him to suggest something personal like a ring or some lingerie or a new scarf when a woman rushed up to him. She wrapped her arms about his neck and kissed him happily on the cheek.

"How wonderful to see you, Sean!" she gushed. "You're

looking as handsome as ever. I just love that mustache."
She reached out and stroked it.

He didn't flinch, though he did flush, and he hadn't
hugged her back. I'd have bitten her finger.

"What are you buying me?" she asked. "Not a blender,
I hope? You can give that to Airy. For me, nothing with a
plug. Just lots of bling."

It was, of course, Jolene.

THIRTEEN

I turned, making believe I hadn't seen either Sean or Jolene. The last thing I wanted was to be pulled into one of Jo's bizarre scenarios. I was foiled when she saw me, though how she saw me with her face buried in Sean's neck is a mystery to me.

"Merry!" she called, her arms still wrapped around Sean. When she lifted one hand to wave at me, Sean broke free. He almost vaulted the counter he and Jolene were standing beside, and watched Jo like a hare might watch the fox from whose clutches he had just escaped, fearful of the next pounce.

I sighed and pushed my cart next to Sean. The poor man was almost hyperventilating.

"Hi, Sean," I said. "We met over spilled Coke the other night, remember?"

He took a second to glance at me. "Oh, yeah. Hi." He scooted past me as Jolene began to make her way around the counter.

"Don't worry, Sean, my love," Jolene said breezily. "I was happy to see you, but I need to see Merry."

But Sean had a few more guts than I thought. He stood straight and tall with me and my shopping cart safely between him and Jo.

"I don't know what your problem is, Jolene," he began. "But I love my wife, and she loves me. You can make both of us miserable if you want. You're very good at it. You make me squirm like no one I know—and that's not a compliment. I don't know how to handle you, and I admit it."

I glanced at Jolene. She was listening with a very serious expression.

Sean continued. "You know how to make Airy lose her temper and behave in ways that aren't characteristic of her. I'm not quite sure how you got this power over us, but be certain we know that you have it, and that we will try and overcome it. And know that no matter what you do, you won't break us up. You may have killed your own marriage, but we won't let you kill ours."

Sean looked at me. "Be careful, Merry. She's a dangerous friend. We know."

I nodded. The man was right.

He looked back at Jolene. "I'm sorry for you, Jolene. I really am. You're a sick lady."

He turned and walked away.

I looked at Jo to see how she had taken this little lecture. To my surprise, she was smiling, a nice, friendly, uncomplicated smile.

"He's a good guy," she said. "I'm glad for Airy."

I blinked. I would never understand this woman. Never. I doubted she understood herself.

"Oh, by the way," I said as I turned my cart toward checkout, "when you picked up your dry cleaning from the car, you left your scarf. It's at my place now."

She shook her head. "No, I didn't." She waved a scarf at me.

"Well, then we've got an extra." I started walking.

"Wait, Merry!" She hurried after me. "I was serious when I told Sean I needed you."

I stopped. "And I'm supposed to believe you came to Kmart to find me?"

"I did," she said. "I called the paper, and Mac told me you'd be here. When I saw Sean, I got distracted."

"Well," I said very ungraciously, "you found me. What do you want?"

"I want you to go out to the house with me."

I stared at her, no doubt with my mouth hanging open. "Forget that, Jo. I've already gone to two too many empty houses with you."

"But the police have released Arnie's body. We're getting ready for the funeral, and I've got to get him a suit and all."

"So go," I said, starting up again.

She took hold of my cart and forced me to stop. She looked me in the eye and said, "I can't go alone. I can't possibly."

"So ask someone else." But I was weakening and hated it.

"Who, Merry? Tell me that. I don't have anyone I can ask but you."

"How about your dad?"

"Are you kidding? It'd kill him."

I thought that was overstatement, but I didn't really know for sure.

"Then—" and I took the plunge "—how about Reilly?"

"Reilly?" She acted all surprised. "What in the world made you think of him? I hardly know him."

"Cut the lies, Jolene." I made my voice cold and hard. "If you can't tell the truth, I can't help you. Now let go of my cart."

She dropped her hand, and I surged ahead. I took my place in line and was soon surrounded by harried last-minute shoppers who had no agendas in which I figured. I glanced over my shoulder once to be sure Jolene was gone and saw no sign of her. I sighed in relief, but unfortunately I was premature. She fell in step beside me as I wheeled my paid-for stuff toward the door.

"Don't get mad," she said when she saw my face. "Just stop a minute and listen. Please."

Mom, I thought as I stopped just beyond the door, you should have taught me to be mean instead of polite.

"You've got to go with me, Merry. You've got to. I can't go alone. The very thought makes me sick." She wrapped her arms around her middle.

"Jo, it's only an empty house." But I knew that wasn't so.

"Merry, please. You're so good in a crisis."

"What?"

"You are. You know who to call and what to do and how not to touch stuff and everything."

"911 and don't touch are hardly signs of genius."

"It'll be dark soon."

"So go tomorrow."

"I have to have the clothes at the funeral parlor tonight so they can get ready for the service on Monday. We want the burial done before Christmas."

"It's too late for me to go. I have a date at six."

"We'll be back way before then," she assured me. "We're just going to pick out a suit, shirt and tie." She started walking toward her car. I didn't follow.

"What's wrong?" she said.

I studied her for a minute before I answered. She had her big hair back today, and her face was rouged and powdered to perfection. Where I had on jeans and a sweater, she wore royal blue slacks with a royal blue tunic with black swirls running from right shoulder to left hip. Even her gloves and scarf were royal blue. The coat was the leather and fur one.

"Jolene, why can't you bear to tell the truth?"

Anger flashed across her face as she backed up a step. It was a sign of her desperation that she didn't stomp away. Instead she became the haughty ice princess. "My personal life is none of your concern, Merry."

"It is if you keep pulling me into it, Jo. You can't tell me I'm wonderful in a crisis but too untrustworthy to know about Reilly. You can't selectively lie to me and expect me not to resent it. Life doesn't work that way, at least not life that I care to get involved in."

"You're such a Girl Scout." Her tone was scathing.

"If you mean I have strong Christian principles and I try to live by them, you're right. I make no apologies for that."

We stood staring at each other. I truly felt sorry for her, but I refused to let her gain any power over me. I would not become her next Airy.

She broke first. "Oh, all right. If that's the way you're going to be, I can play that game, too."

"Jo, I will not play games with you. I will not take on a role to match the circumstances. I don't want to manipulate people for some hidden purpose. I want to be consistent and dependable, not devious and deceitful. I want be true to myself and the person God wants me to be. If I do go with you—and I'm not saying I will—it will be because I want to help you, because I choose to be kind, not because you trick me."

"Well, then what's your problem?" she said, all chirrupy and happy. I knew she thought she'd gotten her way. "Go ahead and be nice, Merry. Go ahead and help me. It sounds to me like we both want the same thing. Let's put your things in the car and go." She reached into the cart to grab a couple of bags.

I put a hand on her arm. "Not so fast, Jo. Tell me the truth."

She loosened her grip on my tree balls and clasped her royal blue fingers together. "Okay, the truth." The next words came out in a rush. "I'm scared to go to the house alone."

I frowned my disappointment. "I don't blame you, but we both know that's not what I'm talking about."

She spun on her blue suede heel and strode away. I shrugged and began putting the packages in the backseat.

"You don't understand," she said, beside me again.

I paused with a bag of fairy lights dangling. "You're right. I don't understand."

"His family hates me, and my family hates him. They always have." Her voice was ragged with emotion.

I gave her my full attention. "Why?"

"They think I'm nasty and mean and no good for him. Mine think he's nasty and mean and no good for me."

Sounded like a match to me.

"We've known each other since we were little kids. Every time he visited his grandmother, we got into a fight. Sometimes he'd win, sometimes I would. I gave him more than one shiner, and he gave me more than one bloody nose. Right up to junior high we were still kicking and punching."

I could see how the two families, coming to the defense of their own child, would quickly develop deep feelings against the other child.

"In junior high, things changed. We decided we loved each other, and that scared our families as much as the fights, maybe more. 'You're too young. You don't know what love is.' We were too young and we didn't know what love was, but that didn't make any difference. It was always Reilly and Jolene. We went together all through high school and beyond.

"We used to have roaring fights just so we could make up. In fact we had one just before I met Arnie again at that New Year's Eve party. Reilly was in the Marines then, and he was home on Christmas leave. We had a fight over something I can't even remember. I probably thought his Christmas present wasn't expensive enough and wanted him to trade up. What I do remember is that he wouldn't give in to me. Before that I could always work on him until he did whatever I wanted. But not that time. He was developing a steel I couldn't bend, and I was absolutely furious at him. So I went after Arnie. I thought it was fun to cut in on Airy and fun to spite Reilly."

"But the fun didn't last," I said.

"I knew I'd made a terrible mistake within a week of the wedding, but I was too proud to say anything. And there was the money."

"Ah, yes, the money."

"It almost kept us together. We had a lot of fun spending it and planning how to spend it. But then Reilly came home, and she popped up."

"How long have you been involved with Reilly?"

"Since the first day he came back to Amhearst about a year and a half ago. We've just kept it secret. It was easier."

"And I bet you liked the mystery and danger, didn't you? Let's see how many people we can fool. But Jo, you can't play games like that all your life."

"I can if I want to," she snapped.

"How does Reilly feel about all this cloak-and-dagger stuff?"

Jolene didn't answer.

"He doesn't like it, does he?"

"He wants to get married." She sounded distressed.

"And you don't? I thought you loved him."

"I've always loved him. Always."

"Then what's the trouble?"

"None of your business." Her tone was flat and hard.

"See you later, Jolene." I turned to get in my car.

"If I marry him, I'll have to put his needs first," she mumbled.

"What did you say?" I looked at her in astonishment.

"If I marry him, I'll have to put his needs first."

I hugged her. "Jolene, there's hope for you yet!"

She smiled self-consciously. "But what if I can't do that? What if I make him as miserable as I made Arnie?"

"Jolene, it couldn't have been that bad."

"Oh, yes," she said. "It was worse than you can imagine. The really ugly thing is that I liked getting him to storm out of the house in a fury." She stared at the ground. "I'm not a very nice person, Merry."

"Oh, Jo. You think Reilly doesn't know that? All those bloody noses and the tempestuous fights and dumping him for Arnie and your clandestine affair—he already knows."

"I want to be nice," she whispered. "I want to love Reilly forever. I want him to love me forever. But I don't know how to make it all work."

"God can help you, Jo. You just have to turn to him."

"I'm so miserable that only God can help me?" She looked utterly despondent.

I laughed gently. "We're all that miserable, girl. That's what Christmas and Jesus are all about. Now get in the car," I said, gesturing to the front seat. "Let's get this trip over with."

"Really? You'll help me?"

"I said I would if you told the truth, remember?"

Jolene hugged me and ran around the car. As I drove, I realized that knowing the truth about Jolene and Reilly didn't change any of the circumstances. Whether it would change any attitudes or hearts remained to be seen.

"Jolene, why do you do it?"

"Do what?"

"Stuff like back in Kmart."

"You mean tease Sean?" She grinned. "It's so much fun."

"I don't understand that. Why is it fun to make people uncomfortable or unhappy?"

"Sean knew," she said.

I thought back over that conversation. "I'm not quite sure how you got this power over us, but be certain we know what you're trying to do," he'd said.

"Power?" I guessed.

She nodded. "Power. There's something very satisfying about making people do what you want."

"Jo, you're crazy. You've got all these people you've

known all your life, and you're reduced to asking me to go with you. Don't you see something wrong here?"

She squirmed a little in her seat, but she didn't respond. I wasn't surprised. How much truth could I expect her to face in one afternoon?

We drove a little bit farther in silence. It was quarter after four now, and the evening was beginning to close in. I would be happy to get in and out of that mansion before it was full dark.

"Oh, no!" yelled Jolene, scaring me half to death. "Look at that!"

She pointed to the side of the road, and I saw a car pulled onto the shoulder and an older lady climbing up a bank on her way to the car.

"It's Mrs. Samson!" Jolene said.

"Mrs. Samson, Master Spy?" I looked in my rearview mirror. "I need to see her peering out between the curtains to identify her. Shall we stop to help her?" I began to pull off the road.

"Don't you dare stop," Jolene said. "She hates me."

"So you've said before. Maybe if we stop, she'll appreciate it and start to like you. After all, if you and Reilly ever get married, she'll be your grandmother-in-law."

Jolene groaned.

"And she may need us."

Our car had just stopped when the headlights of Mrs. Samson's car snapped on and her car begin to move. She pulled onto the road very carefully and drove past us without a second glance.

"That's Reilly's car she's driving," Jolene said. "I wonder how she talked him into letting her use it. She's not the world's best driver."

Out of curiosity I backed up to the place where Mrs. Samson had been and looked out across the cornfield that bordered the road. "What was she doing out here?"

"Bet you this is where she hit the deer," Jolene said.

"Probably. Did you ever hit a deer?" I pulled onto the road and depressed the accelerator. It was getting darker by the second.

Jo shook her head. "I've been lucky so far. I keep waiting for it to happen though. Some day one's bound to get me."

"It's scary when it happens." I shuddered as I thought of that big body sliding across the hood toward me. "Very scary."

When we reached Arnie's house, we climbed out and stood staring at the unlighted structure looming in the gathering gloom.

Now this, I thought, is scary.

Jolene grabbed my arm. "I can't do this. Who cares how we bury Arnie? He sure doesn't."

"Come on," I said, telling myself to be brave. "Sooner in, sooner out."

We walked to the house, struggling to stay side by side on the brick walk wide enough for one. Neither of us wanted to be first because we remembered too well what the first person had found last time. And neither of us wanted to be last because we both knew that the boogeyman carted off the last guy in line.

We finally reached the porch and stood looking at each other. I thought my face probably looked every bit as strained as Jolene's.

"The keys?" I whispered.

"Right," Jo whispered back. She reached into her gigantic black bag and began rooting.

Strictly out of curiosity, I depressed the tongue of the great brass door latch. It gave under my touch and the door swung silently open.

It was all I could do not to scream. I was in every Halloween movie I'd ever seen. I almost heard the weird laugh and the clanking of chains. I almost saw the disembodied hand reach out for me.

Then reason returned, and I wanted to slap Jolene. "You set me up again! Well, I'm not playing along this time!" I turned to stalk back to the car, now mad at myself as well for being so gullible.

Jolene made a slight groan and began sliding to the ground. I watched her go dispassionately. She ended up in a heap in front of the open door.

"Oh, that's great," I said. "Pretend to faint. That's sure to impress me."

"I'm going to throw up," she whispered. She started heaving, great spasms shaking her body. She struggled up onto her knees and crawled to the edge of the porch, retching the whole time. Suddenly I understood that she wasn't acting. She was petrified to the point of illness. I dropped to my knees beside her just as her stomach emptied itself into the boxwoods.

"Oh, Jolene, I'm sorry." I was smitten across the heart with guilt.

She moaned.

"Wait here. I'll be right back." I rushed into the house, flipping on all the lights until I found the powder room. I grabbed a towel from the rack, wet it, and rushed back to Jolene.

She was sitting propped against the house looking utterly spent. I knelt and held out the damp towel.

"Thank you," she whispered and started crying. "You're so good to me. I don't deserve it. Thank you. Thank you. You're so good."

Now I really felt guilty. I had screamed and accused, and she was thanking me. She shuddered. "When that door opened, I had never been so scared in my life. I knew we were going to die."

I realized with intense relief that she hadn't heard a word I'd screamed at her. Fear had made her deaf.

Thank you, Lord. I won't let it happen again. I promise.

"Come on," I offered her my hand. "Let's get this over with."

I pulled her to her feet, and after leaning against the house for a couple of minutes, she nodded her head.

"Okay," she whispered. "Let's do it."

We walked into the front hall, and I looked around. There was fingerprint dust all over things, and furniture had been moved during a police search. My eyes were drawn to the kitchen door where I knew the disorder would be greatest, but not for anything did I want to enter that room again.

We turned toward the steps and began a slow ascent. The master bedroom was our goal.

"Arnie had a navy pinstripe suit that I always liked," Jolene said. "Let's get that. And a white shirt and his yellow power tie."

"That sounds good. Do we have to get underwear, too? And socks and shoes?"

"I don't know," Jolene said. "I never had to do anything like this before. I'm trying to remember what the funeral guy told me."

"We'd better take them," I said. "If he doesn't need them, no harm done. But if we don't take them and he needs them…"

"We'll take them," Jolene said. "I'm not coming back here ever again. Not ever."

I stared at the marvelous verdigris iron bedstead with a canopy of what looked like hand-tatted lace while Jolene went into the closet. I tried to imagine what it was like to sleep in such a fairy-tale bed and to wake up each morning in the blue-and-green luxury of this room. The walls were hung with wonderful impressionistic watercolors, misty and inviting. This was a room carefully designed for relaxing, for forgetting life's troubles.

"Shall I get some underwear and socks?" I called as I

walked to Arnie's tall bureau. "Or do you want to make a selection?"

"Go ahead. You pick." Jolene's voice echoed eerily from the depths of the walk-in closet.

I opened a drawer and found more pairs of socks than my father had owned in his entire life. I chose a pair of navy ones with little cranberry insignia all over them. In another drawer I found piles of silk underwear. I knew it was silk because I read the label. I didn't know men wore silk underwear. Certainly those in my family didn't. I took a pair of boxers and a T-shirt.

"Should he wear any jewelry?" I asked as I looked at his collection of rings sitting on top of the bureau.

"I don't think so," Jolene called. "He hardly ever wore them. He just bought them when we first got the money, and we were spending it on anything. That was before we learned its limits."

I turned from the bureau toward the bed. "Speaking of the money, where—"

The words caught in my throat as I stared at the table beside the bed. It was a picture of the two of them. Arnie stood tall and muscular in jeans and a red polo shirt. Snuggled against him, laughing at the camera, was a girl in jeans and a purple T-shirt. She was slim and tanned and wore her long blonde hair caught up in a ponytail.

"The little tramp," hissed Jolene.

I jumped the proverbial mile. She had walked up beside me without my hearing. Thick rugs are great for sneaking around.

"She's Arnie's girl? The one who broke up your marriage?"

Jolene hesitated. "I can't say that she broke up our marriage because there were others before her. But she's the one he finally fixed on. Their affair lasted for over a year."

I looked again at the smiling face of Lonni Allen

Bushay. I traced a crack in the glass across the lower left corner just above the fluted brass frame.

"I did that," Jolene said proudly, pointing to the crack. "The night I threw it at him."

Throwing things at people was beyond my ken, so I said, "Do you know how old she is?"

Jolene shrugged. "Who cares?"

"She's seventeen."

Jolene shrugged again. "That sounds like Arnie."

"And she's pregnant."

"What?" Jolene had finally heard something that shocked her.

"She's due in a couple of months. They were going to get married as soon as she turned eighteen, about a month before the baby would be born."

Jolene stared at the picture. "I wonder," she said slowly, "what this does to his money. What do you think?"

But I barely heard her. I was lost in memories of my conversation with Lonni.

Then my father went nuts. He screamed. He shouted. He threatened to blow his head off or run a knife through his heart or hang him by the neck until dead.

Had Harry Allen followed through on his threats? Had he come out here and shot Arnie?

And the argument that Elsa, the secretary, overheard in Harry Allen's office. It wasn't Commies that Arnie and Harry Allen were arguing about. It was Lonni.

Did Sergeant Poole know all this? He was certainly questioning Harry Allen. I knew that because of the briefcase comment. But did William understand about Arnie and Lonni?

Jolene studied my face. "What's wrong with you?"

"I may know who murdered Arnie."

She grabbed my arm. "Who?"

"Her father threatened Arnie, and he and Arnie had a terrible fight the day before Arnie was killed."

"The slut's father? But that's Harry Allen Bushay."

I nodded, surprised she knew.

"But how could he possibly do something as awful as kill Arnie? He's too nice a guy."

"If you think someone has hurt your baby daughter, you can do almost anything," I said just like I knew what I was talking about. But then I'd seen my dad give Jack the evil eye on more than one occasion.

Jolene looked skeptical. "She's hardly a baby. And he was hardly hurting her. This was a full-consent romance."

"But daughters are always their fathers' babies, to be protected at all costs. Why do you think your father doesn't like Reilly? Because he thinks he's not nice to his baby girl."

"Maybe," Jolene said. "But right now I need to know what color shoes. Brown or black?"

I followed Jolene around the abrupt corner in her mental road. "With a navy suit? Black definitely. And don't forget a belt." But I still thought Harry Allen was a good suspect.

While Jolene went back to the closet for the shoes, I wandered into the master bath. The Jacuzzi-type tub was big enough for four, though why you'd have four in your bathroom I couldn't imagine, and the vanity counter, miles long, held two sinks. The shower stall was silvered, and I found myself staring at myself. What a depressing sight. I needed to get home and do something with this hair before Curt came.

Was it silvered on the inside, too? Did you have to stare at yourself while you bathed? Weird thought. I pulled the shower door open and almost dropped my teeth.

Staring at me, a horrified expression on her face, was Airy Bennett.

FOURTEEN

Why neither Airy nor I screamed is beyond me. We just stared at each other, equally appalled.

I finally found my voice. "What are you doing here?"

She put her finger to her lips as she peered over my shoulder, fear large in her eyes.

"Don't worry. I won't give you away. I don't want to witness what Jolene would do if she knew you were here."

Airy sagged in relief.

"Hey, Merry," Jolene called from the next room, her voice way too close.

"No!" Airy looked terrified.

I pushed the shower stall door almost closed but didn't click it. I stepped to the sink. Just in time. Jolene appeared in the doorway.

"I've got Arnie's black shoes. Let's get out of here. The place still gives me the creeps."

"In a minute, Jo." I was pleased to hear that my voice barely shook. "I going to use the facilities while we're here. You go on down."

She didn't look pleased. "Just hurry, okay? I need to set the alarm and make sure the place is properly locked up when we leave. We're just lucky that we were the ones who found that unlocked door." The bathroom door clicked shut behind her.

I waited a beat, then pulled the shower door open again. I looked at Airy cringing in the corner. "Was it unlocked when you arrived?" I whispered.

She nodded and stepped out of the shower. We listened for a couple of minutes, but I couldn't tell whether Jolene had gone downstairs or not. The rug deadened the sounds too well. I flushed the toilet, then peered cautiously into the bedroom. The closet light was off, and so was the overhead. The only one remaining on besides the bathroom was the upstairs hall. When I heard the click of Jolene's steps across the parquet floor downstairs, my tension eased slightly.

I glared at Airy. "Why are you here?" Theft never crossed my mind where she was concerned.

She said with desperation, "I don't want Sean to know I was here. I'm afraid of what will happen if he knows. He won't understand!" The last was a cry from the heart.

"He's not the only one who doesn't understand."

"I can't find it." She started to slide down the wall in despair. "I can't find it."

I grabbed her none-too-gently by one arm and hauled her upright. "I don't care whether you can find it or not, whatever it is."

"But if I don't find it, they'll know I was here. Sean will know I was here."

"When?" I asked, going after a fact I felt I could get my hands on. "When were you here? Do you mean now? Tonight?"

She shook her head, mouth stubbornly closed.

"Shall I turn you over to Jolene?"

Terror leaped to her eyes. She pulled her arm free from my grasp and pushed me with all her might. Her move was so unexpected that I went flying. My elbow hit the tiled floor first, taking the brunt of my weight. Talk about hurt!

Airy pulled the door open and was out the room and across the bedroom before I struggled to my feet. Holding my elbow, I raced after her into the upstairs hall. She looked back just as I burst through the bedroom door. I launched myself at her legs. We tumbled to the floor and lay panting, trying to get our breath.

"Are you okay, Merry?" Jolene's voice floated up the stairs. "What was that noise?"

"I'm fine," I said, trying not to gasp too audibly. "I tripped." Sort of.

"Merry, be nimble. Merry, be neat," she chanted. "Merry tripped over her own big feet."

"Charming," I called, rolling my eyes.

Jo giggled, pleased with herself. "I'm taking the suit and shoes out to the car. I'll come back to set the alarm."

"Good idea," I said. I heard the front door open and close.

I sat up and looked at Airy, still lying full out on the hall floor. All the stuffing had been knocked out of her.

"Okay, now tell me what in the world you've been talking about."

Airy rolled over onto her back. "I don't want to lose Sean."

"I don't want you to lose him either, but what makes you think you will?"

"I came to see Arnie."

That didn't seem like grounds for divorce to me unless— "When?"

"After Jolene and I had our fight."

"The day he was killed."

"See why I don't want anyone to know?"

No, I didn't see. Just because you came to see someone didn't mean you killed him. "Why did you come?"

"I wanted to ask him how I should handle Jolene. He must have handled her well because he ended up with the house and the money when they split."

"Half the money. And I'm not so sure he handled her very well at all."

"Oh."

"Was he dead when you got here?"

"She used to make up poems like that about me," Airy said. "You have no idea how I hated it."

"You were a kid. Of course you hated it. But now you're an adult, so you'd better face a few issues. Was Arnie dead when you got here?"

She nodded, her face strained. "I rang the bell but he didn't answer, so I tried the door. It opened, just like tonight, so I came in. I called his name, but still no answer. I thought maybe I'd misunderstood his secretary when I called his office. Maybe she hadn't said he was working at home after all. I thought that I'd just check the kitchen to be sure he wasn't on the phone or something." She stopped and swallowed. "It was awful!"

I nodded. "I know." We were both silent for a couple of seconds. Then I asked, "So what happened next?"

"I got out of there as fast as I could. I didn't want anyone to know I'd been anywhere near him, not with our history. Too many people remember the fool I made of myself when he married Jolene, screaming and crying and making all kinds of threats. I didn't realize until later what a favor she'd done me, not until I met Sean. I'm always afraid that people think Sean was my second choice and a poor second at that. But that's not so. Sean is so much more wonderful than Arnie that I can't even explain."

I nodded, thinking of Jack and Curt. "But I'm still missing something here. Why did you come back here tonight? Whatever made you take such a risk?"

"Because I can't find my scarf."

"Your scarf," I repeated. Suddenly I saw Jolene's bedroom and my bedroom and our closets, and things went click.

"I thought maybe I left it here," she said. "When I saw Arnie, I dropped everything, purse, scarf, gloves, on the table. I made myself feel for his heartbeat and I felt his carotid artery." She shuddered. "He was dead."

"And you knew this when we met at McDonald's that night." I thought of her white face and distress when Curt mentioned Arnie's death. "Airy! I was so worried for you, you little actress!" I snarled the last two words.

"I know. You were so sweet." And she had the nerve to smile at me. She pulled herself into a sitting position and leaned against the hall wall. "Anyway, when I was sure Arnie was dead, I grabbed my things and ran, but I could never find my scarf again. I must have dropped it here, and I'm afraid someone will recognize it. But I can't find it, and I don't know where else to look."

It was lying at home on my bureau, but I didn't mention that fact. "What if the police have it?"

"I don't care if they do. They won't know where it came from. It's Jo I worry about. She gave it to me the Christmas of that infamous New Year's Eve party."

"Ah." And Jo had seen it and not recognized it. "So you broke into Jolene's house looking for it." I gave her a hard-eyed look. "And mine."

Her face turned scarlet. "I was desperate."

I tried to work up some sympathy for her, but I kept remembering my feelings of apprehension and invasion.

The front door opened, and Jolene clicked into the foyer. "You ready, Merry?"

"Be right down," I called.

I looked at Airy. Did I want to report her to the police? Or more pressing, did I think she had something to do with Arnie's death?

I could see Airy coming to Arnie for advice. I could see her finding him dead. I could see her panicking. I could see her trying to protect her back rather than risk Sean's lack of understanding. I couldn't see any reason for her killing Arnie.

I decided that when I called William Poole to tell him that Harry Allen had a beaut of a motive, I would tell him about Airy. He could deal with it as he felt best. In the meantime, how were we going to get her out of the house if Jolene set the alarm?

I took Arnie's underwear and socks and put them on the hall table. I indicated to Airy that she should wait right where she was. I went down the stairs, turning off the hall light as I went. I found Jolene by the front door pushing a number pad.

"What activates the alarm?" I asked. "Pushing the numbers or closing the door? Or both?" I hope, I hope.

"Both," she said. "Let's go."

We went out the front door and Jolene reached for the latch to pull it tight.

"Wait a minute," I said, putting my foot on the doorsill. "I think I left Arnie's socks and underwear upstairs." I searched my empty pockets.

"Merry!" Jolene wasn't pleased.

"Go on," I said. "Here are the keys. Start the engine and get the heat going. Then turn on the headlights so I can see when I come out. I'll only be a minute."

Sighing and shaking her head, Jolene accepted the keys and started toward the car. I went back inside, flicked on the foyer lights, and pushed the door almost closed. Then I raced upstairs, turning on the upper hall light as I ran. I grabbed the underwear and socks and Airy, too.

"Come on. This is your only chance."

We hurried downstairs and I turned toward the kitchen. She froze.

"I can't go in there. I just can't."

"You don't have a choice." I dragged her with me.

We crept through the dark kitchen to the back sliding glass door, both taking care not to look toward the spot where Arnie had lain. The cloying, butcher-shop smell of blood made me feel sick at my stomach. In the light seeping from the front hall, I found and flicked up the lock on the door. I pulled, but the door refused to slide open.

"Burglar bar," Airy hissed and bent to lift it free.

The door slid open at last, and I pushed her out.

"Get lost." I pulled the door shut, threw the lock, dropped the burglar bar in place, and raced back to the front hall. I was flipping off the upstairs hall light just as Jolene walked in the front door.

"Ready?"

"Ready."

We walked outside together and pulled the door firmly shut, engaging the alarm on the beautiful, sad place where a person and a marriage had died.

As we backed out of the drive, I scanned the shrubbery, but I didn't see any sign of Airy. If she was smart, she was crouching somewhere out back until we were well out of sight. When we turned the corner, I glanced back for a last look at the mansion.

"Funny, isn't it, how it looks like the front hall light is still on?"

I finally got home fifteen minutes before Curt was due for our dinner date. I spent most of the time trying to revive my hair, drooping big-time. I was pulling up the zipper on my red dress when the front doorbell rang.

Curt took one look at me and actually whistled. I don't think anyone had ever whistled at me before, at least no one who counted. Construction workers don't count, at least not unless you're dating one.

I glowed and we stood staring at each other. It was a wonderful, ridiculous Hallmark moment. Then he extended a plastic Kmart bag to me.

"What's this?"

"I thought you might like them."

One by one I pulled out tree ornaments wrapped in tissue paper. I opened each like it was a priceless treasure because in a sense each was. The first was a clear glass ball with an angel flying inside.

"That one was always my favorite tree decoration as a little boy." Curt ran his finger softly over the glass. "I just knew this was what angels really looked like."

The next treasure from Curt's bag was a cross-stitched sprig of holly with red berries and ribbons on a cream background, the initials JCE in the corner.

I fingered the initials. Joan Carlyle Eldredge.

Curt smiled sadly. "She made it her last Christmas."

I laid it reverently on the coffee table next to the glass ball.

There were two matte white tree balls with Christmas scenes reminiscent of Currier and Ives painted on them.

"You did these?"

"No. My mother."

"No wonder you're so talented." I placed them beside Joan's work.

Next I extracted a felt cardinal, a chickadee and a partridge without his pear tree, all stuffed and wearing hand-crocheted hanging loops.

"Mom," Curt said. "She liked to make something new for the tree every year."

"Oh, Curt." My eyes were full of tears. "They're wonderful!"

I pulled out the last bauble and opened it. I gasped as I stared at a small picture in a little gilt frame with a red ribbon hanger.

"It's me!"

The picture was a line drawing bordering on caricature. My wild black spikes were there, my eyes, my smile, my chin. The marvelous part was the economy of strokes presenting a complete individual.

I went to my tree and hung the little piece of art front and center.

"So everyone will be sure to see it." Then I threw my arms around him and hugged my thanks. "All that's missing is one of you to keep it company."

He ignored my hint, helped me on with my red coat and we walked to the car arm in arm. We held hands all the way to Maddie and Doug's. Then I climbed into the backseat with Maddie, and Doug, with his extra-long legs, sat in the front with Curt.

I had never been to Dilworthtown Inn before, and it was all I'd heard it would be. The service was excellent and the food delicious. I basked in the rosy glow of Curt's gift and the pleasure of good food and fine company, at least until I told the tale of Airy in the shower stall and our rush to get her outside without Jolene seeing her.

"I just pushed her out the back door and ran for the foyer," I said. "I hope she found her way home."

"How do you get yourself in fixes like that all the time?" Maddie asked, laughing.

"I've never known anyone who has such strange things happen to her," Doug said. "Knowing you has added a whole new dimension to our lives."

Curt said nothing. He just withdrew from me like he had the other morning at Mr. Hamish's. Pulled away. Retreated. Doug and Maddie didn't seem to notice anything, but then he talked and laughed with them as animatedly as before. It was me he ceased to respond to.

My rosy glow faded, and though I smiled brightly, I felt hurt and confused. Had I been right? Was I falling in love with him when he was falling out with me? Then why the tree ornaments?

When both Doug and Maddie excused themselves for a few minutes, I put my hand on his. "What's wrong?"

He looked surprised. "What do you mean?"

"You've done it again, just like the other morning. You're here but you're not."

He lifted his coffee cup. "You must be mistaken. Everything's fine."

But it wasn't. He'd let his hand sit like a log rather than

turn it palm up and clasp mine. When we left, he put his hand on my back to guide me, and when we had to wait in the parking lot for a car to back out, he rested his hand on my shoulder. But he didn't stand close. I could have been any woman being treated politely by any man.

I climbed into the backseat beside Maddie. "Do you two want to come back to my place and help us decorate my Christmas tree?" I didn't know whether I wanted them to say yes or no because I didn't know whether I wanted to be alone with Curt or not.

"That sounds like fun," Maddie said. "We'd love to. It's much too early to go home."

I put all our coats on my bed and watched Whiskers climb up to inspect them. I felt a perverse pleasure when he climbed onto Curt's camel topcoat and circled and circled. It would serve Curt right to wear cat hair.

Maddie and I let the guys fight with the lights even though we ended up with more lights on the left side of the tree.

"Don't worry," Maddie whispered. "You can restring them tomorrow."

I pulled a dining-room chair up to the tree and slipped out of my heels. "I'm going to put my new gold angel on the top."

I climbed onto the wooden chair and reached for the top of the tree. As I did, I felt my feet, slick in their hose, slip. "Oh, no!"

Curt leaped toward me and grabbed me around the waist. I ended up with my arms around his neck and my feet dangling inches from the floor as he pressed me against him. My angel dangled down his back.

He held me for a split second, looking at me with that distant expression in his eyes. Then, almost as if a little switch somewhere had been thrown, a marvelous smile lit his face.

"All I can say," he said as he put me back on the chair, "is that I'm glad you had nothing liquid in your hands." And he held me steady while I put my angel in place.

Just that easily he was back. Just as easily I welcomed him.

Maddie and Doug left shortly before eleven, but Curt stayed awhile. We turned out all the lights except the tree and sat on the sofa, me resting against Curt, his arm across my shoulders. Whiskers came out of the bedroom and climbed up beside me. He curled against my side and began to purr. The three of us sat companionably, mesmerized by the tree.

I turned to face him. "Aren't you glad I got you to celebrate at least a little bit of Christmas?"

He looked at me, his eyes warm. "I am."

"Will you come for dinner Christmas Day? You can help me learn to cook a turkey."

"I will, and with pleasure."

Sighing happily, I turned back to the tree. Curt put his hand on my head and guided it until I was resting on his shoulder.

"And it came to pass in those days," Curt said, "that there went out a decree from Caesar Augustus, that all the world should be taxed."

"And this taxing was first made when Cyrenius was governor of Syria," I said.

"And all went to be taxed, every one to his own city. And Joseph went up from Galilee, out of the city of Nazareth, to the city of David, which is called Bethlehem, to be taxed with Mary, his espoused wife, being great with child."

I continued the story. "And so it was, that, while they were there, the days were accomplished that she should be delivered. And she brought forth her firstborn son, and wrapped him in swaddling clothes, and laid him in a manger, because there was no room for them in the inn."

"And there were in the same country shepherds abiding in the fields, keeping watch over their flocks by night. And, lo, the angel of the Lord came upon them, and the glory of the Lord shown round about them, and they were sore afraid."

Whiskers stirred and rearranged himself, his chin

resting on my knee. I laid my hand on his head and said, "And the angel said unto them, Fear not, for, behold, I bring you good tidings of great joy, which shall be to all people. For unto you is born this day in the city of David a Savior, which is Christ the Lord. And this shall be a sign unto you. Ye shall find the babe wrapped in swaddling clothes, lying in a manger."

"And suddenly," Curt continued, "there was with the angel a multitude of the heavenly hosts, praising God, and saying, Glory to God in the highest, and on earth peace, good will toward men. And it came to pass, as the angels were gone away from them into heaven, the shepherds said one to another, Let us now go even unto Bethlehem, and see this thing which has come to pass, which the Lord has made known unto us."

"And they came with haste, and found Mary, and Joseph, and the babe lying in a manger."

We looked at each other and grinned.

"Not too bad," I said.

We were quiet a minute. Then Curt said softly, "Amen."

FIFTEEN

Dawn and I met for lunch at Ferretti's after church Sunday.

"How's Pam?" I asked. "Is she okay?"

Dawn waved her hands back and forth. "So-so. It's hard for her right now. She's convinced she did the right thing, but she misses David immensely. 'My belly's empty and my arms are empty,' she told me yesterday."

"Poor girl. Will she ever get over it?"

"Yes and no. She'll move on with her life. Hopefully she'll go back to school and graduate. Maybe she'll marry some nice man and have more kids. She'll have a full life, especially if she continues to follow the Lord. But there will always be that baby out there growing into a man, and she'll always wonder what he's like, if he's okay, if the people who adopted him have done a good job in raising him."

"Maybe some day she'll search him out." I welcomed my grilled cheese sandwich.

"Maybe." Dawn studied her tuna on wheat toast like she'd made a mistake ordering it. "Sometimes finding children or birthparents is a good thing. Sometimes it's traumatic. We always tell our girls that if they ever decide they want to find their babies, wait until they've grown. There's just too much emotion involved to put a child or a young teen through it. And we encourage them to go through a third party in case the children don't want to be found."

"Why wouldn't they want to be found, to meet their mother?"

"Because they have another mom, one they've known for eighteen or twenty or more years. Some don't want the confusion of a second mother."

I ate a forkful of coleslaw. "Sandy Rasmussen called me."

Dawn nodded. "I thought she might. You'll like her. She and Karyn are renting an apartment at Sweet Meadow."

"She's a single mom?"

"Oh, no. She has three other older children at home with their father. He's a doctor, a pediatrician. He's a very nice guy. He tries to get down to see Karyn and Sandy at least every other weekend. He usually brings one or more of the older kids with him. I think they're all arriving this afternoon for the holidays. If things go as expected, they'll be here for the birth, too."

"I wonder if they'd all talk with me?"

"They might. You can always ask."

I looked at my little tape recorder whirring on the table between us. "You know, there's more to this whole issue than the quick story Mac wanted. I need to talk with him about a series."

"You need to talk to me about what?"

I looked up. "Why, Mac, imagine seeing you here. I think you know Dawn Trauber?"

"Sure he knows me," Dawn said. "We've met several times before. How are you, Mac? Want to join us?" She slid over, totally unaware that she was making his day.

Mac, grinning like an idiot and uncharacteristically tongue-tied, slid into the booth beside her.

The waitress appeared. "Can I get you ladies any dessert? How about something for you, Mac?"

"Ah," teased Dawn. "She knows Mac's name. I bet all the ladies know Mac."

I watched in amazement as he flushed a brilliant crimson.

"I'll take a spaghetti," Mac said. "No garlic bread."

The waitress looked startled at the last part of the order, but she wisely said nothing.

"We'll wait dessert for Mac," Dawn told the waitress, and I wanted to laugh out loud at Mac's delighted expression.

Dawn looked at me. "Would you like to interview Pam? She's willing."

"Are you serious? Would I ever! But how do you feel about that?"

"I think it would be good for her right now. I think the more she talks about David, the better it is."

"Why'd you change your mind?"

"Because I can trust you."

I was overwhelmed and speechless.

Mac grinned at me. "Not much shuts her up, Dawn. You've accomplished a great feat here."

Dawn grinned, too, then sobered. "Pam's not my greatest concern, though, believe it or not. I'm worried sick about Lonni. Something's wrong—besides the pregnancy, I mean. And she won't talk to me about it."

Mac and I looked at each other over his salad.

"What?" Dawn demanded. "Do you two know something I don't?"

"Merry knows it all," Mac said.

Little did he know. I hadn't had a chance to tell him about Arnie.

"Do you know who Hunk is?" I asked Dawn.

"Do you?" Mac asked, startled.

I nodded.

"Who is it, and how did you find out?" he demanded.

"Yes," Dawn said. "Who is it? If I hear that ridiculous name one more time, I'll puke."

Mac blinked and looked at Dawn. "Puke?"

"Yeah, you know," Dawn said. "Barf. Toss. Hurl."

"Please." He looked pained. "I'm eating." His dish of spaghetti steamed enticingly before him.

But it wasn't that Mac was unfamiliar with the word. I suspected he knew every synonym Dawn did and more. It was the fact that Dawn said a slang word referring to a bodily function. How high, I wondered, was the pedestal he had her on?

Dawn returned to the subject we were discussing. "Tell me what you know about Lonni."

"Hunk is Arnie Meister."

"You're kidding!" I got great satisfaction in seeing Mac's disbelieving expression.

Dawn looked hesitant. "I don't think I know him."

"The guy who was murdered a few days ago," Mac said.

Dawn sat back in her seat and stared at us, appalled. "That's what she saw in the paper the day you first visited."

"Right. And she thinks her father might have done it."

"Harry Allen? No way." Dawn was emphatic. "I wish all fathers were as supportive of daughters in trouble as he is."

I thought of her intense anger. "She does not see it that way."

"You don't really think he did it, do you?" Dawn asked Mac just as he put a forkful in his mouth. "Not Harry Allen!"

Mac chewed manfully until he could speak. "It's hard to imagine."

"I need to learn more about this Arnie," she said.

"Go ahead, Mac. Tell her everything we know." I gathered my gloves and scarf and slid out of my seat. "I've got to call Sandy Rasmussen and set up an interview before her family gets here. By the way, Dawn and I think that His House and its residents need a series, not a single article. Right, Dawn?" And grabbing my tape recorder, I left.

I called Sandy Rasmussen as soon as I got home and we set up an appointment for tomorrow, Monday, at 10:00 a.m. at my place.

"There's no way we could talk around here," Sandy said. "Karyn's dad and brother and sisters are getting here late this afternoon. They had to be at home this morning to be in the choir for the Christmas service. They left right afterwards and should get here this evening. Thankfully the weather isn't bad."

"How's Karyn doing?" I asked.

"Better than I am," she answered, laughing. "She could deliver anytime."

"A Christmas baby," I said and gave Sandy directions to my place.

Then I made another phone call and issued another invitation. I smiled at another acceptance.

I worked on my His House articles for the rest of the afternoon. I was just putting my laptop away when the phone rang.

"Merry, are you coming to Arnie's funeral tomorrow? The viewing's at noon, the service at one."

"Sure, Jolene, I'll be there."

"June?" It was Mrs. Luray on an extension. "Will you come to our house tomorrow evening? We're having our annual Christmas Eve open house, and I especially want you to come. You're Jolene's nicest friend."

"Thank you, Mrs. Luray." How about Jolene's only friend? "I'm going to the Christmas Eve service tomorrow night with a friend. What time is your open house? Maybe I can come over afterwards."

"We'll be here from eight to midnight," she said. "Why don't you bring your friend? There's always room for one more." She sighed. "Arnie won't be here this year, though. I'm so sad that he and Jolene Marie are getting a divorce."

There was a little silence while I tried to figure out how to respond to that one.

"Okay, Mom," Jolene said, her voice a mix of frustration and sorrow. "Say goodbye to Merry. You'll see her tomorrow."

"All right, Jolene," Eloise Luray said. "Goodbye, June, dear." And there was a click.

"Sorry," Jolene said. "She gets more impossible all the time."

"Is there an open house tomorrow evening? Or does she just think there's one?"

"There's one. It's a bit awkward this year, coming only hours after the funeral, but what can we do? She's been looking forward to this for months. Dad says we have to let her do it because she won't understand if we don't. We'd have collapses galore."

"He's probably right."

"Yeah, I know. Please come and bring Curt. Mac will be here, too."

"Jolene, I know it's none of my business, but have you thought about your parents going to some sort of a retirement facility where your mom would get the appropriate care?"

Jolene snorted. "I've been talking about a setup like that for years, ever since Mom started to fail so dramatically. I finally got Dad to put their names on the waiting list at Tel Hai over in Honey Brook. He's been called three times about a cottage becoming available, and he's turned them down every time. It's driving me as crazy as Mom. Now let's change the subject before I get all depressed. How was your date last night?"

I quickly gave her the short version of my evening.

"What's your family think of this new man in your life?"

"They haven't met him yet, but they've heard enough about him. They even sent him a couple of Christmas gifts after I told them he doesn't have a family."

"That's so nice." She sounded wistful. I knew she was thinking about her family's animosity toward Reilly.

"Jo," I said hesitantly, "would you and Reilly like to go to the Christmas Eve service with Curt and me? Or do you have to be at the house to help your mother?"

"No, she won't let me help her. Mrs. Samson comes over, and the old ladies rule the kitchen. I might as well still be ten years old."

"Well, then, will you come with us? You can see me play in the bell choir."

"You play in a bell choir? I'll tell you, Merry. You're amazing."

"That's what Curt says, but I'm not sure it's a compliment."

"Let me talk to Reilly and I'll let you know, okay?"

In the background Mrs. Luray called, "Jolene Marie, dinner's ready."

"Don't hang up, Jo," I said quickly. "I've got a weird question for you."

"Ask it fast. She'll be here pulling the phone from my hand if I linger."

"Where did you and Arnie get your money?" I said it in a rush because it was such an impertinent question.

To my surprise she began to laugh. "Are you serious? I thought everyone knew, though come to think of it, you probably hadn't even heard of Amhearst that long ago."

I was totally confused.

"We won the state lottery," she said. "Can you believe it? Twelve million dollars."

"You're kidding! People you know don't win those things."

"I know, but we did. Fifty thousand a month for twenty years. Remember that certificate hanging on the refrigerator? I made that for Arnie the week we won. We each put down half the money for the winning ticket, so we split the jackpot evenly. I guess I ought to have made him a new one that read $25,000 when I left."

"You actually won the lottery." It boggled my mind.

"Yep. Fortunately Harry Allen sat Arnie down and talked to him about the realities and limitations of the money. 'You haven't got a family,' Harry Allen said. 'So

I'm talking to you like your father would if he were here.'
He was great. Otherwise I think we'd be in a terrible financial mess. Lots of these millionaires end up declaring bank-
ruptcy. It's not like you ever have twelve million in your
hand, you know."

"Do you get Arnie's half now?" Now there was an impertinent question.

"I thought I might. After all, we're not divorced yet. I
even went to our lawyer to ask him about it."

"And?" I said when she stopped talking.

"And Arnie made a new will a couple of months ago. It
seems when the little slut got pregnant, he named her and
the baby his beneficiaries. They each get three million—
or what's left of it. We've already gotten two years of
payments. Only eighteen to go."

In the background Mrs. Luray called her to the table again.

"I've got to go before Mom faints," Jo said. "See you
tomorrow."

The next morning I went into work early, then drove
home in time to meet Sandy Rasmussen at my apartment.
I made us some tea and put out some crumb cake. I plugged
in the tree to lighten the mood.

Sandy looked incredibly weary, great circles under her
eyes testifying to countless sleepless nights. "It's wonderful having Dan and the other kids here," she said. "I'm
not alone."

"If being here by yourself with Karyn is so difficult,
why did you bring her here instead of staying back in
Massachusetts?"

"She's thirteen. Thirteen! She has her whole life ahead
of her. We felt we couldn't prejudice everyone against her
at this young an age."

"You think people today would treat her badly? Isn't
there more compassion and understanding than fifty or a
hundred years ago?"

"Sure there is, and philosophically everyone would agree that she shouldn't be penalized for such a tragic situation, but let's be realistic. Who in middle-class America wants their thirteen-year-old daughter hanging out with another girl that age about to have a baby? These girls have barely put their Barbies aside. Do you think they want Karyn at their kids' slumber parties? And the boys! What would they think of her?"

I flinched mentally.

"So Dan and I decided to take her away to save her in the long run."

"How did you ever hear about His House?"

"Dawn came to speak to a women's meeting at our church. I don't know how they ever heard of her or His House, and I don't care. We think it was God taking care of us before we even knew we needed that care."

"How did such a thing happen to Karyn?"

Sandy stalled by sipping her cup of tea. She fiddled with her napkin, tearing at the edges until they looked like the fringe on a rug. Finally she took a deep breath.

"I struggle every time I talk about this because I feel such seething resentment toward the boy. He was a friend of our sixteen-year-old son. He came over one day when he knew Zach was out. Karyn had a crush on him, and when he asked if he could come in and spend time with her, she was delighted. At first he sweet-talked her, kissed her, but when she got afraid and asked him to stop, he forced himself on her."

Sandy's voice was shaking almost as much as her hands. "When I got home, she was in bed, bundled up to her neck, crying, her eyes huge and scared. 'Am I still a virgin?' she asked. 'I want to be. Am I? Can I be again?'" And Sandy began to cry.

I sat there, my throat tight, my eyes filled with tears.

"You'd think I'd be cried out, wouldn't you?" she asked. "Nine months of tears, an ocean."

"What do you plan to do about the baby, keep it or give it up?" I asked.

"I don't know," Sandy said hopelessly. "I'm as confused today as I was the day we found out Karyn was pregnant. This is my grandchild. How can I give away my grandchild? But how can I keep her? The whole reason for living in Amhearst for these five months has been to protect Karyn. If we suddenly come home with a baby, people will know where it came from." Her hands fluttered helplessly in the air. "I'm exhausted from going around in mental circles. I keep asking God to show me what's right."

"How does Karyn feel?"

Sandy laughed without humor. "We've been going to Faith Community, and I decided we should work in the nursery every Sunday so Karyn would get used to babies. She can't easily go to Sunday school with the junior high kids, so we take nursery during the Sunday school hour. Good training for her. A few of the facts of life."

I thought of the nursery at church, full to bulging with often screaming little people. It seemed an eminently suitable place for a little girl to learn about some hard baby realities.

"At first Karyn thought it was a great lark. Then as cold weather set in, so did colds and runny noses and crankiness. Just last Sunday she was holding a crying little guy about fifteen months old when he had a very loose bowel movement. I thought Karyn would die. 'Mom, he got it all over me!' I made her clean him up before she could clean herself up. 'That's babies,' I said. 'They can't help it.' 'Not mine,' she said. 'Mine's going to be cute like her.' And she picked up the cutest little poppet who promptly threw up all over her."

I couldn't help laughing. "Poor Karyn."

"I just started law school," Sandy said urgently. "If we keep the baby, I'll have to drop out permanently, not just for a semester. I can't do four teenagers and a baby and law school. Is it horrible of me to want to go to school instead of raise this baby?" Her eyes were tragic. "But she's my grandchild!"

The doorbell rang, and I went to let Maddie in.

"Sandy, this is my friend Maddie. She and her husband have been thinking about adopting."

"Merry!" Maddie said, aghast.

"Maddie, this is Sandy. Her thirteen-year-old daughter is about to have a baby. They haven't yet decided what they plan to do."

The women looked at each other with interest and discomfort. I picked up the teapot.

"Let me get some more hot water for Maddie." And I left them. In the kitchen I leaned against the counter.

Dear Lord, please don't let me have made a terrible mistake. This is miracle season, isn't it?

SIXTEEN

I sat on the end of the fourth row at the Christmas Eve service. Curt sat beside me with Jolene and Reilly beyond him.

"What are you doing?" Jolene had hissed when I led the way up front. "I want to sit in the back!"

"I have to sit up front because of the bells." I pointed to the tables set with our music, gloves and instruments.

She scowled as she slid into the pew. "I'm never going anywhere with you again."

Reilly just looked at his beloved and smiled. Her bad temper didn't seem to faze him at all, but then after all the years he'd known her and all the questionable behavior he'd seen from her, I guess he was used to her.

We stood to sing "O Come All Ye Faithful" and I heard Jolene whisper in pleased surprise, "I know this!"

We were singing "It Came Upon A Midnight Clear," when Jack appeared in the aisle beside me. "Move over." He gestured with his hands.

I moved. And Curt, Jolene and Reilly moved, too. The Domino Principle. I found myself scrunched between the two men, here in the front of the church where everyone could see me.

Dear Lord, why me? Why now?

Out of the corner of my eye, I saw Jolene lean forward and grin. At least she was enjoying herself.

I was so flustered it took every ounce of concentration I possessed to play my bells correctly. I only forgot to change to C sharp at one place, and hopefully no one but Ned realized the temporary musical clash was my fault.

When we stood to sing "Hark! The Herald Angels Sing," Curt looked down at me and smiled. We know about angels, the smile seemed to say. I smiled back and moved closer to him. He took my hand.

When we sat, Jack slid his arm across my back, resting his hand on my far shoulder. Short of telling him to keep his crumby arms to himself, something that didn't go over well in most church services, there was little I could do. I spent the rest of the meeting with Curt holding my hand and Jack putting his arm around me.

After the service we swarmed into the aisles like everyone else. Somehow Jolene elbowed her way to my side in no time flat.

"That was the best Christmas service I ever went to," she said, and I didn't think she was referring to any spiritual blessings she received. "I didn't know church could be such fun. Like I said before, Merry, you're amazing."

I made a face at her and turned as my name was called. It was Sandy Rasmussen.

"Hey, Sandy. Merry Christmas." I gave her a holiday hug. I felt a little awkward seeing her because I didn't know how she felt about my springing Maddie on her this morning. She had been very polite when she left, but it could have been merely good manners.

"And Karyn." I hugged her, too. "How are you doing?"

"I don't think I'm feeling too good. It's hard to sit so long."

"Merry," Sandy said, "I want you to meet Dan and the kids."

We shook hands all the way around, and I was pleased to see Dan standing with his arm around Karyn.

"Sandy told me about your interview today," he said.

"Especially about meeting Maddie. I don't know if anything will come of it, but it moved Sandy out of the quagmire of doubt where she's been drowning these last few months."

I looked at Sandy. She nodded. "I was mad at you at first. How presumptuous, I thought. But then as I talked with Maddie, and then as the three of us talked, I realized you were trying to help us."

"I was," I said. "I love Maddie, and I care what happens to this young lady over here." I gave Karyn's hand a squeeze.

Out of the corner of my eye I saw Curt get swept past me in the crowd. "I'll see you outside," he said as he swirled by. Then Jack passed. "I'll see you in the foyer," he called.

I turned back to the Rasmussens to find Karyn watching me in fascination. "They both sat with you, didn't they? One on each side. Which one is your boyfriend, Merry? I think they're both cute."

Blushing, I said, "I've got to go put my music away," and made my escape.

I was putting my bells in their velvet case when I felt an arm slide around my waist. Curt or Jack? I was afraid to look.

"Thanks, Merry."

With relief I realized it was Maddie. I turned to hug her. "You're not mad at me?"

"I was at first, but the longer I talked to Sandy, the more excited I got. Did you know she asked me back to their apartment where I met Karyn? Just as a friend of her mother's, nothing more. Doug and I have been talking ever since."

As Doug joined us, she said, "I don't know if anything will happen, but thank you for caring."

Thank you, Lord. Thank you!

She looked over my shoulder. "Hi. Are you ready?"

I turned. The Rasmussen clan stood there.

"They're coming over for a late supper," Maddie said.

I watched them walk up the aisle together.

It is miracle season, isn't it, Lord?

Jack was waiting for me when I walked into the foyer.
My heart dropped. I didn't want a confrontation. I wanted
to feel toasty and warm and hopeful about the Reeders and
the Rasmussens.

"Merry, I'm leaving in about five minutes for Pittsburgh." He grinned his most engaging smile. "If you come
along, you can still be home in time for Christmas."

"Oh, Jack, I can't. You know that. Work and all."

He studied me for a minute. "Do you even want to go
home? I mean, if you could, would you?"

I glanced over Jack's shoulder and saw Jolene and
Reilly standing by the front door waiting for me. I saw Curt
spot me and break into a broad smile. I saw Maddie and
Sandy talking like old friends as they bundled the kids
outside ahead of them.

And I knew. I didn't want to go home because I was home.
Amhearst was where I belonged. Sure, I'd miss Mom and Dad
and Sam. Sure, I'd miss the familiar fun of our extended
family. But if I went home, I'd miss Amhearst more.

Jack saw the answer in my face. A flash of sadness
darkened his eyes. Then his usual carefree smirk returned.
He leaned over and kissed my cheek.

"Merry Christmas, Merry girl. I'll see you next year."

He turned and walked toward the door, past Jolene and
Reilly, past Curt. At the last possible moment, he paused
and stuck out his hand to Curt. The two men eyed each
other, nodded and shook.

Jack left.

The crowd at Jolene's house surprised me both in its size
and diversity. I don't know why I expected it to be only the
few people I knew in common with Jo, but it wasn't. There
were friends of Mr. and Mrs. Luray as well as several relatives of the Lurays and Mrs. Samson. Most of them were
a maze of faces that came and went through the evening.

"Reilly," Mrs. Samson called when we entered the living room. Wearing a highly practical, thoroughly unseasonal apron of orange and yellow tied around her ample middle, she rushed to Reilly's side. "Where have you been? You're late."

"We went to the Christmas Eve service, Grandmom." He planted a kiss on her withered cheek.

"At a church?" The disbelief and horror on her face were almost comic. "You didn't!" You'd have thought he told her he'd gone to Sodom or Gomorrah.

"But we're here now." He smiled. "So let the party begin."

Mrs. Samson reached out a hand and caressed his cheek. "You are my most precious possession, Reilly," she said.

"I know, Grandmom, and I love you, too, but I'm not your possession. I make my own choices." Casually he reached out and rested his hand on the nape of Jolene's neck. She looked at him and smiled. He looked at his grandmother. "Do you understand?"

Mrs. Samson looked at Jolene with loathing, then turned her back and marched to the kitchen.

"Thank you, Reilly," Jolene said quietly, sliding her arm around his waist. "Now let's get some food."

I watched Jolene and Reilly with interest. A public declaration was being made, no question about it.

Jolene led us to the dining room where the table was stretched by extra leaves to truly impressive length. A gaudy red-and-green plaid tablecloth covered the table, and candles in a centerpiece of greens shed a soft light over the bounteous and mind-boggling array.

Curt and I filled our plates and carried them to the living room. There wasn't a seat to be found. We wandered into the hallway and found a deacon's bench against one wall. We grabbed it and enjoyed a private dining corner where we could actually hear each other talk.

The doorbell rang as we sat there, and I got up to answer it. Mac came in, Dawn on his arm. He looked at me and smirked as he helped her off with her coat. Dawn saw me and smiled.

"The bells were great again," she said. "Weren't they, Mac?"

"You were at church?" I blurted to Mac.

"Don't drop your dinner over it," he growled as he steadied my plate, which was bending under the weight of too much food. "I just hope it counts for something with my mother and God. Now where's Eloise? I have to give her a Christmas kiss and a poinsettia."

"Here I am, dear Mac," Mrs. Luray bustled into the hall and held out her cheek for his peck. "This is Jolene's boss, June. He thinks he's gruff and tough, but he's not."

I nodded. "He's my boss, too. Remember?"

There was a brief struggle in the fuzzy depths of Mrs. Luray's mind, and the saner part won for a change. "Of course," she said with her sweet smile. "How silly of me. If you work with Jolene and Mac is Jolene's boss, he's yours, too." She turned to the unsuspecting Curt. "Is he yours?"

"No," Curt said. "I don't work at the paper. I'm self-employed."

Mrs. Luray reached out and patted his hand. "Well, I hope you get a job soon."

Mrs. Luray turned from the bemused Curt to Dawn. "And who's this lovely lady, Mac? Your girlfriend?"

"This is Dawn, Eloise," Mac said.

"No, dear boy." Mrs. Luray glanced out the window beside the door. "It's night-time. Dawn's hours away. Now let's get you two some food."

We'd barely started eating again when the doorbell rang for the second time. Before I could answer it, Harry Allen Bushay let himself in with a rush of cold air, followed by a petulant and unhappy Lonni.

"Just be polite, Lonni. That's all I ask," he muttered. "We don't need a scene to ruin everyone's Christmas Eve."

Then he saw us and became all smiles as he slid out of his coat.

"Curt and Merry." He took my hand. "I must thank you for the food project article and picture. Both were very well done."

Lonni noticed me for the first time and frowned. "What are *you* doing here?"

Had I been feeling especially sensitive, I'd have collapsed like a sand castle at high tide. "I work with Jolene. Remember?"

Mrs. Samson came bustling into the hallway.

"Lonni, my baby, how are you?" She grabbed the girl in a fierce hug.

"Careful, Grandmom," Lonni said, struggling to break free. "You'll squish the baby."

Grandmom? I stared at Lonni and Mrs. Samson.

"Oh, honey girl," Mrs. Samson said, placing her hand against Lonni's cheek. "You're my prized possession."

"Yeah, I know." Lonni sounded unimpressed. She handed her jacket to Harry Allen and headed for the dining room.

"Hi, Mom." Harry Allen kissed Mrs. Samson on the forehead. "How's my favorite mother-in-law tonight?"

I blinked. Never in a million years would I have made that connection.

"I'm fine, fine," she said absently, watching Lonni. "I'm glad you brought her."

His eyes followed his daughter, too. "It was a fight. She did not want to come, believe me. She's become terribly hostile to me in the last few days, and I don't know why."

"Don't worry." Mrs. Samson waved her hand like she could shoo Lonni's tantrums away as easily as she could shoo a fly. "Whatever it is, she'll get over it."

Harry Allen didn't look convinced.

"By the way," Mrs. Samson said. "I got my annual Christmas call from Eileen this afternoon."

"Oh," Harry Allen seemed unmoved at the mention of the woman I assumed was his long-departed wife. "How's she doing?"

Mrs. Samson looked disgusted. "She's still living with that horrible cowboy. She did say they want to get married, finally! So I expect you'll get a letter from some Wyoming lawyer one of these days about a divorce. I tell you, Harry Allen, you're more my son than she ever was my daughter. Now let's get you some food."

With a nod in our direction, Harry Allen followed Mrs. Samson as she almost raced to the dining room.

"He's her son-in-law," I said to Curt.

"Apparently."

"And Lonni's her granddaughter."

"Yep."

"That means Reilly must be Lonni's cousin."

"That sounds about right. Want some more to eat?"

"Talk about a small world." And I began to think furiously.

"Yo, Merry." Curt waved his hand before my eyes. "More food?"

I blinked and looked at my plate. It was still full of food I wasn't certain I could eat. "Thanks, no, but you go get some more if you want. I'll just wait here."

I took his empty plate and slid it under mine to keep mine from collapsing. Curt walked down the hall to the dining room, braving the cacophony of conversation and music. I sat in our relatively quiet corner, eating absently and thinking for a few more minutes. Then I got up, ready to take our dirty things to the kitchen.

As I passed the living room door, I heard Jolene say to Reilly's father, "The funeral went very well, thanks, Mr. Samson. Lots of our old friends from high school came."

I had thought the funeral depressing, without hope and impersonal since the minister who led it hadn't known Arnie.

"It was a nice service," Harry Allen agreed as he joined

them. "Given all the unusual circumstances surrounding it, I doubt it could have been better."

The people near me fell silent a minute, thinking about murder and young death to a background of "Jingle Bell Rock."

"I wasn't allowed to go," Lonni suddenly announced loudly to the room at large.

"Easy, Lonni." Harry Allen watched her with worried eyes.

"And I knew him better than any of the rest of you!" she cried.

"Of course you knew him," Mr Luray said. "He was Jolene's husband." He was too busy serving coffee refills from an insulated pitcher to feel the emotional currents flying around the room. "Just don't mention the funeral in front of Mrs. Luray, okay? She's having a hard time accepting Arnie's death."

"*She's* having a hard time?" Lonni exploded. "What about me?" And she started to weep. "What about me?"

Mr. Luray looked shocked.

"You shouldn't have brought her, Uncle Harry." Reilly moved toward Lonni. "It's too raw. Come on, Lonni, honey. Let's you and me go somewhere quiet."

But Harry Allen reached the girl first and tried to hug her. She screamed and jumped back.

"Don't touch me!" She wrapped her arms protectively about her stomach and the baby. "I hate you! You killed him!" She broke and ran, heading for the hall stairs, Reilly right after her.

Harry Allen stood frozen in the middle of the room, his face gray, his shoulders stooped. While Nat King Cole began to sing about chestnuts roasting and Jack Frost nipping, everyone shifted uncomfortably, uncertain where to look.

I felt sorry for Harry Allen, especially since just twenty-four hours ago, I was willing to cast him in the role of villain myself. Now with my new information I knew better.

The tense silence was broken by Eloise Luray who had come into the room in the middle of Lonni's tirade. "Harry Allen, you didn't kill anyone, did you?" She didn't wait for an answer. "Of course you didn't. But did you know that someone killed Arnie? Jolene thinks I don't know he's dead, but I do." She smiled sweetly at her daughter.

Jolene had been watching Reilly follow Lonni but turned to her mother. "You're smarter than I thought, Mom."

Eloise Luray preened. "Now there's lots more food on the table, everyone. Harry Allen, why don't you go get some? It'll help you feel better. Besides, you're too nice to kill anyone. It was someone not very nice who killed Arnie." She took Harry Allen's arm and led him out of the room.

In the silence that followed, the Mormon Tabernacle Choir sang the "Hallelujah Chorus." Suddenly there was lots of shuffling and coughing as people became busy with their food and drink. I was no different. I took a bite of Jello/pear salad I had no room for.

As I looked down at my plate, I saw on the floor the backpack/pocketbook Lonni had dropped when she dashed from the room. It had dumped itself at my feet. I set my plate on an end table, stooped and scooped up lipsticks and a compact, keys and tissues, pens, a date book and a huge blue wallet, a brush and hair spray and slid them all back into the black leather bag. The last thing I picked up was a framed picture that had fallen facedown.

I turned it over automatically as I rose, and there was Lonni in her purple T-shirt leaning against Arnie in his red polo shirt. Their smiling faces were captured in a fluted brass frame with a crack in the glass in the lower left corner.

I elbowed Jolene. "Look."

Her index finger traced the crack in the corner. "That's from the bedroom at the house." She frowned. "The kid must have been there last night after we left."

"Maybe," I said. "But what if she was there when we

got there? That would explain why the door was unlocked."
I fished in Lonni's pocketbook and drew out three keys.
"Do any look familiar?"

Jolene pointed to a large gold key. "That's the front
door, I'll bet anything. And of course, if she had a key, she
had the alarm code." She smiled sourly.

I put Lonni's purse on the hall table and picked up my
dirty dishes. I pushed through the swinging door into the
kitchen. I found a large trash can lined with a giant plastic
bag. I dumped our paper plates in with the rest.

It was comparatively quiet out here with the sound
muffled by the door, an oasis for splitting eardrums. I
relaxed into the quiet, wondering how soon Curt and I
could leave. As I turned to reenter the fray and find him,
Mrs. Samson pushed through the swinging door, bringing
Gene Autry and Rudolph with her.

"Oh," she said. "Jolene's friend." She made it sound as
if I had infected the party with a terrible social disease.

"I have enjoyed the food so much," I said with my most
charming smile as I edged toward the door. "You and Mrs.
Luray have done a magnificent job."

"Thank you." She looked surprised. "*Someone* I know
never says thank you."

There was no doubt who that someone was. In fact at
that exact moment she pushed through the swinging door,
Gene's voice now on foggy Christmas Eves. Soon we
could have our own party out here. Not a good idea.

"I need something cold to drink," Jolene announced.
"The temperature must be at least eighty in there." She
pulled the refrigerator door open. "Want a beer, Merry?"

I shook my head. "But I'd love a Coke."

Soon Jolene and I stood side by side, leaning against
the kitchen counter enjoying the cold bubbles sliding
down our throats.

"Say, Mrs. Samson, we saw you the other day out near

Arnie's," Jolene said, obviously trying to have a conversation with Reilly's grandmother. Too bad this was the first topic that popped into her head.

I bumped her elbow and she almost dropped her beer. "Let's get back to the party," I said brightly.

"Watch it, Merry," she said. "In a minute." She turned back to Mrs. Samson. "You were looking for something, weren't you? At least that's what we thought." She pointed to herself and me. "Did you find it? Did you drop it after the accident or something?"

"You must be mistaken," Mrs. Samson said. "I haven't been out that way for a long time."

Jolene shook her head. "No mistake. You were driving Reilly's car. I'd know it anywhere."

"Let's go join the others, Jo," I said, taking her arm.

She pulled free. "Nah, I want to stay out here a bit longer. It's cooler."

"Then let's go out in the backyard. It's really cool there."

"Oh, I remember now," Mrs. Samson said. "I was looking for the deer I hit."

"I thought you killed it," Jo said.

"There were others with it. I wanted to make certain they were all right."

Jo looked at Mrs. Samson strangely. "You didn't think they'd still be there, what, four or five days after the accident?"

"You're right. They weren't." She laughed in a strained manner. "Silly of me, wasn't it?"

Suddenly Jolene got very still, and my heart sank. "What day was your accident?"

Mrs. Samson said nothing.

"The day Arnie got killed? And what time of day? Midafternoon?"

"Jolene Marie, shut up!" I hissed. As usual she ignored me.

"Did you know about Arnie and Lonni? Did you hate him as much as you hate me?"

I grabbed Jolene by the arm and began dragging her toward the door. "We'll see you later, Mrs. Samson."

"Merry, she—"

"Shut up, Jo." I pushed her ahead of me, trying to get her through the swinging door. "We'll discuss it later." But I wasn't fast enough.

The feel of the little gun pressed against my spine was chilling.

"Stop," Mrs. Samson ordered, but she didn't need to say it. I had stopped. "You, too, Jolene, or I'll hurt your friend."

Jolene looked at me curiously.

"She found what she was looking for when we saw her," I said. "She's got it pressed to my spine. And it isn't a gun that needs cocking. The slightest pressure on the trigger, and I'm gone or paralyzed."

At precisely that moment the door swung open again and Eloise Luray bustled in to "Silver Bells."

"Oh, how nice," she said, smiling happily. "Jolene and June have come out to help us. Aren't you such sweet girls."

Jolene looked desperately from her mother to me to Mrs. Samson.

"Eloise," Mrs. Samson snapped with all the crack and snarl of a bullwhip. "Get back in there and check on the coffee. You know that's Alvin's job and he forgets to make more. Everyone needs another cup."

Mrs. Luray's face fell. "Oh. I'm sorry. I thought I was supposed—"

"Go, Eloise. And don't come back out here until I call you. And keep everyone else out, too."

Lip trembling at her scolding, Mrs. Luray went back into the dining room.

As I watched the door swing shut, I contemplated my chances if I threw myself to the side or tried to whirl around and disarm Mrs. Samson. Because of the type of gun she had, the gun that had shot Arnie, the gun she had thrown in the field when she hit the deer after she killed Arnie but before the police came about the accident, the gun she had gone back to retrieve, because of that gun, I had no chance of escaping injury or death. For the moment, she had me.

"Now turn the kitchen lights off, Jolene," Mrs. Samson ordered.

Jolene had her typical response to an order. "No."

Mrs. Samson placed the little gun under my chin so Jolene could see it. "Lights off."

Lips clamped in fury, Jolene flicked the lights off.

"Now slide that cabinet in front of the door. I don't want any unexpected visitors."

Jolene put her shoulder against a white wooden cabinet about four feet tall and pushed. It creaked and protested for a minute, but finally it slid across the door.

"Now get over there and open the cellar door."

"No," Jolene spat.

"I shot someone before, Jolene," Mrs. Samson said. "I'll do it again."

"No, you won't. You'd get caught. There's people out there who'd hear."

"But you'd be dead," Mrs. Samson said. "And Reilly would be safe. Just like Lonni's safe."

"No wonder Mr. Samson never came back from Korea. He thought dying was preferable to living with you!"

I squeezed my eyes shut and moaned as I felt the gun skitter across my neck. "Jolene, just open the door."

Suddenly Mrs. Samson grabbed hold of my hair and yanked. I had been leaning to one side, trying to get away from the gun, and she pulled in that direction. I overbalanced and knocked into the trash can. Garbage and I sprawled all over the floor, and I had a fleeting sad thought for my new green velvet dress.

Before I could regain my feet, Mrs. Samson lunged at Jolene. Jo screamed and turned to run, but Mrs. Samson's hand flew out and she brought the gun down on Jolene's temple. Jolene fell where she stood, blood gushing from the laceration caused by the blow. Mrs. Samson, careful to stay out of the blood, went down beside her to kneel with the gun at the unconscious woman's throat.

"Don't try anything," she said to me, her voice quiet and even. "I would love to shoot her."

Slowly I stood, but I held my hands in front of me in a placating gesture.

"Now you open the cellar door," she ordered.

I moved cautiously to the door located on the inside wall between the stove and the entrance to a pantry. Slowly I pulled it open.

"Now take her to the top of the steps."

"Mrs. Samson, you don't want to hurt Jolene. Reilly will hate you for it."

"Reilly bought me this gun. Did you know that? He took me to the target range and taught me to shoot it. He thought it wasn't safe for me to live alone with no protection." She raised the gun and pointed it at me. "I'm very good with it."

I didn't doubt her. There was an aura of comfort about the way she handled the weapon that supported her claims.

"Take her to the top of the steps."

Sighing, I took the still bleeding Jolene under the armpits and pulled her toward the steps.

Head wounds bleed excessively, I kept telling myself. It's not a sign of the severity of her injury but of surface blood vessels. Jo is really all right.

"You can't get away with hurting us or killing us," I said.

Mrs. Samson smiled. "Getting away is not my goal."

I stood at the top of the cellar steps, Jolene propped against my leg, a dead weight. "What now?"

"Turn around."

"What?"

"Turn around!"

"So you can shoot me in the back? No, ma'am."

"I have no reason to shoot you. I barely know you. I had a reason to shoot Arnie. Look what he did to Lonni. And I had a reason to shoot Tony."

I blinked in confusion. "Who's Tony?"

"My husband."

"The one who died in the Korean War?"

"That's what everybody thinks. But he came home, planning to divorce me so he could marry his Korean girlfriend."

Paradigm shift. "So you shot him?"

"I did."

"And nobody noticed?"

"Nobody saw him but me. He made sure of that. He knew everyone would pressure him not to return to her, so he didn't tell anyone he was coming. He only saw me because he needed my signature on the divorce papers."

"But what did you do with his body?" As I understood murder, and I didn't understand it all that much, the disposal of the body was one of the hardest parts of the crime.

"I put him where all bodies go," she said.

"In a cemetery?"

She nodded.

"But who did the funeral director think he was burying?"

"I buried him."

"What?"

"I'd been to a funeral at this little cemetery outside Coatesville near the reservoir. I noticed a huge pile of dirt near the back of the property, loose dirt left from the graves, I guess. There was also old flower arrangements and baskets dumped there. Not that I was looking for a place to bury someone then. But I remembered it when I had Tony lying at my feet."

"So you went out and buried Tony in that dirt pile?"

"I did. As far as I know, he's still there."

I stared at this old woman, trying to imagine her fifty-five years ago, young, strong and scorned, spurned for another woman. "Didn't anyone see you? At the cemetery, I mean."

"I went at night. It was summer. All the trees and shrubs were full, and I didn't think the people at the closest house, which wasn't very close, would ever see or hear anything." She shrugged. "I was right."

Jolene chose that moment to groan and slide onto her side. Her eyes flickered.

Mrs. Samson glanced at her briefly, then without warning ran straight at me, gun hand extended.

I flinched, stuck my hands out in front of me to protect myself, and took an automatic step backwards. My left hand struck her gun and knocked it flying. I was as surprised as Mrs. Samson. The gun hit the floor, fired once and spun under the refrigerator across the room.

Victory's ours, I thought. We'll get her now!

But that involuntary step backward did me in. I'd stepped onto air. I lost my balance and fell down the cellar steps. I hit my head on the stair railing and my back on a step. I hit my cheekbone on a railing support.

Everything went black.

SEVENTEEN

I lay, groggy, trying to remember what had happened to me. I turned my head to the right and saw darkness, to the left and saw darkness. Overhead was darkness, too.

Maybe I was asleep. But my eyes blinked and I knew they were open. You don't sleep with your eyes open.

I reached beneath me and felt a smooth, hard, cold surface. I knew that I knew what it was called; I just couldn't remember right this very minute. I reached above and felt only air. Well, I was in a large, open space.

I tried to think where that space might be, but my mind was leaden and dull. I rolled on my side, and leaden and dull instantly metamorphosed into brilliant stabs of pain. My elbow! With a great groan, I rolled onto my back again, but the pain had cleared my mind somewhat. I remembered falling on that elbow in the bathroom at Arnie's house.

But this wasn't Arnie's house.

Now how did I know that? I concentrated, trying to follow logical thought patterns. I knew this wasn't Arnie's because, because—Jolene and I had left there last night!

Yes! I felt as proud as a kid who's just finished his first chapter book by himself. I tried again. I knew this wasn't Arnie's house because, because—I went to church with Curt and Jolene and Reilly—and Jack?—tonight and because I went to an open house at the Lurays after church.

And I knew this wasn't Arnie's because I knew who killed Arnie.

With a shudder I remembered Mrs. Samson and her little gun. I remembered dragging an unconscious, bleeding Jolene across the kitchen, standing at the top of the cellar stairs, and falling backwards into the cellar.

Well, there was no great problem then. I could get out of the cellar. All I had to do was climb back up the stairs. I rolled onto my side, the one without the sore elbow, and pushed myself into a crawling position. Even that little bit of movement was all it took for my head to explode. I saw red and yellow stars just like in the comic strips. I groaned, nauseous and afraid to move.

Concussion. I huddled miserably on my knees, waiting for the clamminess, the nausea to pass. I pushed myself up with my good arm until I was upright on my knees. All I felt was a minor case of *mal de mer*. I was making progress. I put one foot flat on the floor, then rested from the enormous effort this move had required. I realized suddenly that I was sore not only in my elbow but all over. The tumble down the steps had beaten me up but good.

I was trying to work up the fortitude to block out the pain and the courage to stand upright when I heard a muffled explosion. I turned toward the sound and saw a narrow band of light flash high in the air.

That's the door. I must get up to that door.

But the staircase, open on both sides, might as well have been Everest. Even if I clung to the wooden railing that marched up one side, the thought of scaling such a steep incline was overwhelming.

As I stared at the door, I realized my concussion was worse than I thought. I had begun hallucinating. I watched, fascinated, as my mind conjured up liquid fire which rolled under the door and began falling, falling in a molten sheet, tumbling, running, sliding down the steps toward me. I watched from my knee, enchanted as one stair step, then another and another became ledges over which the fiery fluid flowed.

It was the most beautiful thing I had ever seen. I needed to stand so I could see it better. I pushed myself upright and stood weaving, mesmerized by the reds and golds and the flickering blue. Drops of flame plunged off the edges of the steps to splash in fiery raindrops on the concrete and flatten into tiny flickering pools. If I could have clapped my hands in pleasure, I would have, but my right arm hung limp, made useless by the re-injured elbow.

It was now that somewhere in the deepest part of my mind, an alarm began to sound. Something wasn't right. I raised my good hand to my head, trying to think.

At that moment the cellar door ignited, bursting into hungry, devouring, roaring flames. Then the top step came alive, no longer merely a burning sheet of—what? Gasoline? Kerosene? It crackled and burned, its wood feeding the ravenous fire. The second step flared. Black smoke, far blacker than the cellar, began billowing, mushrooming across the ceiling with terrifying speed. And heat. I could feel heat traveling with the smoke, pressing down from above. The third step ignited. The railing. The rafters.

This was no hallucination!

"Help! Help!" I screamed. "Curt! I'm down here! Get me out!" The roaring, rushing of the flames ate my voice.

Oh, God, get me out!

There should be windows somewhere down here. All cellars had windows high on the walls. Crouching low because of the smoke, I searched frantically.

There! Wasn't that a window with the shine of a distant streetlight cutting through the dirt and grime that darkened the glass? I lurched toward it as another stair burst into fire. The smoke roiled about my head like an angry serpent, undulating, rippling, convulsing. I knew that it would poison me, devour me if it could.

Oh, dear God, help me!

I ran toward the window. It was small, but I wasn't very big. If I could get up to it, I could get through it. If I could get up to it.

God, how do I ever reach a window that high in the wall? And what can I break the glass with once I get there?

I was concentrating so hard on the window that I wasn't watching where I was going. I tripped and lost my balance, falling forward onto a large flat surface. It was a table and the fact that I could see it so clearly terrified me. The fire had gained so in intensity that the once-dark cellar was awash in light.

I heard a crash and spun to see pieces of a rafter falling, spreading the fire to the old furniture and the bags of newspapers on which it fell. I slipped under the table for protection, and as I did, I spotted a line of paint cans against the outside wall.

I groaned. All I needed was for them to blow.

I felt a curious mental prodding, and I looked at them again.

They'll break glass! *Thanks, Lord.*

I grabbed the closest can and taking a deep breath close to the ground, stood and put the can on the table. Pushing the table with all my strength, I shoved it under the window. I bent for another deep breath, then climbed awkwardly onto the table, favoring my poor right arm. I grasped the paint can in my left hand and rammed it with all my strength into the window.

The glass shattered with a satisfyingly loud report, and I put my arms up to protect my eyes from the flying shards. Fresh cool air, rich in oxygen, poured in.

"Yes!" I yelled. I was reaching toward the window and my escape when a roaring like a thousand waves crashing on a rocky shore stopped me. I spun to see the fire mush-rooming across the ceiling, lunging at me, rushing for me, its greedy tongues ravenous. When I broke the window, I had created a chimney, and its draft worked all too well.

I dropped from the table to the floor, devastated as I understood that I could never get out of that window before the flames reached it.

Crying, I crouched and ran away from my window, away from my salvation.

But if there's one window, shouldn't there be two? Three? *Dear Lord, there has to be!*

The air currents were alive as the fire reached and burst through the broken window and began licking up the outside wall of the house.

Didn't anyone see that? Didn't anyone hear the fire? Smell the fire?

Didn't anyone miss me?

I saw a second window but only because its glass re-flected the fire burning its wooden frame. Suddenly the window shattered from the heat and with a great woosh! the flames dove to and through it.

I huddled in the farthest corner beyond tears and, certain I was going to die, hugged myself against the chill.

Against the chill? But the room was superheated.

I concentrated fiercely and knew that I wasn't crazy. Cool air hit my back and streamed past me. I spun around and cried out. Stairs! Concrete stairs! They rose to a Bilco door, those slanted cellar doors that open up and out.

Oh, God! Thank you!

I scrambled into the tiny alcove and pressed my face against the cool metal. I sucked in great drafts of fresh air. My head cleared and I began pounding on the doors.

"Help! Help! Curt! God! Somebody!"

Suddenly someone pounded back from the outside.

"Help me!" I shouted. "Help me! Open the doors!"

"Merry! Oh, thank God, it's Merry!"

"Curt! Open the doors!" I glanced back over my shoulder and saw nothing but fire and smoke. "Hurry! Hurry!"

I heard the doors rumble and groan as people struggled to lift them. I felt them heave and shudder, but they didn't open.

"Merry!" It was Curt. "The doors are locked on the inside! You have to unlock them!"

I started to cry again. "I can't," I bawled. "I can't."

"Come on, sweetheart! You can! Oh, God, help her do it!"

Hiccupping and sniffing, I ran my hands back and forth across the inside of the door, searching for a handle, a latch, anything. All I felt was a smooth surface. Suddenly I rammed my hand painfully against the latch.

"I found it! But it's stuck!"

I pulled. I pushed. I shoved to the right, then to the left. And I came as close to sheer panic as I ever had. Safety and freedom were so close! So close! And the fire was, too. A paint can exploded and the can sailed across the cellar streaming fire behind it.

"Open!" I screamed. "Open!"

"Keep trying, Merry." It was Mac sounding insufferably calm on the safe side of the door. "Dawn's out here holding a prayer meeting for you. They're going to sing 'Amazing Grace' in four-part harmony any minute now."

I giggled and gulped and the panic receded.

"Turn the latch counterclockwise," Curt called to me. "Mr. Luray says to turn it counterclockwise!"

I wrenched at the latch counterclockwise, and I felt a movement.

"Yes," I screamed. "It's moving! Tell Dawn to keep praying!"

I twisted harder, making the most of my one good arm. Again and again I felt the latch give ever so slightly. Then there was a terrible, grinding screech of metal and the latch released completely. It was so sudden that I almost fell over, down the stairs, and into the fire.

I righted myself and gave a mighty heave at the same time Curt gave a mighty pull. The doors exploded into the wonderful, sweet night air. I stumbled up and out into Curt's embrace as the oxygen-rich air surged in a low sweeping arc down the concrete stairs to rise inside the cellar, feeding the flames until they burst through the floor to join the fire already devouring the rest of the house.

I clung to Curt and couldn't stop shaking. His arms locked around me.

Thank you, dear Jesus! Thank you!

Suddenly Curt yelled, "No, Reilly! No!" He let go of me so quickly I almost fell. He grabbed wildly at Reilly who stood on the steps of the Bilco door, his arm over his face as he searched the flames.

"She's not there, Reilly! She's not there!" I called, but I wasn't sure he heard over the noise of the fire.

Curt grabbed him by one arm and Mac by the other, and they pulled him away from the house.

"Reilly, son." It was Mr. Luray, his face haggard and scared. He rested his hand on Reilly's sleeve. "You can't go in there. You can't. We can't lose both of you."

"But she's not in there," I repeated. "I was in the cellar alone."

"Then where is she?" Reilly's voice was raw with anguish.

Suddenly Mrs. Luray stood beside me, staring with rapt face at the flames eating her house. "Isn't it pretty, June? Isn't it beautiful?"

I slid my arm around her and gave her a squeeze. For once it was a good thing that she didn't understand real life anymore.

I turned to Reilly. "I don't know where she is. The last time I saw her, she was lying semiconscious on the kitchen floor. Then I fell down the stairs."

"Nobody was in the kitchen when we cleared the house," Curt said quickly. "I checked."

I glanced at him. He must have seen the blood, but he didn't mention it.

"How did she get hurt to begin with?" asked Mr. Luray. He looked at me with eyes as full of pain as Reilly's. "What happened to her?"

I didn't want to tell him. The answer would just inflict more pain on these already hurting people.

"Please, Merry, we have to know," he said, and of course he was right.

"Mrs. Samson knocked her unconscious."

"Grandmom knocked her unconscious?" Reilly was incredulous.

I nodded. "She used the gun she shot Arnie with."

There was a small minute of frozen disbelief when the roar of the fire was the only sound. Then Lonni screamed, a cry of great anguish. "Grandmom? Grandmom shot Arnie?"

"Shush, baby." Harry Allen pulled his daughter into his arms. "Shush, baby."

This time Lonni clung to him. "Daddy," she sobbed, "how could she? How could she?"

Sirens sounded and suddenly the street and then the yard were alive with men shouting and running. We moved back near the alley, clustered for comfort.

My mind was running as quickly as the firefighters, spinning and tumbling with my own mad ideas.

"Reilly, where does your grandmother keep her car?" I asked.

"She got her new car today," he said. "It's in the garage." He pointed to a garage facing on the alley.

"Is it?"

As a group we turned and ran.

"Where are we going, June?" Mrs. Luray asked, holding back as she tried to look over her shoulder at the fire.

Reilly reached the garage first and lifted the great door. The garage was empty.

"Listen. I have an idea, but it's crazy."

"It's the only one we've got," Curt said. "Go on. Tell us."

I took a deep breath. "Just before I fell downstairs, Mrs. Samson told me the strangest story. She said she killed her husband—"

"She killed Tony?" Mr. Luray interrupted.

"Tony," Mrs. Luray said. "He was a nice man. Very handsome. He died in the war."

"He didn't. He came home wanting a divorce so he could marry some Korean woman he'd fallen in love with. Mrs. Samson shot him rather than deal with the embarrassment. Then she buried him in a dirt pile in some little cemetery outside Coatesville by the reservoir."

"It's too bizarre to be true," Harry Allen said skeptically. "People don't do things like that. She was nasty and critical, but…"

"But what if it is true?" Mac said. "I've been a newspaperman long enough to know that people will do just about anything given the right circumstances. If William Poole were here, he'd say the same thing."

I could see Mac's newsman's mind turning. He wanted everything I'd said to be true. It was a fantastic story, and it was all his! (I didn't count.) It was sure to make the wire services, and he could break it before TV even knew it existed. The editorship might just become his permanently.

"It's true, all right," I said. "Remember, I saw her. I heard her. And I think she took Jolene out to that little cemetery."

"Here, Reilly." Mr. Luray held out a car key. "Find out if Merry's story is true. Find out if Jolene's out there at that little cemetery. That's my garage." He pointed to the next building on the alley.

Reilly rushed to the Luray garage and threw the door open. A brand-new Jeep Grand Cherokee stood there.

A gift from Jolene, no doubt. No wonder her dad drove her to work in iffy weather.

Reilly ran to the driver's side.

"You can't go out there alone," Mac yelled. "It's too dangerous." He grabbed Dawn by the hand and jumped in the backseat.

I looked at Curt and found him watching me. He had that distant look again. "I'm going, too," I said.

He blinked once, twice, then nodded. "I know." He turned and yelled as Reilly backed out of the garage. "Wait for us!"

We climbed in beside Reilly, and Curt had barely shut the door before we tore down the alley. Reilly screeched around the corner and burst onto Houston Street. A policeman at the fire to help with crowd control saw us careen off and took chase. I guess he thought we were speeders at best or criminals leaving the scene of an arson at worst.

I managed to snap my seat belt, but it was Curt's arm around my shoulder that held me steady as we rushed through the night. I looked to make certain he was belted in too and saw that he still wore that distant look. What had happened to the desperation and love I'd seen when he pulled me from the cellar?

He felt my glance and smiled kindly. Kindly!

Reilly hit a pothole, and I groaned and grabbed my arm.

Instantly the distance left Curt. "Are you okay?" he asked, his forehead wrinkled in concern. "I never should have let you come along! You're in no shape to be caught up in this danger. Whatever was I thinking? You need to go to the hospital."

I didn't answer. My mind was much too fragmented and fatigued to deal with his mixed signals. Besides, it took all my energy to hold on as Reilly tore along Business 30, empty at midnight Christmas Eve, and ran every red light he met all the way through Coatesville. He went around the corner at Route 82 North on two wheels, then cut to the left and raced through Rock Run. He barreled along the narrow, twisting macadam road smack in the center. The police were right behind us, lights flashing and sirens blaring.

Oh, Lord, please don't let there be anyone coming toward us!

I glanced back at Dawn and knew she was praying exactly the same thing and just as hard.

Suddenly Reilly wrenched the wheel left and hit the brakes so hard we all would have gone through various windows if it weren't for seat belts. We stopped inches from a heavy chain that blocked our way as it stretched across the access road to the tiny cemetery. Parked beside the chain was a brand-new red Accord.

"Grandmom's car," Reilly said grimly.

He threw the Cherokee in reverse, backed clear of the chain, and threw the Jeep into drive. We bounced off the road and into the weeds, shrubs and small trees at the edge of the woods, completely circumventing the chain.

"Three cheers for four-wheel drive," muttered Mac. His eyes were bright with the excitement of the chase.

The Jeep lumbered back onto the access road as the police pulled up beside the Accord.

A bullhorn cut the night. "Stop! Police!"

Reilly kept going. As he rounded a curve in the road, the headlights limned an unforgettable tableau.

A mound of earth, red and loosely packed, rose about seven feet, a small mountain of soil collected from graves that never needed all their fill after they received their contents. Caught shovel in hand was Mrs. Samson, a freshly turned, much smaller pile of dirt at her feet. The beginnings of a small tunnel in the large dirt pile showed her handiwork.

Lying in a huddle off to the side about ten feet was Jolene, her red Christmas outfit a bloody slash in the dark forest.

Reilly jumped out of the Jeep and raced toward Jolene. The rest of us climbed out more cautiously.

"I don't think she's got her gun anymore," I said. "I think it's under the refrigerator, but I don't know. But I do know she won't shoot Reilly. The rest of us maybe, but not Reilly. He can run anywhere he wants." I took a shaky breath. "We'd better be careful."

Behind us the police crashed through the underbrush yelling, "Stop! Put your hands up!"

Reilly dropped to his knees beside Jolene and felt her throat.

"She's alive!" he cried, his voice thick with tears of relief. He bent to kiss her cheek. He straightened and gently brushed her hair from her face. "It's all right now, Jo. I'm here."

I wanted to cry. Without thinking, the four of us surged forward with relief. When I saw one of Jo's legs move, I did cry.

Blinking at the tears, I turned and limped toward the police.

"We need an ambulance right away," I called. "There's a badly injured woman up here."

A light blazed in my face, and I raised my hands defensively. "I'm not dangerous," I said foolishly. "We need your help."

"Merry?" said a surprised voice. "Is that you? What happened to you? You look awful!"

"William! Oh, William! How wonderful!" I threw my arms around his neck in relief, only to feel my knees buckle as my right elbow protested vociferously at such careless treatment. I clutched it to me and swallowed against the pain.

"Merry!" His concern was comforting, but I waved it away.

"It's Jolene Meister up there. She's been injured. She needs an ambulance."

He turned to run back to his cruiser. "And we have a murderer cornered up there, too. You might want some backup."

I hurried to Jolene as fast as my aching body would allow.

I lowered myself to the ground so that Dawn and I sat one on either side, each holding one of her hands, our legs stretched along her body to try and offer some warmth. William brought a blanket to cover her with and another to throw around my coatless shoulders. I hadn't been conscious of the cold before, but now I immediately began to shiver.

While we waited for the ambulance, Reilly, flanked by Curt and Mac, tried to reason with his grandmother.

"Grandmom." He held out his hands toward her. "The police need to talk to you."

"I don't want to talk to them."

"You have to, Grandmom."

"Don't tell me what I have to do, Reilly Samson. No one tells me what I have to do." With that, she lifted the carving knife she'd been holding and rested its point against her throat. "If the police come near me, I'll use this on myself since I can't use it on her."

Reilly jerked. "Grandmom, put that knife down!"

"Don't tell me what to do." Mrs. Samson said it slowly, through clenched teeth. Reilly quickly and wisely changed the subject.

"What happened to Jolene, Grandmom? How did she get hurt?"

"I knocked her out." Mrs. Samson's voice was as calm as if she were talking about going to the store for a loaf of bread.

"But Grandmom, you can't go around hurting people like that!"

"She deserved it. She hurt you!"

"Grandmom!"

"She did! You know she did."

Reilly nodded. "You're right. She hurt me when she married Arnie. Both she and I regret that act deeply. But that doesn't mean you can hurt her back."

"She's no good, Reilly. Like Arnie was no good and Tony was no good."

"Grandmom!"

"Listen to me, Reilly. It's not too late. Get away from her. You mustn't love her!"

"It's too late, Grandmom. I do love her. I've always loved her."

"I love you, Reilly."

"Grandmom!"

"You're my most prized possession."

Reilly's hopeless sigh slid sadly through the night and his shoulders sagged. "You've still got it wrong, Grandmom. I'm not your possession."

Into the small silence that fell Mac spoke. "Hey, Mrs. Samson." His voice was perky and full of interest.

The old woman jumped and the knife wobbled dangerously. It was almost as if she saw him for the first time. "Who are you? What are you doing here? Reilly!"

Mac put out his hand to keep Reilly quiet and kept talking, ignoring her agitation. "How come you didn't kill Jolene before you brought her here? Wouldn't it have been easier?"

Mrs. Samson stiffened. "Just who are you to question me?"

I was afraid he'd say, "*The News* editor" or "Jolene's boss," and make her furious because he was on the wrong team. But Mac could be cagey when he wanted to be.

"I'm Reilly's friend," he said. "I'm just curious. That's all. I don't mean to get you mad at me."

Mrs. Samson stared at him a minute, though I doubted she could see any more than a silhouette backlit by the Jeep's headlights and the police cruisers' red and blues. "I didn't want to get blood on my new car," she finally announced. "Reilly helped me buy it."

"But wasn't she sort of bloody from when you knocked her out?" Mac asked conversationally.

"I cleaned her up. I wiped the blood from her face and

made certain she rode in the trunk on some newspapers. They're sort of messy, but the car's okay."

"Good thinking," Mac said, and Mrs. Samson preened.

As he talked, the ambulance pulled quietly up the cemetery road as soon as the police cut the chain. The emergency techs came swiftly to Jolene and Dawn and I moved aside. At least she did and I tried to, but I'd turned stiff on the cold ground. Eventually Dawn had to pull me to my feet and help me out of the way. We stood watching as the EMTs stabilized Jo, then lifted her onto a gurney and quickly put her into the ambulance, anxious to leave the scene before more trouble erupted. As the door slammed, I saw one of them was already slipping an IV into her arm.

When the ambulance was gone, William Poole stepped into the circle of light thrown by the Jeep's headlights.

"Mrs. Samson," he called.

She had been watching the men work over Jolene, her expression bitter. She seemed so focused on her hatred that she hadn't noticed the sergeant. She appeared shocked when she saw his uniform.

"Who are you?" she asked.

"I'm Sergeant Poole of the Amhearst police, Mrs. Samson. I'd like to ask you to give me your knife."

"You can't make me," she said.

Suddenly a dozen officers stepped forward, forming a loose circle around her. Mrs. Samson looked totally disconcerted.

"Grandmom," Reilly called. "Please give us your knife." He began walking slowly toward her, one arm extended. "Please don't hurt yourself. I don't want to feel any worse than I already do."

"It's that Jolene that makes you feel bad," Mrs. Samson said, waving the knife for emphasis. "I love you."

"Then give me a hug. Please. I need one." He reached out and gathered his grandmother into his arms. As she hugged him back, the knife hanging over his shoulders, Curt reached out and quietly took it from her unprotesting fingers.

When Reilly stepped back, Sergeant Poole and another officer were there, and each took one of her arms. As they led her away, she called, "Reilly, I love you. You're my most prized possession. Don't ever forget. I did it for Lonni and you."

Curt had to drive us to the hospital to see how Jolene was because Reilly couldn't stop shaking. I don't think he even realized he had tears streaming down his cheeks.

EIGHTEEN

I wrestled my first-ever turkey into the oven at two o'clock Christmas afternoon for dinner at six. It was a small turkey, more the size of a large roasting chicken, but handling it with one arm in a sling was still a challenge. I set the timer carefully even though the bird had one of those little plastic doodads that pop up when everything's done.

This dinner was important to me. It was to be the backdrop for a talk with Curt, a talk he wasn't yet aware we were going to have, a talk I had to have before I went crazy. I was hoping that if dinner went well, so would the talk, sort of like if you smiled for the photographer, the picture had a better chance of being good. The catch was that for either my metaphorical picture or my very real conversation to turn out well, there had to be something worthwhile to photograph, to discuss.

I'd spent a lot of time thinking about Curt during the small hours of the night after I'd finally gotten home. I'd tried to sleep, but every time I rolled over, my elbow woke me. Finally I gave up, plumped my pillows, and sat, stroking a blissfully snoring Whiskers. As I sat, I thought. And thought. When Christmas Day finally dawned, I was weary but determined. Then I surprised myself by falling asleep for several hours.

Now, somewhat rested, I peered into the oven at my turkey. I was basking in self-worth when my phone rang. It was probably Mom calling to wish me Merry Christmas.

It was Maddie. "Good news!" she said, excitement spilling down the phone lines. "Karyn had her baby about two hours ago."

"How wonderful! Is everybody okay?"

"Mother and daughter are fine." Suddenly Maddie was crying. "They let me be in the delivery room," she said. "It was Sandy, Karyn and me. And they let me be the first to hold her."

"Oh, Maddie! Merry Christmas. What's her name?"

"Holly Claire. Karyn wanted Holly because it's Christmas, and Claire has always been my favorite name. Oh, Merry, nothing's for sure yet. There's so much legal stuff that none of us know much about and counseling stuff and all. But pray for us? Please pray!"

When I hung up, I was crying a bit myself.

I went to the hospital to visit Jolene after I was certain the oven wasn't going to incinerate my turkey when I turned my back. I'd had enough incinerations to last a lifetime. I shuddered when I thought of the rubble that was all that was left of the Lurays' home. They had lost everything. Everything, that is, except Jolene.

She was going to be all right. She had a non-displaced fracture of the skull, the doctors said, from the blunt instrument trauma, but there were no further complications like blood clots or anything. She would not need surgery if the CT scan was normal, as they expected it to be. She probably would have amnesia of the event but they thought little if any other effect.

When I got to her room, she was lying flat, tubes and wires running to all sorts of machines. Reilly, scruffy and unshaven, sat in the chair beside the bed holding her hand. Mr. and Mrs. Luray sat on two other chairs and watched TV.

"June, look!" Mrs. Luray called to me, pointing to the screen. "It's my favorite movie."

Mr. Luray, face drawn and pale, smiled sadly at me. "She's never seen it before," he said.

I gave both a hug, then turned to Jolene.

"Hey," I said as I leaned over and gave her a light kiss. "Merry Christmas."

She opened her eyes for a few seconds and smiled vaguely at me. Then her eyes dropped shut and she slept.

"She's been asleep most of the time," Reilly said. "But she's doing very well."

"How about you? You've had a pretty brutal time of it."

"I'm okay," he said. "She'll be all right—" and he looked at her with such love that tears came to my eyes "—so how can I be anything but fine?"

But I knew—and he knew—it wouldn't always be fine for him. He'd always know that his grandmother had murdered his grandfather as well as the man who might have been his cousin-in-law. She had also tried to kill the woman he loved. But most heartrending and difficult would be his Judas hug that had turned Mrs. Samson over to the police. That there was no choice for him would not do much to alleviate his guilt.

I left almost as soon as I arrived. I had come not for Jolene or Reilly or the Lurays. They didn't need me. I had come for myself, and I felt free now to enjoy my first Amhearst Christmas.

Mr. Luray, his steps dragging, walked me to the elevator. "We're going to Tel Hai Retirement Community as soon as there's a cottage available," he said softly. "In the meantime we're staying with relatives." He sighed. "I've known we should do something like this for a long time, but I was always afraid of what it would do to Eloise. Now there's no choice."

"I think that's a wonderful decision, Mr. Luray." I gave him a quick, one-armed hug and kissed his wrinkled cheek. He smiled faintly. "Do they know how the fire started?"

"Adele Samson did it. The fire officials said she made a crude incendiary device out of a plastic milk jug and kerosene with a dish towel for a fuse. Apparently she filled the jug halfway—if she'd filled it all the way, you wouldn't have stood a chance—lit the kerosene-soaked wick, and fled, taking Jolene with her."

I tried to imagine Mrs. Samson dragging Jolene across the darkened lawn to the rear garage. My mind boggled.

"The bomb exploded a few minutes after they had gone."

I nodded. "I heard the explosion," I said. "And I saw the flash of light under the door. I thought I was hallucinating when the fire came rolling down the stairs."

Mr. Luray patted my shoulder awkwardly. "Thank God you're all right." And he gave a mighty sniff.

"You are a sweet man to care so much about me," I said and kissed his cheek again. The elevator came and I stepped on. "Merry Christmas."

When I got home, I was relieved that the oven was still behaving and the turkey was smelling ever more wonderful.

On the way to the bedroom to change, I checked my table setting. My only tablecloth, a white, wrinkle-free number, looked festive with the red napkins and the poinsettia and red candle centerpiece. My mismatched silver didn't dampen the posh effect too much, and my Kmart goblets looked much better than they were.

As I forced my injured arm through the arm of my prettiest red sweater, I grimaced, but it was worth the pain for the color it brought to my face. Of course, the color was somewhat undercut by the large, rapidly darkening bruise splashed across my left cheek. I pulled on a pair of black slacks, knowing black was an absurd choice with a black and white cat in the house. But Mom and Dad had sent them to me, and I wanted to feel close to them.

The doorbell rang, and my heart jumped. I put my comb down with shaking hands. Did realizing you loved someone and needed to talk always make people candidates for antacid tablets and cardiac care?

Curt came in on a gust of cold air, tall and handsome, his hair in ringlets, his eyes shining through his glasses. In his hands he held a flat rectangle which could be nothing other than a picture. But when I turned from hanging up his coat, he was no longer holding it. Neither was it under the tree.

I eyed him uncertainly.

"It smells wonderful in here," he said, sniffing the air appreciatively. He was warm, gracious and distant.

I smiled tentatively and led the way to the kitchen. I looked in the oven.

"The little doodad's up," I said. I reached for my oven mitts and pulled the turkey from the oven. I put it on the counter to rest. I looked at Curt and he looked noncommittally, politely back. My heart became a lump in my chest. That's when I knew I'd never be able to eat dinner without clearing the air first.

Oh, Lord, I'm so scared. What if he truly doesn't care anymore? What if he's only here because I'm just marginally better than an empty house?

Don't worry. I care. And I'll always care. Remember the Babe.

I took a deep breath as I let the truth of God's love ease my fear.

"Come with me," I said. "We need to talk."

He followed me warily to the living room.

"Sit." I pointed to the chair. He sat or rather perched on the edge, a long-legged, bespectacled bird ready to fly away at the slightest provocation. I sat on the sofa facing him.

"You're driving me nuts, Curt!"

He looked somewhat startled, but his look of polite disinterest didn't change.

"You have become the most frustrating, the most irritating, the most maddening, the most—" I paused, searching for another word. "The most aggravating man I know."

His face became a study in surprise and wounded offense. At least the look of bland boredom was gone. "I'm irritating? I'm aggravating? I'm frustrating? Me?"

"Yes, you!" I pointed a finger at him. I noted with dismay that the nail and cuticle were still sooty in spite of all the showers, shampoos and food preparation they'd been through.

"Listen, lady," Curt said through clenched teeth. "I'm not the one who goes around trying to get herself killed all the time. I'm not the one who risks life and limb regardless of other people's feelings and fears. I'm not the one who ties other people's innards into knots on a regular basis." He was on his feet, glaring down at me like I was suddenly the villain.

Well, I wasn't. Not in my script.

I got to my feet, too, and stood, hands on hips, chin raised defiantly. "Don't try and make me the problem! You're the one who keeps offering affection and then withdrawing it. Which is a million times worse and more hurtful than anything I might do." I felt tears prick and I blinked furiously. I would not cry. I would stay in control. This was, after all, my confrontation. "I don't know anymore whether you love me or not."

There. I'd said it, though it sounded a bit more plaintive than I meant it to. And I also meant to clamp my mouth shut at this point and let him feel like a heel. Instead, I kept going. "I mean, here I am, falling in love with you, and there you are, pulling back."

He started to speak, and I put up my hand. "Not that I blame you for pulling back. I don't. I'm a mess. I know that. But Curt," I looked at him, as open and naked and vulnerable as ever I'd been my entire life, "you can't have it both ways." And I started to cry in spite of myself.

"Oh, Merry!" He wrapped his arms about me and held

me so close it would have hurt if it hadn't felt so comforting. I laced my good arm around his waist and held on, too.

After a couple of minutes, I stepped back. Or tried to. Curt only let me retreat to arm's length as he kept his hands on my shoulders. Then he reached out and gently traced my bruised cheek.

"I haven't had anyone to love for a long time," he said. "And I do love you. That fact isn't open for question. You make me feel like no one ever has before—which is part of the problem."

"That's good," I said. "That you feel like that about me, I mean."

"It's frightening," he countered with unexpected vehemence. "What if I lose you, too?" There was anguish in his voice.

"Is that why you withdraw?" I thought about the times he'd pulled back. It had been when I hit the deer, when I went with Jo to Arnie's at night, when we chased a murderer. In other words, when I had been in potential danger.

"I keep thinking that if I don't get too close, I can't get hurt again." He looked embarrassed.

"Just like if you don't celebrate Christmas, the loneliness won't strike?"

He stared, startled.

"But it hasn't worked, has it? You've still been lonely, right?"

He nodded.

"Pulling back from me won't work either, Curt." I drew him down to the sofa so we faced each other. "Loving isn't that easy to control."

He leaned forward and kissed me softly. "Tell me about it."

My heart soared at the kiss, but I made myself stick to the point. "You've got to decide whether we're worth the risk that loving entails."

"I just want to take care of you. To keep you safe."

I bristled a bit. "I can't take care of myself?"

"Don't make more of my comment than was intended. You do that, you know."

I ignored him. "You don't need to be my savior. I already have One."

He looked at me, exasperated. "Merry, you don't understand. I don't *need* to be your savior, except maybe for my peace of mind. I *want* to. I want to take care of you, to protect you. Maybe it's a guy thing. I don't know. Maybe it's just me. All I know is that anything that concerns you, hurts you or distresses you, I want to fix. Not because you can't fix it and I can, but because I love you."

I reached out and laid a hand on his cheek. "Poor Curt. To have fallen in love with me."

"I've talked to the Lord about this unsought turn of events quite a bit, believe me."

"And what does the Lord say?"

"That you're perfect for me."

He looked so woebegone that I laughed. "If it's any consolation, I love you more every day."

He took my hand and held it. "Just as I am, protectiveness, fears and all?"

I brushed a dark curl back from his forehead, enjoying the way it wrapped itself around my finger. Our eyes met, and I spoke from my heart. "I'll take you just as you are—" he smiled "—if you'll take me just as I am."

"Risky," he said.

"Scary," I agreed. "But worth it?"

In answer he got up from the sofa and reached behind it. He pulled out the flat package he'd brought with him.

"So that's where it went," I said.

"I was trying to decide whether to give it to you or not. I was trying to decide where I stood on the risk factor."

"And now you know?"

"And now I know—though I think I've always known deep down." He offered me the gift.

I tore off the wrapping paper, and my breath caught in my throat. I was looking at a painting of two hands entwined, lovers' hands. Curt's hand and mine.

"When did you do this?" I asked, knowing the power of the picture told me much more than his words ever would.

"This morning."

I blinked back my tears. "You did know."

"I guess I did."

I laced my fingers in his to mimic the picture.

"I love you," I said. "Always."

"At any risk," he agreed.

* * * * *

Dear Reader,

One of the themes running through *Caught in the Act* is that of adoption. It is a theme dear to my heart. My mother was an adopted person, given to my grandparents when a sixteen-year-old had her out of wedlock. In a nice piece of family history, the baby who became my mother was delivered by my great-grandfather, her adoptive grandfather.

In those days, adoption was often not discussed. My mother knew nothing of her adoption until she was around twelve, when a kid at school got mad at her and told her he didn't care what she thought because she was only adopted.

When she mentioned the boy's comments to my grandmother and asked if he told the truth, Grandmom said only, "Yes, you were adopted." That was it. Years later, Mom found her adoption certificate and a letter from the agency to my grandparents.

Our sons are adopted, too. Because of a severe case of endometriosis and a run-in with cancer in my midtwenties, I, like Maddie, was unable to have children. God gave my husband and me two boys who are now young men with families of their own. One knows a lot about his beginnings and has met his biological family. One knows very little, and all efforts to make contact with his birth mother have been rebuffed.

I like to remember that Jesus was the adopted son of Joseph, that Moses was adopted by Pharaoh's daughter as part of his preparation for leading the Exodus, and that when we trust in Jesus, we become the adopted children of the God of the universe.

All I can say is thank God for adoption.

Gayle

QUESTIONS FOR DISCUSSION

1. Merry's life is full of little frustrations, from her car calamities to her Curt/Jack embarrassments. Is your life full of frustrations both big and little? How do we find peace in the middle of frustration—or worse? Read Philippians 4:4–7.

2. Airy refers to Jolene as Princess Jo. What gives Jolene the princess complex? Do you know people as self-absorbed as Jo? Are you raising your children to be so inclined? What does Philippians 2:3 offer as the answer to self-absorption?

3. What is your reaction to the way Dawn deals with the girls who come to His House? Would you deal with such situations differently? How? Why?

4. Read Philippians 2:5. How does this verse apply to Dawn's clients? Is adoption always/ever the answer?

5. Maddie faces one of a woman's worst fears: sterility. Why does she hate the holidays?

6. Do you know women in situations like Maddie's? Have you asked awkward questions or inadvertently made the pain worse? Is adoption always/ever the answer?

7. Jolene and Merry have a very telling conversation in which Merry says, "Life can't be put in categories or compartments where you act one way over here and another way over there....You can't selectively lie to me and expect me not to resent it. Life doesn't work that way." Do you know people with the tendency to lie easily? Read Colossians 4:6 and compare this model to Jo.

8. In Philippians 3, Paul writes about forgetting what's behind and straining toward what's ahead. Curt has no Christmas decorations in his house. Why?

9. How does Merry help Curt in a practical manner? Have you ever been in a situation where moving on is hard?

10. Curt and Merry see the risk in loving. They also see the need to accept each other just as they are. In a marriage are there limits to acceptance? If so, what are they? How do you think I Peter 4:8 applies?

REQUEST YOUR FREE BOOKS!
2 FREE RIVETING INSPIRATIONAL NOVELS
PLUS 2 FREE MYSTERY GIFTS

Love Inspired®
SUSPENSE

YES! Please send me 2 FREE Love Inspired® Suspense novels and my 2 FREE mystery gifts. After receiving them, if I don't wish to receive any more books, I can return the shipping statement marked "cancel." If I don't cancel, I will receive 4 brand-new novels every month and be billed just $3.99 per book in the U.S. or $4.74 per book in Canada, plus 25¢ shipping and handling per book and applicable taxes, if any*. That's a savings of 20% off the cover price! I understand that accepting the 2 free books and gifts places me under no obligation to buy anything. I can always return a shipment and cancel at any time. Even if I never buy another book from Steeple Hill, the two free books and gifts are mine to keep forever.

123 IDN EL5H   323 IDN ELQH

Name	(PLEASE PRINT)	
Address		Apt. #
City	State/Prov.	Zip/Postal Code

Signature (if under 18, a parent or guardian must sign)

Order online at www.LoveInspiredSuspense.com

Or mail to Steeple Hill Reader Service™:

IN U.S.A.: P.O. Box 1867, Buffalo, NY 14240-1867
IN CANADA: P.O. Box 609, Fort Erie, Ontario L2A 5X3

Not valid to current Love Inspired Suspense subscribers.

Want to try two free books from another series?
Call 1-800-873-8635 or visit www.morefreebooks.com

* Terms and prices subject to change without notice. NY residents add applicable sales tax. Canadian residents will be charged applicable provincial taxes and GST. This offer is limited to one order per household. All orders subject to approval. Credit or debit balances in a customer's account(s) may be offset by any other outstanding balance owed by or to the customer. Please allow 4 to 6 weeks for delivery.

Your Privacy: Steeple Hill is committed to protecting your privacy. Our Privacy Policy is available online at www.eHarlequin.com or upon request from the Reader Service. From time to time we make our lists of customers available to reputable firms who may have a product or service of interest to you. If you would prefer we not share your name and address, please check here. ☐

LISUS07

Love Inspired ®
SUSPENSE

TITLES AVAILABLE NEXT MONTH

Don't miss these four stories in June

GLORY BE! by Ron and Janet Benrey
Cozy mystery

An unexpected windfall had greedy church choir members
preparing for a battle. Emma McCall wanted no part of it...
until a VW Bug appeared on her porch. No one would take
her complaint seriously—except the handsome deputy police
chief.

WHERE TRUTH LIES by Lynn Bulock
The Secrets of Stoneley

Miranda Blanchard spent her life as a prisoner to her
debilitating panic attacks. But Pastor Gregory Brown became
a steadying force in her life as she and her sisters worked to
unravel the mysteries that plague their family.

SHADOW OF TURNING by Valerie Hansen

Her Ozark hometown had always been a safe haven for
Chancy Boyd. But now a series of crimes threatened her, and
a deadly tornado—her worst nightmare—was racing toward
the town. Only "storm chaser" Nate Collins could help her
face her deepest fears.

CAUGHT IN A BIND by Gayle Roper

People don't vanish into thin air. Yet that's what happened to
the husband of one of Merry Kramer's coworkers. And in his
place? A strange corpse. Could Merry's search for the scoop
spell doom for this spunky sleuth?